LETTERS TO Zell

LETTERS TO Zell

a Novel

CAMILLE GRIEP

47NORTH

Published by 47North, Seattle

www.apub.com

Amazon, the Amazon logo, and 47North are trademarks of Amazon.com, Inc., or its affiliates.

ISBN-13: 9781477829622
ISBN-10: 1477829628

Cover design by Cyanotype Book Architects

Library of Congress Control Number: 2014957280

Printed in the United States of America

For Ashlee:
This is a story because of us and friends like us and friends not like us. This is a story because the years of our friendship now outnumber the years without. This is a story because I love you.

Once Upon a Time

From the Desk of Cecilia Cinder Charming
Crystal Palace
North Road, Grimmland

Dear Zell,

We were all waiting for you at the Swinging Vine so we could start our book club, when poor DJ dropped your note off with the first round of wine. You won't be surprised to learn Bianca went off like a confetti cannon, pelting him with accusations of cowardice and collusion.

All this drama to let us know you left to manage a unicorn preserve? I thought that sort of rural charity work was only for indulgent royalty out West. You said in your note, "I've always dreamed of making a difference." Since when? I know you love animals, but this is a bit more involved than leaving a saucer of milk out for stray kittens.

How did you expect we'd react? Laugh? Cry? Lament your departure to the half dozen tipsy, dancing princesses in the corner of an otherwise empty wine bar? I almost expected you to come through the door, doubling over at your own practical joke.

It was a long time—too long—before anyone said anything at all. And then it was clear your note was real. That you and Jason have actually departed to start a new life in the country. That you were already gone, having avoided those "messy good-byes" you're so opposed to, ever since Mother Gothel banished you to the edge of the Realm after she caught you two mid-canoodle.

Once Jason found you out there in the boonies, I know it was hard trying to reconcile the broken, blind man with the one you fell in love with back in the tower. You had to be the strong one, raising the twins on your own during the hardest years.

I understand that leaving lets you focus on your relationship and your family. But why not tell *us* your solution? Did you think we were too shallow to understand?

Perhaps I should have seen such an audacious move coming. It seems like just yesterday you and Jason returned, but really it's been years. After the drama of his homecoming and your wedding was over, I suppose I got wrapped up in my own engagement and the dwarves announcing Bianca's recovery—and, of course, Rory's ongoing quest to mold Henry into a prince worth waking up for. It's no wonder you needed some space away from everything and everyone. I get why you left, but I still can't see why you kept the decision to yourself. No discussion, no apology, just good-bye.

The other girls were as baffled as I was. Rory used her signature narcoleptic detachment to defend your actions as "romantic." Bianca threatened to enlist the dwarves to retrieve you.

What am I supposed to do without you? You and I didn't start out as royalty—me the little cinder girl and you Rapunzel, prisoner of the Tower. We complemented our eccentric princesses, the four of us a perfect team. Now we're like a three-legged goat. Or something.

The thing is, I had no idea that you wanted anything other than the life we're currently living. When did you experience this big revelation? When did you decide to allow yourself to follow through?

We've all lived beneath the weight of our Pages for so long that wanting something of our own volition feels dangerous. We aren't like the lucky ones waltzing around as they choose. You and I had to live out unpredictable stories penned by a capricious author. It's true we're free now, but I've never dreamed of admitting I still want more than what I already have.

I can't figure out if you're brave or crazy or selfish or brilliant. Maybe all of those. You've always been ahead of the curve.

Then there's Bianca, whose Pages don't end until she's married and Valborg is executed for those four counts of stepmotherly attempted homicide. Pages always seem to be the most trying right before they're finished. Worse, Bianca doesn't want to be a queen. She doesn't want to live in a castle. She wants to travel the Realm—and beyond, Outside—just like her father is doing. She talks big about young Human women wasting time at universities, chewing on their pens and debating whether a chair is really there, but under all that bluster, I know she'd rather do that than sit listless on an ebony throne.

And now here you are, traipsing off into the sunset. Bianca tried to act like she didn't care that you'd gone, but she spent the remainder of the night trashing the romance novel you'd chosen for book club. I'd fill you in, but I'm sure you'll be hearing about it directly from her.

I'm not sure how late I stayed after everyone else left, but it must have been pretty late because I was still sitting there when DJ shooed the last of the prance-cesses (get it?) out the door.

The girls had left a glittering mess from one end of the bar to the other. "Damned pixie dust," DJ muttered. "Not everything needs to sparkle." Those dancing ditzes have such a terrible reputation as a group, but I guess I don't know anything about them as individuals—not the six in the bar, not their six sisters. What are the chances that all twelve are intolerable? There's a fourth spot in the book club now, so I could find out. We could even ask the new girl in town, the one from Swan Lake telling everyone about her mattress problem. I'm almost mad enough to fill your spot.

Instead of kicking me out as well, DJ asked why I was pouting. I told him that you had moved to the country to save the unicorns, focus on your family, chase your dreams, grow tomatoes, maybe compost.

He said, "Well, good for her. Those kids could use some fresh air and a change of scenery."

I told him he was right because he probably is, and I'm sure I won't be angry with you forever. And maybe you'll get there and reconsider and come back to us after all.

But when I got home, I *was* still mad at you or maybe just sad at you, so I rummaged up another bottle of wine from the deserted cellars. I figured I'd work up a batch of scones while I unwound. I know princesses aren't supposed to bake, but baking helps me relax. Edmund was in Wonderland again, going over the new plans for the Bunny Byway (to avoid further collisions with curious children), and the kitchen staff always clears out around nine or so.

You know what the best part about the kitchen is? My brooding stepsisters wouldn't set one mutilated foot in there for fear of being seen, nor would my nosy stepmother. Also it smells good and it's nice and warm.

Last night it was maybe too warm.

I fell asleep at the long table, head resting on a half-full sack of oats. At some point, Rosemount, returning from jestering, removed my very well done scones from the oven, and bustled me to my chambers. Even though I had the whole bed to myself, I had harried, black dreams.

Dreams interrupted, of course, by my stepmother.

"Cinderella! Time to get up."

It didn't feel like it could have possibly been a time consistent with morning. I should have asked Edmund to install a secret passageway in my chamber. Or a moat filled with alligators. Or a better lock. But instead, the door swung open and Duchess Lucinda of Everland swept in wearing a crisp, white dress, inlaid with an intricate pattern of black silk.

When I was small, I thought her flair for drama, her style, and the way she carried herself was so beautiful. Actually, I still think so—no one evil is ever so simple—but that morning I wasn't yet ready to see anything, beautiful or otherwise.

Lucinda stared at me. "Why in Grimm's name do you still have yesterday's dress on? What kind of skulking about have you been doing? Are you trying to bring ruin to our house— after all we've been through, all we've accomplished?"

I tried hard to make the room stop spinning, but she was so loud. Her voice reverberated off the stones on the wall, the floor. I should have asked for a trebuchet. A terrier. A trapdoor. For a moment, I imagined how her face would contort as she fell through the floor, black petticoats swishing around her head. I smiled.

"You think this is funny, do you?"

Vertigo. I opened my mouth to speak and instead out came a veritable torrent of red wine and bile.

They'll be talking about it for weeks. I *almost* feel ashamed.

Love,
CeCi

Important Fucking Correspondence from Snow B. White
Onyx Manor
West Road, Grimmland

Z,

You silly bitch.

First, you made us read *The Cake and the Damned* for book club just because those glittering, gallivanting Glindas did, and then you couldn't even bother to show up? We all gathered at your favorite froufrou bar, and you didn't come? You sent a note? I'd address your epistle line by line, but I got a little carried away and burned it with one of DJ's ridiculous ambiance candles. We had to get your address from Fairy Records.

So DJ drops the note on the table and CeCi reads it to us. Everything seems too loud. Especially DJ's choice in music. I say to him, "Hey, can you turn that earsplitting dubstep shit off?"

"Why didn't you say so?" he sings. "Everybody likes house music better anyway." He flutters his fingers, and the volume goes up on something equally reprehensible. At a table over in the corner, a half dozen voices start to squeal, "We love this song!"

There isn't enough port in my glass. In fact, there isn't any port in my glass, so I wave it in the air. The universal signal for more. But DJ is too busy showing off his dance moves. If he's going to convince Grimmland he's a highfalutin' sommelier instead of a barkeep like the generations of DemiJohns before him, he's going to have to make some changes in his repertoire.

Patronizing as usual, CeCi motions to my glass and says, "Careful with that stuff, it makes you obnoxious."

"What's your excuse, then?" I ask her.

Rory rearranges her petticoats and clears her throat. "Ladies, this always happens at book club. Someone starts talking about something else, and we never discuss the story. Perhaps we can talk about *The Cake and the Damned*, instead?"

"Fine," I say. "This pandering drivel is the single worst piece of literature I've ever had the misfortune to lay eyes on. It is, in fact, so abominable I fear I've been mentally impaired by reading it."

I wish you had been there, Zell, so I could have thrown the book at you. Instead, I slam it on the bar for emphasis. Rory jumps off her stool because she's strung tighter than a cheap harpsichord. She spills her wine and CeCi's wine and so we're *all* out of wine and I suggest Rory try drinking a little more frequently, you know, for her nerves.

CeCi isn't finished being sarcastic. "Okay, Bianca, tell us how you really feel about the book."

"Do you have specific complaints?" asks Rory in a timid little mouse voice.

"Nobody wants to read shit like this. It isn't how life works. There's no such thing as True Love and soul mates and perfect perfection. My ass. Love isn't anything like this. Life isn't anything like this! What is this author thinking? We *are* the Fairy Tale. We know better."

At this point, I pause to inquire of anyone who will listen as to whether DJ is still serving alcohol at this particular establishment.

Rory seizes the moment to argue with me. "Maybe, in this person's experience, True Love *was* magical."

"Magic has nothing to do with it," I tell her. "A relationship should be based on mutual interests, trust, friendship. Come on, CeCi, back me up here."

"In the book," Rory insists, "Star wanted Sabian to love her, she just didn't know it yet."

I can't comprehend how she can possibly be so naïve. "It's irresponsible storytelling. Love can certainly include the occasional experimental romp in handkerchiefs or a playful smack on the behind with a riding crop, but it doesn't involve isolation and belittlement. Star is already worthy of Sabian. What does she have to reinvent herself for?"

"Maybe she wants to change," Rory mumbles. "You said yourself love is compromise."

"I meant eating your eggs scrambled instead of poached on Wednesdays and Saturdays, not giving up everything you are and becoming someone else. What kind of love is that to want?"

Rory squirms in her seat and CeCi frowns. I continue, reminding them none of our parents had healthy relationships and at the very least we should attempt to learn from their abysmal examples.

After my mom died, my dad immediately traipsed out to find another woman, one so obsessed with herself she tried to kill me. And look at your parents, Zell. Your father was so eager to regain your mother's approval that he traded you for a *bunch of goddamned lettuce*. Those weren't relationships based on True Love. I'm half tempted to go Outside and ask this author just what her malfunction is. If this literature is the future of Human imagination, we Fairy Tales are seriously fucked.

DJ mercifully sails over with more wine, and I grab him by his velour collar. "You have to put something else on the speakers."

"Oh, honey," he sighs at me. "Do you object to all popular music or just happiness in general?"

"Anything else, okay? I'm trying to be reasonable here."

A moment later, something slower, yet still strange and cacophonous, floats over our heads. Sometimes I think DJ's ability to run Human electronics with magic is useful (the blender, for instance, has its advantages), but often I want to throw that CD player into the frog pond.

I start to say something, but he levels a long, jeweled finger at me. "You asked for *anything else*, sister, so zip it."

And I do zip it because I remember it's your fault we aren't at Shambles listening to rock and roll or at Ma Kettle's sucking down those dastardly carbs everyone's so scared of. But I'm getting distracted. Back to the book.

CeCi says, for maybe the first time ever, "I think Bianca has a point."

Both Rory and I struggle to stay on our stools. "You do?" I cough.

She nods. "I agree. Love is hard work, not magic. There's no secret formula, there's no right person; it just takes a certain amount of chemistry and then working your ass off. Being honest about who you are and what you want and then hoping for the best. The magic part comes later. At least in my experience."

"Magic, eh?" I poke her in the arm. "Is that what they're calling it these days?"

She flushes red. "I didn't mean it like *that*."

Rory asks if we're absolutely sure things didn't happen that way in the book.

"It positively didn't happen that way in the book." I stand up, and the Twirling Twits in the corner stop talking and stare. "Instead of making each other stronger, Star and Sabian hobbled one another. Sort of like Zell and Jason—practically joined at the hip."

So before either of them tells you, yes, I said that. I think you are making a terrible mistake. I think you're just like that book. I think you couldn't face real life here and you're running away. Who wants to work at a glorified zoo, cleaning up unicorn shit every afternoon? It's not like it smells nice or glitters in the sun.

I guess you think this is the way you're going to salvage your marriage. You think you owe Jason because he never stopped looking for you. You think he owes you because you got knocked up. He thinks he owes you for healing his sight. Love—and friendship, for that matter—isn't a game of reciprocity.

You act like you have things figured out just because you're a few years older than the rest of us. (Well, not Rory, technically, but still.) Just because the two of you chose to be together at seventeen doesn't mean that you have to choose to be unhappy for the rest of your lives. You completed your Pages. You're free now.

I envy that freedom, Zell. I don't want to get married. It feels like a waste of time—opportunities flying past—while I plan this sham of a wedding. I chose William because, if I am being forced to do this, at least it's to *my* friend on *my* terms.

That said, if you miss my wedding, I swear on my own glass coffin you'll be dead to me. And your stupid unicorns, too.

B

Princess Briar R. Rose
Somnolent Tower Castle
South Road, Grimmland

Dearest Zell,

I don't know why Bianca and CeCi are so upset over *The Cake and the Damned*. It's just a book, after all. What do they have against love, anyway? What I wouldn't give for that kind of love. The kind of love you simply know in your heart will be forever.

Just take you and Jason. You'll be so happy in faraway East of Oz. Especially with your perfectly romantic past. You met, fell in love, were cruelly separated. You: alone, at the edge of the Realm, pregnant, hungry, hopeless. Him: blind and lost. He stumbles into your wilderness, you heal his eyes with tears of joy, and you all return to Grimmland. Now that is a story. *That is True Love.*

Even though Bianca says that you would have fallen for the first eligible bachelor who climbed through your window, I know better. I know it was fate. It hasn't happened that way for me, true, but there's still time. One day, Henry will enter the room and see me at just the right angle. He'll think to himself, *I've never realized how in love I am with Briar Rose, my Sleeping Beauty.*

Bianca and CeCi both swore they were going to write and give you a piece of their mind, but I imagine they left out the little plot they've hatched to venture Outside.

I should back up a bit. You see, CeCi has been hanging out in the kitchens lately, and two nights ago—the night we got your note—that silly jester told her how Outside one can take lessons to be a certified anything. Tailors become fashion designers, planners become engineers, and, most importantly, cooks become chefs.

Since then, she hasn't been able to talk of anything besides becoming a real chef (and some silly chasing one's dream nonsense). Her preoccupation unfortunately coincides with Bianca's burgeoning recklessness, which worsens the closer she gets to her wedding.

I had hoped CeCi would come to her senses after her hangover was cured. (The story about Lucinda's new gown quickly made its way round to my servants' quarters.) Instead, Bianca seized the opportunity to declare we would all attend a cooking class as a bridesmaids outing, even though she's about as interested in cooking as DJ is in country music. I'm not sure why I agreed to go—someone responsible had to chaperone.

Thinking our outing was to be an informal affair, I was enjoying five extra minutes of sleep when CeCi turned up attired as though we were attending a party, blond hair coiffed and complexion perfect, as if she'd been up for hours. As for Bianca, she managed to secure some sort of Outside clothing from Rumple's tailoring shop. We spent the entirety of the walk from my castle to Solace's Clock Shop arguing whether her arms were inserted through the correct openings. I maintain to this minute that she put the outfit on wrong, because it didn't cover very much of her. Bianca informed us she'd been reading something called *Cosmo*, and that we could kindly *go fuck* ourselves.

It had been some time since I'd seen Solace, probably not since CeCi's wedding. She looked as lovely as ever—as beautiful as a rabbit woman can be. She hasn't aged a bit, still soft and shiny. I suppose that's a perk of being the Godmother of Time.

Though Solace radiated a contagious and cheering sort of calm, the shop itself was crammed far tighter than it once was, with new clock portals to who knows where. There was scarcely room to walk, and moreover it was difficult to hear above all the *bing*-ing and *bong*-ing and *chime*-ing and *tick*-ing and *tock*-ing. Bianca wended her way to the front desk and proceeded to yell something about an "essential errand."

"Your friends are welcome to travel, Snow White." Solace smiled. "But residents with unfinished Pages are discouraged from traveling Outside."

Bianca leaned back and crossed her arms—the same sort of posture she uses when we disagree with her. "*Discouraged*, Solace? *Discouraged* sounds an awful lot like your sister's rhetoric."

Solace frowned. "As you well know, I believe travel to be a liberating and essential rite of passage. However, there are dangers. It's an unnecessary risk while your Pages are incomplete."

Bianca's eyes narrowed at the rules plaque on the wall adjacent. It read:

Rules and Regulations:

1. Keep hands to oneself when walking through the clocks.

2. No one shall travel unaccompanied.

3. Return within 24 hours of your departure date. Please consult your clock bracelet.

A not-very-nice sort of smile spread across Bianca's lips. "The rules say I can't go *alone*. And I'm not going *alone*."

"Figueroa will have my ears if I let you go."

"Since when did she start ordering you around?"

Solace gave a heavy thump of her hind foot. "If you don't fulfill your Pages, Snow White, it will wreak havoc upon Grimmland, not to mention the entire Realm of Imagination."

"Okay. Fine. Can we skip the melodrama?"

"If," Solace said reluctantly, "you were to go with your friends, they would have to vouch for your safe return. It isn't a burden any of you can take lightly."

Bianca turned and widened her eyes at us. "Don't volunteer all at once or anything."

"We'll make sure she gets back." CeCi's voice was tight.

When Solace looked at me I nodded, though I wasn't sure that vouching for Bianca was safe to do in any Realm—Imaginary or Human. Solace's eyes stayed on mine too long. At first, I wasn't sure what more she wanted of me.

"This is serious," said Solace. "It would be a hundred years before things could be set right again."

"Oh," I started. Of course. I should have known she'd bring up Fred. He wanted so badly for our stories to end together, but it took one hundred years of sleep and all of Solace, Figgy, and Malice's powers to keep the Realm from ripping apart. My entire palace atoned for Fred's mistake. When I woke up, everything around me had changed, and Fred was gone. I completed the new Pages Figgy gave me. What more can I do?

"Keeping us here," I said, "won't undo what happened with Fred."

Bianca let out a relieved sigh. "If it helps, I've read all of my father's travel journals."

Solace looked at her in a rather piteous manner. "The Outside is very different from here, Snow White. I fear you may be unprepared."

"Then you'll be glad to learn I've also been subscribing to

magazines through the Pigeon Post. I know exactly what I'm doing. And if I get stuck, I'll totally send you a postcard."

A breeze crossed the room and blew a sheaf of papers from the counter between Bianca and Solace. Solace's brow furrowed as a clot of feathers floated though the window.

"You think this is funny, Snow White, but you have a lot to learn." Solace returned the papers to the counter. She looked at Bianca very intently. "Still, perhaps traveling can help you accomplish that very objective."

Bianca smiled like a cat who'd eaten a fat bird. It was then I knew that, even if not today or tomorrow or next year, we were almost certainly doomed.

"If you are late to return, I will not be able to assist," Solace said, binding our wrists with clock bracelets. "If you stay beyond the chime, the binding magic that allows you to pass through the portals will begin to decay. Once it is gone, you will become as if you were a Human or any other sort of being who cannot pass into our Realm. Now, are you prepared for your journey?"

Earlier that morning, the question had been a simple formality. At that moment, with Solace awaiting an answer, I wanted nothing more than to go back home and have tea. All three of us nodded.

"I assume you have currency?" asked Solace, her paw hovering over a large ebony lever.

"My father left trunkloads from when he came back from his last trip." Bianca patted a leather satchel slung over her shoulder and bounded forward.

We passed the open mouths of portals leading to other places in the Realm of Imagination—Wonderland, Neverland, Toad Hollow, Fantasia, Atlantis. I trailed behind, following the other two into the looming black grandfather clock at the end of the shop, through a brightly lit hall of blue sky and cloud, to the Outside.

The trip was far more exciting than the yawns I'm experiencing now would suggest. However, I've gone on so long already, and I'm overdue for my nap. I'll write again tomorrow. Don't worry. We're home safe.

Always,
Rory

From the Desk of Cecilia Cinder Charming
Crystal Palace
North Road, Grimmland

Dear Zell,

I'm sure you've already heard the news from Rory. It's not as if it's a secret, though I'm sure Solace meant for us to emerge Outside less conspicuously than we did. Bianca and I made it out quietly enough, but Rory, so busy gawking at the sky, stumbled and caught the attention of a group of nearby children.

A particularly sticky-looking boy pointed at us with a dripping fudgesicle. "How long did it take you to learn how to just appear like that?"

"Do it again!" said another boy.

I looked around to try and understand where we'd emerged. The structure in front of us didn't seem to be the typical wardrobe or outhouse or saloon one arrives at within the Realm. Instead, we faced a squat and bulbous manor with a sign that read "The Magic Castle." Overgenerously labeled (it was a manse, at best), the building also lacked a visible door.

"Where did you come from?" asked a redheaded girl.

"Grimmland!" Rory volunteered.

The girl scrunched her forehead. "Is that like Disneyland? We went there yesterday."

"She means south," Bianca said, elbowing Rory in the ribs. "We're from the south."

"You don't sound like you're from the south," said the fudgesicle boy.

The little girl looked at my gown. "How come you two are dressed up like princesses?"

I tried to keep from rolling my eyes. "We were just at a fancy costume party."

"Yes," Rory added, with cheerful vapidity. "A fancy party here at the, um, Magic Castle."

"That means they're real magicians," said the second boy. "Only real magicians are allowed inside. You have to know the magic words."

"Tell us the magic words!" said the first boy, brandishing his fudgesicle. I took a step back.

This was probably pure entertainment for Solace, venting us into the courtyard of a monument to Human wizardry. Of course the children were right—we had arrived by magic, just not the sort of Human illusion they believed in.

"How come your friend isn't dressed up?" The girl pointed to Bianca, who was stuffing bits of cleavage back into her top.

"She's in disguise," Rory said.

"Are you *sure* you aren't princesses?" the little girl whispered.

Rory leaned down and smiled beatifically. "Do you like princesses? Would you like to be one?"

The little girl twisted the toe of her shiny shoe against the ground. "I don't know. I'm kind of tired of princesses. There were a lot them at Disneyland. I saw Belle and Jasmine and Ariel and Cinderella and—"

Rory jumped in front of me. "She doesn't know any better, CeCi"—as if I'd been a breath away from sliding the little pedant into my gingerbread oven and consuming her limb by limb. No one but Lucinda calls me that humiliating nickname.

"Let's get out of here before we catch something," I grumbled. Rory began waving good-bye, but the girl was already distracted by a rectangular object in her palm.

Bianca pointed to a line of motor vehicles, like they have in Toad Hollow. "We have to find one that's yellow or has checks or says *taxi* on the side." She strode past a group of gawking young men. "You snap your fingers at them like this." Some of the drivers held up their middle finger at her.

We piled into a taxi and asked to go to the cooking school. This caused some confusion as there is apparently more than one cooking school. Luckily, our coachman possessed a rectangular device like the redheaded girl's, used primarily for talking to people who aren't next to you. Like Valborg the Vain's mirror, it also answered questions. Of course it's much smaller. And less evil. The driver told us it was called a *cell phone*, then asked if we were Amish. I wasn't quite sure how to answer.

It didn't matter. We were finally Outside, making our way to a cooking class. Maybe it's foolish, but this was a dream come true. And even if I had tried to talk myself out of it, you know how convincing Bianca can be.

Outside was even more hectic than I pictured from Bianca's father's diaries or her *Cosmo* magazines. And it was certainly nothing like Rory's novels—especially the old ones that claimed that the land had once been empty, the hills full of plants instead of houses, and the sky blue like home instead of greyish yellow. But who knows? The grass might have been purple and the sky orange once upon a time, for all we know. We are taught to believe deeply in books, but there are some things they just won't tell you.

After a lot of nattering between Bianca and Rory, the driver dropped us on a boulevard named Sunset. Bianca went inside the school and returned to tell us our class would start later that evening but first—according to the "jackass" inside— we all needed new clothing. Rory pointed out that she'd known

Bianca's outfit was inappropriate. Bianca responded by telling Rory she could stuff it or receive Human clothes for her next thirty birthdays.

We walked back past a bumpy dome called the Cinerama, past tall buildings and short buildings and about a hundred places that served those cheeseburger sandwiches Hansel and Gretel introduced at the café a few years ago. Bianca bought us new clothing from a store with mannequins in the window. I didn't mind ditching my gown because it was heavy and hot in the sun but Rory, as you might suspect, was temporarily despondent at the loss of her high, lacy collar.

"Don't be such a twit," Bianca told her. "Are you telling me you sleep in your gowns, too?"

"A *dressing gown*, of course," Rory said. "Like everyone else."

"Not me," Bianca laughed. "CeCi?"

I shrugged.

"Oh!" Rory let out a high-pitched squeal. "You terrible, lewd things!"

The cooking class itself was incredible. As usual, everyone fell in love with Bianca's deep laugh and carefree ease. We had trouble finding another taxi at the end of the night, but Rory had been so paranoid about getting back on time, we ended up staying only half a day.

But now that we're home, I want to be Outside again. I want to feel all the heat from the sidewalk and smell the exhaust and the cheeseburgers and the wisps of sea air. I want to be in a bright room full of people creating food for each other. I want to forget about undecorated nurseries and meddlesome stepmothers and blind stepsisters, the obligations of court, and the weight of a tiara—if even for an hour or two.

Like you care, anyway. You're probably having all kinds of

fun settling in to your own dream come true. Is that why you're too busy to write anything longer than a postcard?

Until you write a real letter, I'm definitely staying mad at you. Sad at you. Both.

CeCi

Important Fucking Correspondence from Snow B. White
Onyx Manor
West Road, Grimmland

Z,

Thanks to Rosemount and his big yap, CeCi's been mooning over this cooking class business, so I said, screw it, let's go see what the big fucking deal is.

Besides, we can't expect CeCi to be satisfied flouncing down to that poor excuse for a cooking school on Drury Lane for "Muffin Stuffin Saturdays" the rest of her life.

And before you tell me to be less incautious (like Rory does five times a day), I have my father's maps and his money and his diaries and his last letter with instructions on how to navigate all the major kingdoms in (and out) of the Realm.

Going Outside will let us compare notes as soon as he gets back for the wedding. The Pigeon Post will find him any day now, I'm sure of it. And instead of awkward silences or his poor choice in brides, we'll be able to talk about something we both enjoy, about the big wide world and our place in it. Or whatever. We can start a new relationship, one that lets stepmothers named Valborg be bygones.

After sorting things out with Solace, we're off, and I locate a taxi. Rory asks the driver a thousand irritating questions, and we arrive at the class venue around noon. CeCi and Rory are too nervous to go in, so I try the door and it swings open into a high-ceilinged, glassy box of a room filled with long countertops, banks of sinks, and a back wall of oven ranges. I learn several things, herein.

First, being early is not a virtue appreciated on Earth. Second, despite the fact I'm *already* wearing Human clothing, the man at the front desk tells me we won't be allowed to take class that evening unless we find *different* clothing, insisting I'm wearing too little clothing and Rory and CeCi are wearing too much. I try to explain we know how to handle ourselves around open flames. But alas, Humans seem to have an outfit for *every* activity.

The shopping turns out to be pretty fun. The soufflé class, however, is ungodly boring. Add this, stir that, fold this, blend that. To top it all off, the Head of Soufflés makes me put on a pair of ugly rubbery shoes because she's convinced that I'm going to slice my toes off. I ask her why they're so orange and so homely and she mutters something about it being the nature of crocodiles. (I'll have to ask Hook about it the next time I see him at Shambles.)

Rory and I manage the class just fine and neither of us falls asleep. Head of Soufflés shows off her witty repartee when she's not winking at me, and I find myself asking a lot of questions during oven time. Just before she heads back to the front of the room, she slips me a piece of paper inviting me for drinks after class.

I expect Rory and CeCi to be staring at me with some manner of accusation, but when I turn toward their corner of the room, they aren't even paying attention. Rory is clapping her hands at CeCi, who is positively beaming over her perfectly brown dish of pastry pudding. I don't think I've ever seen her look so happy. It's like she's glowing from the inside. Covered with pixie dust.

Part of me feels the same. I'm free here. I can enjoy the attention of the Head of Soufflés and listen to all the silly Humans talk about the books they've read and the music they've heard and the trips they've taken. It feels like anything's possible here. Well, anything but achieving my own cooking milestone.

When I reach the ovens, I pull out a black, smoking mass. Everyone laughs.

B

PS. ~~Hell yeah! My new pigeon Cliff just brought me your wedding RSVP.~~ The three of us have *always* been bridesmaids for each other. My wedding will be the last one, and you just bail without any explanation? You can't make it for one stupid day? There's no "I wish I could be there with the remorse of a thousand flatulent unicorns, Bianca," or "Sorry, Bianca, but you are the least important to me," or "Fuck you, Bianca." Just nothing. Just a check in the box that says, "Regrets."

PPS. What the hell are you doing out there, anyway? Are unicorns too stupid to find their own sustenance—stumbling around like CeCi after a night of drinking? Sometimes I don't know why I bother with any of you.

Princess Briar R. Rose
Somnolent Tower Castle
South Road, Grimmland

Zell darling,

I'm so sorry for cutting off our cooking school tale in my last letter, but lately I've been dropping off faster than a ripe apple. Not a poisonous apple, mind you, just a regular one. Heavy, but medium sized, not overly shiny—

Sorry. Can you believe it just happened *again*? Anyhow, I want to make sure you get the full picture of how thoroughly your departure has kindled our friends' wild imaginations.

CeCi took to the soufflé class like a duck to water. Most of us churned out acceptable dishes, but hers was extraordinary in aesthetic and flavor. Of course I'm the only one who noticed. The woman Bianca dubbed "Head of Soufflés" seemed to embrace her new moniker, not to mention Bianca herself. (This turned out to be fortunate because she was right there with the fire extinguisher when Bianca finally remembered to remove her dessert from the oven.)

Bianca gave her signature half smile and a curtsy to the rapt attendees, and said, "This is why I let my servants cook!" No one would suspect for a moment she's soon to become the queen of anything, let alone Onyx Manor.

We don't have to worry about blending in—the inhabitants of Los Angeles seem to be more than a bit zany. The class was full of all manner of people, men and women, old and young, plump and reedy. The one trait that seemed to unite them was a love of putting all these small things into a big dish and having something completely different appear. I can see how cooking is a kind of magic to some. But, truth be told, as a hobby it makes me yawn.

After the class, the instructor joined us for drinks at a restaurant next door. She tolerated a few of CeCi's questions about how she'd learned to cook and then, despite my repeated throat-clearing, told her about culinary school for people who want to learn to cook as a vocation. After that, CeCi fell silent and would not be distracted by any topic of conversation. Bianca and the instructor discussed absolutely nothing of substance, so I dozed off for a bit, until I began to slide off my bar stool.

Bianca—either oblivious to the woman's interest or in spite of it—didn't mention her wedding even once. I felt sympathy for the soufflé woman's romantic intentions. If only she knew how recent Bianca's obsession with Humans and the Outside was. Had she heard one of Bianca's diatribes about Humans a few months ago, she'd have run for the hills faster than a dormouse.

Finally, Bianca took pity on us and proposed that we locate a taxi—but there wasn't an empty one to be found anywhere. The instructor began to laugh.

"It's Saturday in West Hollywood," she said, as if we were supposed to parse some intonation besides her clear disdain. "Where are you from again?" she asked.

"South," said Bianca.

"You mean Orange County?"

"More south," said Bianca.

"San Diego?"

"Small town. You wouldn't have heard of it."

"Do you need a ride somewhere?" she asked.

"The Magic Castle in the hills," I whispered.

The instructor began laughing again, until we convinced her that we weren't joking. "Either I've had too much to drink or not enough," she said, jangling a set of keys. And so we all climbed inside her tall blue automobile.

On the way she began to glance at Bianca from the corner of her eye—not at all the kind of glances she had been giving her before.

"This isn't exactly the way I saw this evening going," she said.

Bianca looked chagrined. "Of course. We paid the taxi we took earlier. How much do you want?" She fished a wad of cash from her satchel and held it out. The soufflé woman looked at Bianca as if she had turned into Medusa.

"I'm sorry," CeCi said, trying to diffuse the palpable discomfort. "It's my fault for not explaining. We're on a schedule."

"See, we're performers," I added. Bianca, sadly, could not contain a snort. "We do magic tricks." Thankfully, the soufflé woman did not ask for a demonstration.

She let us out at the end of the long driveway without so much as a good-bye. We hiked up the hill and went through the portal as discreetly as we could manage, though we heard gasps from a bunch of suited men puffing on white tobacco sticks nearby.

"What if she hadn't given us a ride?" I said.

"What-ifs are a serious fucking waste of time," Bianca said.

She was right. I know all too well that dwelling on things that didn't happen doesn't do anything but keep you from living.

It's a good bit different than worrying about the future, though. I'll try not to worry about that, and I hope you'll try not to, either. Let's not worry together.

Love,
Rory

From the Desk of Cecilia Cinder Charming
Crystal Palace
North Road, Grimmland

Dear Zell,

I'm sorry about my last letter. I shouldn't have ended it so harshly. I was mad that you weren't there for our adventure and mad that we went at all because I liked going so much and I don't know when we can go again. I'm mad because I feel like I've finally found my purpose and I'll never be able to immerse myself fully.

Sure, I made meals for Lucinda and the twins for years, but she and the girls said my food tasted like donkey piss, and I believed them. I made simple things and I never pushed myself. Now, I feel as if I could be a success. I've never been talented at anything before. Remember the time I tried to help out at Rumple's and cut a hole in the rear of your Aunt Bess's bustle?

I couldn't wait to tell Edmund, so when he came home today, I met him at the gates. He was a little distracted talking about the Queen of Hearts' opposition to the Byway (and everything else, for that matter) and next week's Supporters of Robin Hood meeting, but I finally got him to listen for a moment.

"I want to do something extra special for the two of us."

He put his arm around me and smiled. "I'd love that. What is it?"

"I want to make us a special dinner. Candles and wine and soufflé!"

"That's a fantastic idea. I'll tell the kitchen staff."

"No. Thank you. You don't have to tell the staff. I can do it."

"Cook dinner? Well, of course you *can*. But the great part is that you don't have to. Remember when I told you you'd never have to wait on people again?"

"Well, I just . . . See, I want to do something for us. For you."

And he held my face in his hands like he does sometimes and said, "Darling, toiling away in the kitchens is no longer your destiny. We rescued you from all that, remember."

"But it would be like a gift, Ed."

He stepped back. "I never want you to feel as if you owe something to me or that you serve me in some manner. I'm not that kind of guy. You know that, right?"

"Of course, but I just—"

"All you need to do is be your beautiful self. Besides, we couldn't have everyone thinking I put you back in the kitchens, could we? Come now and see the gifts I've brought you."

They were lovely gifts. They looked very bright and shiny, like things do when you're trying not to cry. Once, he looked up and noticed and asked what was wrong, so I told him I was just happy to see him. That I'd missed him. At least that part was truth.

I did not tell him that he had misunderstood. That I was all at once in awe of the gracious man he is and heartsick that I hadn't managed to explain myself coherently. Then I followed things up by lying, saying everything was fine when it wasn't. That was a mistake because then I had to have sex while pretending that I didn't want to cry.

The point is this: I want to cook. I've never wanted anything more in my life. And then again I don't. I don't want to make a mess. I don't want to destroy the fragile truce between me and my life. Everything is fine just as it is. Do I need to go and upend everything? This is *your* fault for making me think

I could have something else. For making me wonder. For letting me hope it would be okay to want anything other than what I have.

We're princesses, damn it. Our job is to become queens. Our job is to wear pretty dresses and have even complexions and carry on inane conversations with other queens and wear crowns and capes and furs and ride sidesaddle and be demure at dinner. Our job is to love all of these things more than anything else. Our job is to churn out progeny and hand them over to nursemaids. Our job is to enjoy bread pudding when we really want chocolate mousse. Our job is to forget what we want and do what's expected.

I don't understand how you just quit that job, how you pulled on a set of riding breeches, tossed your circlets in a saddlebag, and rode off into the sunset. Bianca says that Jason's mother has petitioned the Fairy Council to have you stripped of your title. When she's done, not only won't you be a queen, you'll be homeless.

You probably think it doesn't matter because you have your new place in Oz, but have you fully thought out the repercussions? I get it. You never want to find yourself trapped in another tower, metaphorical or otherwise. Maybe you don't want another woman—your mother-in-law instead of that old kidnapping witch Gothel—calling the shots. But was it necessary to throw all of your old life away in order to ensure your autonomy?

I think of Darling and Sweetie spending their entire lives trying to become what I am now. They sacrificed their feet, their minds, their own desires to fit into a damned shoe. Then Figgy's filthy starlings took their sight as they left my wedding. Ever since, they've clung to one another, frightened and miserable. They're finally safe, and here I am contemplating risking their futures for a few scones?

I hear them all day, shambling around the hallways, Lucinda yelling at them to do this or that while I consider abandoning all my good fortune for one selfish desire. Don't I owe it to them to just do my job, to be a good princess? How could a ridiculous dream be worth the risk in the end? Please tell me; you seem to know. I miss you.

Love,
CeCi

Important Fucking Correspondence from Snow B. White
Onyx Manor
West Road, Grimmland

Z,

So, now that you can't come to my wedding, you're the most prolific profferer of postcards ever? Or just the penpal who's most curious about my adventures?

Yes, I flirted with a Human. Big fucking deal. I mean, I know what I used to say. But I can change my mind, just like the rest of you, can't I? Humans can't *all* be assholes, right? Head of Soufflés herself can't be responsible for techno music, Chia Pets, *and* pies in a jar.

Besides, here I am, back where that nonsense exists safely between the covers of *Cosmo*. So yeah, maybe I'd like one of those cell phones. But who wouldn't? They're a lot more pleasant than pigeons (sorry, Cliff) but only because they don't shit all over the floor.

Stupid Figgy and her stupid scare tactics. When we were young she told us there would come a time when the Humans died off, their imaginations blinking out like stars, and us along with them. Even if she's right, that day isn't today. It won't be tomorrow, either. Their imaginations seem as healthy as ever.

Case in point: We get Outside and some kid tells Rory about this park full of princesses called *Disneyland*. Head of Soufflés corroborates the tale. Not only is it a real place, they apparently tell Rory's story to little girls—some sort of gussied-up version that's all a pile of cakes and singing birds and Fairy Godmothers warring over evening gown colors instead of philosophy. Their retelling is nicer. It skips over the part where Rory's parents kept her in isolation under lock and key and the part where they burned all of her belongings to play the old "No princess here!" card whenever Malice returned. Most bafflingly, Humans don't even seem to know about the Fred business.

Figgy would say their minds are shutting down—they're forgetting. But I think it's just the opposite—maybe they're too fond of retelling stories, reshaping them to what's safe and comfortable. I should send a strongly worded letter to their equivalent of the *Tiara Tattler*.

Then again, if Rory doesn't want to remember Fred, why would the Humans? He tried to outwit fate with brawn. I suppose that storyline has been done to death Outside. Sure, he saved Rory's life, but only because Grimmland got hit with four seasons at once and Malice had to put everyone to sleep before they wandered outside and were flattened by a flying cow.

Of course Rory would never admit to being in mourning or denial or anything else, for that matter. She acts like everything is just a step away from perfect. You and CeCi think she's got her geese in a row, but she's completely delusional about her own imbecilic imbroglio. I don't know how she can be an expert on everyone else and still miss the fact that Henry is an overbearing, overloud, overwrought orangutan. (And those are his good points.) He's a moron and yet still smart enough to be an effective bully.

I can understand where he gets his bluster, because he probably has to spin the story in his favor just to look in the mirror in the morning. He can pretend he's exactly who Figgy inserted into the end of Rory's Pages—a savior. Here's her kingdom under its sleepy-time spell and most of the guys trying to break in end up in coffins. At the end of the century—and, conveniently, the spell—along comes Henry. He saunters in behind a couple of servants with sharp axes and avoids so much as a bramble scratch.

Picture it: At this point, Rory's already up, but out of it, blinking and rubbing her eyes and trying to sift what she remembers into the right category—dream or reality. She's still in love with Fred and at first she thinks he's her miraculous rescuer.

Then she has the horrible realization that Henry isn't Fred and Fred won't ever come back and she doesn't even have time to be sad about it because she has new Pages to complete. Still, she's alive and the Realm is safe, so who is she to question Henry's unbidden advances?

It isn't as if her parents helped any by offering to bestow their kingdom upon the couple as soon as Henry produced an heir. And then there are Henry's parents, who insisted Henry had saved everyone's life and was owed even more. If ever a wedding deserved its own TV movie, it was probably theirs—or so I gather from reading *Entertainment Weekly*.

Despite all their misguided storytelling, I'm not convinced Humans get to decide when things are over any more than Figgy does. We all—Humans and Fairy Tales alike—stop living when we stop dreaming. So screw Figgy. I'll go and dream where I want, Pages be damned.

And just maybe with whoever I want, too. Yes, Zell, I'm attracted to girls *and* guys. I appreciate beauty in all forms. And I appreciate being appreciated by all forms. Besides, I have a very short time to live things up before I marry my very own Sir Come to the Rescue next month. After that I'll be responsible to a whole palace, and no amount of soufflé will change that.

And while we're on that subject, you've written lots of nice notes, but nary a good excuse for why you're not coming to my wedding. I don't even know why I'm still writing to you, except otherwise I'd have to go share my thoughts with our new friend, Princess Pea Brain (who is *still* talking about her mattress problems). And that's definitely *not* going to happen.

B

Princess Briar R. Rose
Somnolent Tower Castle
South Road, Grimmland

Dearest Zell,

Are you sure you can't reconsider being here for Bianca's wedding? I'm not sure if CeCi and I are prepared to manage this very Bianca-style event all by ourselves.

It isn't even so much the wedding planning, though securing approval for even the smallest detail is impossible. The real problem is that Bianca is so obstinate about love. She already knows there's no way around the fact that she simply must marry William. It's right there in her Pages. If she'd just let herself fall in love with him, everything would work itself out. He must be humoring her with all that friendship and respect nonsense, don't you think? It's so nouveau, the idea that she might live independently once they're married, but surely he can't mean to follow through with such poppycock.

That must be why she hated *The Cake and the Damned* so much. Of course she's angry because she has to follow protocol instead of her whims. No one was around to tell her no when she was young, and no one has had the heart to since she survived the poisoned apple.

I suppose what I'm trying to say is, it isn't as if any of the rest of us got to choose who completed our Pages. Someday Henry will want to be my friend as well as my husband. Despite what everyone seems to think, I already *know* love requires work.

Bianca, on the other hand, chases love away. She and William are already good friends. Love is the logical next step, isn't it?

Instead of welcoming it, she's living out some petulant rebellion, misdirected anger at her abuse by that madwoman Valborg. (Grimm forbid we say anything about her father's role in the whole mess.)

Perhaps the bigger problem is that Bianca is up to her elbows in indebtedness. First, she's beholden to William for his genuine—albeit clumsy—assistance. It would have been so much more romantic if he'd woken her up with a kiss rather than by dislodging the apple she was choking on when he dropped her coffin. But we all know it almost never happens *exactly* the way it's supposed to.

If that debt weren't enough, she's busy petitioning the Fairy Council to rescind the ban on that Huntsman who set her free all those years ago. Bianca claims she was his first and last mark; she insists that he couldn't say no to Queen Valborg, but that he made the right decision in the end.

Then there are the dwarves. They've been good friends to Bianca, and she feels she owes them for her safekeeping. She probably doesn't listen to them, either. They've surely encouraged her to give love a chance. Except for the one with the terrible allergies, they're all coupled up these days—two pairs within the group, one with Goldi, and, since you left, another with Muffet.

My point is that Bianca most likely resents having so many people to please in her life. And all that resentment is just misplaced passion, isn't it?

She says she doesn't want to get married, but what could she possibly know about marriage itself? Her father was constantly back and forth between Grimmland and who knows where. Short trips, long trips, trips when he was with Bianca's mother, trips when he was with Valborg. Her stepmother was not exactly a paradigm of love and communication, either, except with that damned mirror. (If Bianca would only try to read the romance novels I give her, perhaps she'd have a bit more hope.)

Our futures are inevitable, Zell. And yet Bianca is so belligerent about the life she will one day lead. I've tried explaining to her that I could have sulked when I woke up, but instead I tried to accept what happened gracefully.

Bianca has her theories on whether the new Pages Figgy gave me were binding, but in truth, it doesn't matter anymore. They're complete now, and I'm living my life accordingly. Henry and I might not have been what the other expected when the celebrating was all finished, but I'm still trying to make it work, and Bianca should make an effort, too.

I don't mean to sound as if I don't appreciate what Fred did to save me—I wouldn't be writing you this letter had he not tried to destroy my original Pages. It was the ultimate Romantic Gesture, and he paid the price with his exile.

I wish you all could have known Fred. If you had, you'd know that True Love *is* real. The first time we ever spoke, I was filled with elation, an energy—not unlike the way you can feel music through the floor. It was like my whole world was suddenly clearer. And I never wanted to return to the way I felt before.

Once you've been loved a certain way, it's hard not to expect to feel the same again. Though now I suspect that love is a different sensation for everyone and every relationship.

So it seems for Henry and me. Here are the things I know we have in common so far:

Likes:

Wine

Roast beef

Dislikes:

Sharing a bed

Sharing a wardrobe

Versions of how we met

A relationship based on wine and roast beef isn't much to go on. But it is *something*. The point is, Fred's intentions were true, but we still lived lives apart. If Figgy's Pages say Henry is my True Love, then so be it.

I have faith Bianca will come around. If I can just convince her to concentrate on her wedding—on William—perhaps she'll see herself as I do: a princess worthy of a crown. When Figgy hands her that stack of golden, stamped Pages after her wedding, she'll change her attitude.

I wish I could count on CeCi's help, but she was no better after she completed her own Pages. Remember when Figgy handed her the seal of completion and CeCi threw it into the fireplace? I think she was so scared of starting over, she made her new life as close to her old life as possible, even keeping her stepsisters and that terrible Lucinda around.

This cooking obsession of hers isn't any different. She's returning to what's comfortable, despite the fact that it's not queenly by any stretch of the imagination. Edmund's parents have been on their farewell tour, preparing to hand over shared rule of Grimmland to Edmund, William, and Henry, for what seems like aeons. When they find out they're coming home to a daughter-in-law who's traded her scepter for a slotted spoon, they're likely to keel over from shock.

You and CeCi can do whatever you want, running hither and thither. But I'm setting a good example by embracing my destiny—it's supposed to bring me exactly what I want and need. And I'm certain that it will, if I'm patient. It isn't as if we don't all have doubts. My love for Henry is a different kind of love than I had with Fred, but roast beef and wine are just the first step. Soon I think we'll even try sleeping in the same room—well, you know, aside from our scheduled relations.

If I can try, so can Bianca.

Love,
Rory

A Princess Considered

From the Desk of Cecilia Cinder Charming
Crystal Palace
North Road, Grimmland

Dear Zell,

Thank you for the birthday present. I'll find somewhere to display my new unicorn magnet—though I don't have much metal in my room. Having something from your gift shop is certainly very exciting. I would have also liked a long letter detailing everything that's been going on since you got to Oz, but I suppose your days are best left to the imagination.

For example, I imagine that you wake up in the morning and take a walk around the property, feeding the unicorns apples or cubes of sugar as you go. Then, you return to the kitchen, where the staff has prepared breakfast and the sun shines in on the table and highlights the steam from the oatmeal and the eggs. The kids tell you they love you before they leave for the house of

the tutor (who must be the wife of your farrier or groom), and
Jason gives you a long and passionate kiss before the two of you
walk out the door to start your day, hand in hand.

You spend your time greeting your guests and telling them
about your mission and your aspirations. Women bring you
cake and tea and want to spend time with you because you're so
much fun to talk to. Jason shows the men around the property
and they clap him on the back and congratulate him for a job
well done. You gather again for dinner, laughing about the day.
The moonlight sparkles as you count the stars from the window of the children's bedroom. You drink a couple of glasses
of strawberry wine. And at the end of the day Jason loves you
doubly with his hands, his body, in order to see you with his
mind, remembering his former blindness.

If any of that is incorrect, please feel free to elaborate.

Rory and Bianca, of course, came to the birthday dinner
Edmund threw for me, but they gave me their gifts during a
quiet moment in the garden. Rory gifted me the most beautiful apron that she commissioned from Rumple's.

"For your next culinary adventure," she said.

I tried hard not to cry, but it seemed so hopeless. The most
beautiful apron, green with polka dots and a giant thick bow
and ruffles—almost like a dress in itself—and no possibility of
ever using it. "It's so pretty" was all I could choke out. Rory's
face fell from expectation to puzzlement to that horrible, guilt-
inducing concern. You know the look.

Before I could start genuine waterworks, Bianca stepped
between us and shoved a big envelope into my hand. It was a
welcome packet for a yearlong cooking course Outside at Le
Cordon Bleu in West Hollywood—not far from where we took
the soufflé class. A letter inside said that my schooling had met
the admissions requirements, my tuition for the year had been

paid, and there was one last test to take before my enrollment was complete. When I'm finished, I'll have a diploma in the Culinary Arts.

I can't believe it. I have no idea how I'll get the last test completed or how I'll get to and from the classes or how Bianca even managed the application or anything but, Zell, I'm so excited. I'll figure it all out. With everyone's help.

With Bianca's help, at least. I'm not sure Rory is on board with the plan. (She didn't say much, and her eyes got really big before she started gulping air like a beached carp.) We agreed to keep it a secret—well, excluding you—so don't say anything to anyone until I figure out how to break the news.

It was good Rory's apron was so extravagant. Edmund saw me putting it in my dresser after we retired to our chambers.

"What is that?" he asked, uncorking one last bottle of champagne.

"Oh, it's just a gift from Rory."

"Is it a dress? It's very . . . green."

"Not quite." His face registered brief confusion.

"You could give me a fashion show," he said, and winked.

I closed the drawer and turned to him. "Did you have a good time at the party?"

"Of course," he said. "Did you? I was worried when you disappeared, but then I noticed Thing One and Thing Two were also missing."

"Stop," I said, laughing. "You can't call them that."

"Forgive me, your highness." He looked at me intently, waiting for me to meet his eyes. But I was still so overwhelmed.

I gave him a quick smile. "I'm sorry I worried you. We had some, you know, secret girl stuff to attend to."

"Of course. It's silly. I know you aren't skulking around or anything. I guess if I'm honest I just, well . . . Never mind."

"What? No. Tell me."

He took a long sip of his champagne. "I don't want to sound controlling. I'm not. We have friends whose relationships aren't like ours. The fisherman's wife is always fencing his worms because she wants him to take a day off. The shoemaker is always ordering gifts for Gretel from Jimmy Choo and passing them off as his own. The point is, other couples keep things from each other. And I don't want that for us."

"I don't want that, either," I said. I could feel my neck and ears flushing. My gifts were evidence of a crime I hadn't yet committed, but most certainly meant to.

"I can make soufflé," I blurted. "It's hard to do."

"Of course you can," he said, putting his arm around me. "You could make a thousand impossible soufflés. But now let's leave the difficult stuff to someone else."

Zell, I let him kiss me then. I didn't try to argue. We're not speaking the same language right now. Perhaps when I can prove to him, to everyone, that this is more than a hobby to me, they'll be much more amenable to the idea. Right?

To thank the girls for their gifts, I'm planning on cooking a secret luncheon next week. Do you think you could make it? I know things aren't great with your mother-in-law, but at least consider it? We could drink strawberry wine and play Mad Libs for old times' sake?

Love,
CeCi

Important Fucking Correspondence from Snow B. White
Onyx Manor
West Road, Grimmland

Z,

Well, I certainly topped you this year for birthday gift giving. A magnet? Seriously, Zell. I know it might take awhile to build up trade credits in a new town, but what's going on out there? Your postcards are vague at best, and at worst, insulting. You've been a lot of things throughout our friendship, but you've never been cheap before.

I should explain about CeCi's classes. When we were Outside, I asked Head of Soufflés exactly where someone might go to school to become a "real chef." And she suggested this Cord on Blue joint. Solace won't let me go Outside on my own, lest I don't finish my stupid Pages, so I started exchanging letters via Pigeon Post with the Humans at the school. She still has to take a test to finalize her admission—they insist that it be done in person. And we still have to get her those crocodile shoes and some knives and things. Rory already bought her an apron. Oh, and she has that nice magnet you sent that will be, let me think, oh yes, totally fucking useless.

You should have seen CeCi's face, though. She was so happy. She looked free. For a second there I was almost jealous instead of self-satisfied.

Don't worry. It didn't last long.

CeCi has baked soufflés daily ever since we got back. She pays someone in the kitchen to clear off for a couple of hours after breakfast—telling the head cook she doesn't want anyone to see her eating scones.

For her secret thank-you luncheon, we ate cheese soufflé for a first course and chocolate soufflé for dessert. I'm so looking forward to her starting classes so that perhaps a vegetable might eventually join the mix. I admit, the best accompaniment to lunch would have been your sickeningly sweet face, but I guess not even CeCi's birthday rates your presence these days. I hope you're settling in nicely, because your mother-in-law seems to have someone's ear at Fairy Council and they're actually considering your banishment. Not Jason or the kids, just *you*.

Speaking of banishments, I got some good news today about the Huntsman. He's been allowed probationary access into Grimmland. He can visit during daylight hours, as long as he doesn't make trouble. If he doesn't take any more hit contracts this year, he'll be allowed full access again. I feel victory is near and justice will be accomplished. The dwarves say he was an asshole for taking the job in the first place but I say he still saved my life. Plain and simple. Give the dude a break.

You must be receiving letters from Rory, right? Do you think I gave her too many wedding duties? She's only on table decorations and music, but she seems more intense than usual. Maybe it's because Maro, the pea princess, has been hanging around over the past couple of weeks. As pea princesses go, I suppose she's fine. If Rory didn't loathe her so much, I might even see if she fits into that third bridesmaid dress I've got lying around. Unless you change your mind.

CHANGE YOUR MIND, YOU SELFISH COW.

B

Princess Briar R. Rose
Somnolent Tower Castle
South Road, Grimmland

Rapunzel,

You have to come back this instant. If you come back, then this Maro woman will leave because, well, there won't be enough chairs. Or teacups, will there? Or cake slices. Or plates.

CeCi invited her to the soufflé luncheon. We've only known her a little while, and she hasn't lived in Grimmland for more than a couple of months. How do we know she can be trusted? If the rest of CeCi's court finds out about her cooking, there will be *hell* to pay. Did she tell you she hasn't even told Edmund yet? This is all going to blow up in our faces. And no one will be able to say I didn't warn them. No one ever listens to me, though. *Rory's always overreacting, isn't she?* they say. Piffle.

I just have this feeling. Maro told us that the brouhaha about the mattresses was malicious gossip fabricated by the *Tattler*. Also she wears a pair of irritating wooden shoes everywhere— *clop clop clop*. She sounds like a two-legged horse. I must sound out of sorts to you, and I'm not trying to be. I suppose I'm simply not ready for a new addition to our social group. I tried to be nice. I tried to ask good questions, but everyone got mad at me.

"Why aren't you home with your husband?" I asked. Bianca took a big slug of wine and CeCi made a face like I had spit in the salad.

Maro grew flushed around the neck. "You know, we're still having the bedrooms redone. I swear, it's like they haven't redecorated in centuries."

"So you'll go back when they're finished?"

"I'm sure Albert will come fetch me just as soon as things are ready." She picked up her fork.

"But surely your court can handle the repairs. Why isn't he here with you? Won't he want to have relations?"

Maro stammered. Bianca refilled my glass and said, "You'll have to excuse our friend. Sometimes, she can't hold her wine, but she's entertaining as hell." I gave Bianca my best stern glare, but she kept sniggering into her port.

"Aren't you homesick?" I had to figure out why Maro was hedging.

"I suppose so," she answered, a strange smile on her face. "In a manner of speaking. But I've never lived anywhere for long. I guess I've just forgotten how to be homesick."

I probably should have felt sorry for her, but I really did want to know why she wasn't home keeping her husband company. "But you are going back, right?"

"Rory! Give it a rest." CeCi swatted me with her napkin.

Maro didn't answer me. She clopped away to flirt with one of the guards, and helped herself to another soufflé.

I can't explain why I don't trust her, but something about her sets me on edge. It's as if she's expecting something or maybe avoiding something—that's a curious way to behave if you have the option to go back home, lumpy bed or not. Henry and I are still working on the particulars of a perfect relationship, but I wouldn't dream of going to live somewhere else for six months, even if I liked that place very much. And while I can't believe that Maro would also throw away her perfect ending, Bianca lit right up at discovering another adventuring spirit.

Bianca will be getting plenty of practice flitting about with CeCi and her cooking school nonsense. For someone who barely has enough patience to order off a catering menu, it's almost unbelievable that Bianca was able to apply herself to anything as undoubtedly complex as school admissions. I'm just waiting for this to fall through and become CeCi's great disappointment. Even if the classes are legitimate, what happens when someone finds out where they're going? What if Bianca is only using CeCi's classes as an excuse to explore Outside? What if something happens to them? What if someone asks me what's going on? Has everyone gone mad?

I'd love to write more, but my presence has been requested at the Swinging Vine. I will try to be polite to Maro, despite the fact she makes my skin crawl. I know you'd say to avoid her, but that means I'd have to avoid everyone. Please come back so things can be normal again.

Love,
Rory

Dear Zell,

If you had bet me a thousand golden goblets, I'd have never guessed that Rory had the capacity to pour a drink over anybody's head. Maybe there's more going on with her than I thought. Regardless, our Sleeping Beauty officially has it out for the new girl.

Maybe it's just Rory's way of missing you. Or she's scared that I'm trying to replace you. Which is silly. What harm can possibly come of making new friends? When I saw Maro downtown at Gretel's buying bread, she seemed so lonely. Or maybe tentative. Or indecisive. Who knows? But I asked her to the luncheon, and she came. Unlike others who will remain unnamed, she did not complain about my two-soufflé menu.

Maybe you'll understand Maro a bit better if I describe her to you. She's got a toothy smile and a deep laugh. Her hair is that chestnut type of brown that all of us envy, but none of us have—you and I too blond, Rory and Bianca too dark. There's something mysterious about her that I can't quite put my finger on, something interesting, even shadowy. But we've only just met and I suppose I shouldn't rush to judgment. Even though she and Rory didn't get along terribly well at the luncheon, I had no idea things would get even worse.

Maro's most notable fault, I'd say, is that she's a tad overly affectionate. She's constantly clutching my arm or Bianca's shoulder. She plants kisses on lords and ladies and winks madly at anyone who passes by. Last night, she even tried her cleavage on DJ when we were having drinks at the Swinging Vine. He shook his head and said, "Honey, you are barking up the wrong tree." I imagine he and Rolf had a good laugh at that one when he got home—being hit on by the loudest pair of shoes in Grimmland.

Meanwhile, Rory was whispering loudly to me that women like that "can't ever be trusted." I asked her how she knew and she told me that all of her romance novels said so. I told her I'd take it under advisement, but I also told her to relax.

I thought maybe things would settle down afterward, but I should have known better. Maro had just finished her exchange with DJ when she sat back down and asked how long Rory had been awake.

"Five years," Rory answered. I know she hates the topic, though I was still surprised when she drained her wineglass.

"Do you miss your friends from back then?" Maro gave a pitying smile.

"Of course. But I know most of them lived full lives."

"What do you mean, most of them?"

"Well, some of them. I don't like to talk about . . ."

"Oh my dear, I didn't mean to make you uncomfortable. I merely wanted to hear the story. The curse. The daring rescue. The intrigue!"

"Intrigue?" Rory's mouth was hanging open a bit. Mine, too.

"The kiss, darling. The kiss! It's the most romantic story of all time!"

Bianca snorted. "Of *all* time?" She folded her arms in on herself in that indignant pose she takes. "No one actually gets woken up by a kiss, you know. That's all embellishment by the Humans."

"Oh, it's just a figure of speech," Maro said, waving a lazy hand at Bianca, who by this time was scowling.

"Henry came into the castle as I was waking up. I was still pretty out of it. It's not that big of a deal," Rory mumbled.

"Heavens, I hope you don't let him hear that." Maro gave a husky laugh, drawing her hand to her collarbone in dismay.

"Whatever do you mean?" asked Rory.

"No man wants to hear how *unimpressive* he is."

"I didn't say he was unimpressive. I simply pointed out that I was already awake. That maybe it wasn't quite the big production everyone makes it out to be."

"What a quaint little thing you are," said Maro, leaning back. Rory looked up and her eyes had changed from grey to bright blue—you know, like they do when she gets super pissed off—and in one smooth motion, she grabbed *my* wine and poured it over Maro's head.

Maro was prying, sure. I should have seen the conflagration coming. But I didn't.

Rory made for the door. Bianca got up to follow her, but first she stopped, got right in my face, and said, "You. This is your fault. Fix it."

I guess I'll have to keep them apart, at least until they call a truce. I never wanted that from my friendships—little cliques and alliances. Secrets. Secrets from friends, secrets from Edmund. I thought it might be easier to tell him about the classes once I've graduated, but now I'm not so sure. What do you think, Zell?

Thank you for writing that nice long letter. I'm sorry that we've all put so much pressure on you to write, but it's because we love you, and we assume the worst when we don't hear anything. I'm glad you've found a new tutor for the children and very sorry Dorothy isn't working out in the gift shop. I'm sure you'll be better off finding a new helper. She had no right to drink all your hot chocolate then say the preserve was "worse than Kansas"—whatever *that* means.

I'm sure Jason doesn't have any feelings for her, either. But probably the worst thing you can do is assume guilt and push him away without telling him why. If you have any doubts, talk to him. Figure out why it feels that way in reality or in perception. Has he really changed? Have you? Or are you simply still smarting from her insults? Try to take a step back from things. It's very hard for us to give you advice from so far away, but we support you and love you, no matter what.

Love,
CeCi

Important Fucking Correspondence from Snow B. White
Onyx Manor
West Road, Grimmland

Z,

You might want to make a note of this confession, because it will likely never happen again: I think I was wrong.

At first I thought our new pal Maro was all free spirit and traveler extraordinaire, just like me. But there's definitely something else up with her. She has no destination beyond Grimmland, and she isn't particularly eager to get back on the road, either. She's nosy. And those terrible clogs she wears—what is she thinking? I'm not sure I like having her around, but I made fun of Rory for not being nice to her and now I have to try not to be a fucking hypocrite.

I asked the dwarves if there'd been any scuttlebutt about Maro's husband, Prince Albert, or any recent news out of Swan Lake. Then they asked how many months it had been since I read the *Tattler*. They did not care when I told them I had far more important literature to consume of late. Anyway, they said Swan Lake's palace had been in disarray even before Maro's arrival—a spate of fake princesses trying to win the hand of the prince. Maro proved her pedigree by finding that preposterous pea in her bed. Word is she's been high maintenance ever since.

There has to be more to the story, but you can only trust dwarves to investigate rumors so far. It's why they love both mining and the *Tattler*—once they get to the shiny part, they get to quit digging.

What I need is Swan Lake's finest source of gossip. Lucky

for me, she happens to have been my bunkmate at Mary's Little Lambs Sleepaway Camp. Not only is Odette a duchess, she's also Prince Albert's cousin. She'll be sure to fill in the blanks.

I don't have any more time to waste on Maro because I have a fucking wedding to plan. William is annoyed that I've asked *all* of the dwarves to be in the wedding party. CeCi says she wishes she could cater the wedding—in disguise, of course. (I told her absolutely not, never, ever, no. At least not until she knows how to make more than soufflés.) And Rory's been missing in action.

I suppose Rory can be forgiven for wanting to hide after that whole pouring wine over Maro's head debacle. CeCi wants to believe they're even, but I say Maro had it coming with all that "intriguing kiss" nonsense.

Perhaps the most maddening development of late is that I've been informed that whatever punishment I choose for Valborg, it will need to be carried out on my wedding night.

Yes, you read that correctly. The Fairy Council expects me to execute my stepmother on what is supposed to be the happiest night of my life. I guess I should stop being hyperbolic because there's no way it would have been the happiest night of my life even without the meting out of random justice. But still, a wedding reception is supposed to be a goddamned party.

It seems like everyone else's Pages were a lot easier to finish. All of you got married, the end. No crime and punishment following your nuptials. There was the accidental mauling of Darling and Sweetie at CeCi's wedding, but that was because Figgy lost control of her stupid birds, right?

I think about Rory's Pages a lot. I mean, how do we know which parts are real and which parts Figgy added in? What if all this means nothing and all this pageantry—pretending I care what the rest of Grimmland thinks—is just for show? So what if I get lost Outside? Or in the Realm? (Sorry about the smear, there was a big gust of wind through the window and it blew your letter everywhere.)

Anyway, I've proved several times over that I am invincible. Just ask Valborg. You could also ask her simpering mirror, but I already smashed it to pieces and sold the remains to DJ for his new disco floor.

I know all of you think I'm angry and bitter, and you're right, I am angry and bitter. But not because she tried to kill me. I feel sorry for her. Can you imagine the world being so small that it fits into one pathetic mirror? She doesn't have any idea that there's a whole universe out there beyond her skin—the Realm, Outside, and everything beyond that hasn't been dreamed up yet. All she could see was herself.

We're all at risk of becoming imprisoned within our own mirrors. By our expectations of ourselves. We are vain or unkempt, bitches or sycophants, mothers or monsters, queens or servants.

I have no interest in pretending I'm better than anyone else. Which is why if I had my way, I'd ship Valborg's ass to the Snow Queen's North Pole Psych Ward and be done with this silly vengeance bullshit.

When I think about you leaving and CeCi gathering the courage to follow her dream, I'm angry and bitter that I can't do what I want to do. That there's a whole world that defines me and tells stories about me and I am almost completely ignorant of what that world contains.

I'm angry and bitter that I've never looked into a mirror and seen my *real* self staring back. Ugly, pretty, young, old, poisoned, cured—it's all meaningless until I figure out who I am or maybe who I want to become. Right now, I look in a mirror and I don't see anyone of any fucking consequence at all.

I'm angry with the part of myself that believes I owe William for saving me. Bitter because he was so agreeable to the compromise I've asked of him. I resent these Pages of ours, and I resent the Humans for writing them and Figgy for shepherding them into our lives. This isn't fair to any of us. I'm not in love with William, but in order to have a semblance of the life I want, we both have to carry on with this sham. I finish my Pages and William gets his father's crown. We both win.

William knows that I want to travel and he's told me it's okay. Not sticking around to be a proper queen to help him rule feels like cheating, though my guilt is self-imposed. He lets me come and go as I please. He plays a mean game of rummy, and he stocks my office with good bourbon. He's never chosen his parents' side over mine. He lets me keep my father's quarters preserved for his return. He laughs at my jokes. He listens to my opinions about the potential annexation of his lands and people west of Grimmland. This is as good as things get, right? Right?

Speaking of my father, I need to find out where he is. All my letters have been returned unopened. None of the birds can find him. I know he's been gone awhile—probably got caught up in some small village's bleeding-heart activism, or maybe he fell in love again. His last letter is dated the day I woke up. He must have just missed me; he probably thought I'd be asleep for a while like Rory. I can't blame him for taking one of his long, pensive jaunts, like the one he was on when Valborg came unhinged. But I want—no, need—him to be at the wedding. It's all a part of being the best Bianca I can be under the circumstances, see?

Have you heard anything about him in or around Oz?

William says to let it be. He thinks my father is to blame for Valborg. But my father wasn't there—and couldn't have guessed what she'd turn into. Empathy, in this case, is impossible for Will. His family is completely normal.

Good Grimm, your postcards are tacky. How come you can't send me some real letters? I hear you wrote CeCi a long letter. Then again, you also went to her wedding.

B

Princess Briar R. Rose
Somnolent Tower Castle
South Road, Grimmland

Zell,

I apologize profusely for your concern over what transpired at the Swinging Vine. I don't know what came over me. I don't want you to worry a bit or waste a drop more ink on the matter.

In fact, you'll be proud to know I've invited Maro over for tea this afternoon to try and begin our association all over again. A brand new start. I'm going to serve her lunch in the tower so that she can see just how "intriguing" the whole sleep affair was. I haven't been up there since just after I woke up, and I think it would do us both good to have some perspective.

I've decided I've been taking my frustrations out on Maro because she seems to get the things she desires so easily—freedom, friends, admirers, dresses, et cetera. Look how easily she entered our lives. A proper lady has to prove her pedigree, but Maro inserted herself into our circle and no one said a thing. I've decided it has to be because people want to know more about her. She is a walking puzzle, practically brimming with things unsaid—a prime example of that intrigue she seems to like so well. I've never had a shred of mystery about me—my whole life has been fodder for the *Tattler*.

First, it was the plight of a young princess, whose Pages sentenced her to death by spindle prick. Then it was the hubris of Fred, trying to change our future. After that, it was the sleep of the same young princess, while the Fairy Godmothers saved the world from ripping apart. And after Figgy repaired my Pages, Henry's "bravery" was retold and lauded throughout the land.

I don't know what came over me when Maro asked me about it. I should have been happy to tell the story the way Figgy arranged it. I'm sure Henry *meant* to fight through the brambles and wake me up with a kiss. I believe in my Pages, I do. Just because one tiny part didn't happen the way it was supposed to doesn't mean that the rest of the Pages are nullified.

My past isn't Maro's fault. I have to wrest this unpleasantness from inside of me. What if Henry saw me pouring a drink over someone's head? He'd be appalled. Or maybe he'd clap and cheer. I don't think either reaction is what I'm hoping for. What kind of wife and mother (not to mention queen!) does such things in public?

I finally decided on the design for the table decorations at Bianca's reception. They're sculptures, and I think you'd like them because there's something to represent each of us. A souf-flé dish (CeCi) is filled with a mountain of pink roses (my favorite flower), and on top sit the toy unicorns you sent. All of this is accented with white ribbons (an allusion to Bianca's name). I doubt my description is doing the centerpieces jus-tice, but hopefully Bianca will see the symbolism and under-stand how much we all love her and want her to live Happily Ever After, even if she insists on mucking it all up. Don't tell her, but I'm glad I don't have to decorate anything else. All this creativity is taxing.

Oh! I almost forgot to tell you the most important news. I'm going to adopt a pet. You know, for company and char-acter building. As soon as I wake up from my afternoon nap, I'm heading to Pets & Boots. Maybe Puss can set me up with a nice fluffy puppy or a luxuriant kitten or a parrot that I can talk to or maybe a grand, colorful fish in a grand, colorful bowl. I haven't decided.

I'll let you know how it goes.

Love,
Rory

From the Desk of Cecilia Cinder Charming
Crystal Palace
North Road, Grimmland

Dear Zell,

Edmund returned from his latest diplomatic summit in Wonderland three days ago. Negotiations on the Bunny Byway unraveled after the Queen of Hearts beheaded several contractors. As you might suspect, we're both glad he's back. He slept for the entirety of his first day home, celebrated his homecoming for the duration of the second, and this morning we finished catching up and began discussing the future.

He wanted to know what I thought of the design modifications he'd drawn for the Byway and what I'd been doing while he was away. He asked if Lucinda had refrained from meddling, and if Darling and Sweetie had found hobbies yet. (He finds their moping understandable, yet irritating.) He also told me that his parents would return from their Sea of Dreams cruise in time for Bianca's wedding, so he wanted to start work on the closest spare room to ours for a nursery.

I felt ill. The test date flashed in my mind, but how could I bring up the classes when we were destined to rehash a very old argument about the nursery? "Fine. I guess I'll ask Rumple's to send over some samples."

"What's wrong?" he asked.

"Nothing," I lied. I tried to look cheerful, but I must have failed. "Maybe I'm just not excited about yet more gold-striped fabric. Grimm forbid they make anything in silver."

"Let's use the Brave Little Tailor instead. Goldi will find us some nice, boring colors to use."

"Great. I can't wait."

He put his arm around my shoulder. "We don't have to *have* a baby right now, CeCi, we just need to look like we could."

"I know." But I was lying again. I don't understand. Why can't we just tell the king and queen that we may never be ready to have a child?

"Are you sure there's nothing else?" he asked. "You seem so distracted."

Edmund says that sometimes you have to fudge the truth in order to avoid hurting people. That's what we're doing to his parents. I suppose that's what I'm doing by not telling him about the classes. I just have to find the right time, and that time is not now.

You told me a long time ago that you were loved too much when you grew up in the tower—kept too precious. And I get that. But after my mother died, I was so lonely. Every day I wished that something or someone would come and take me away from it all. I dreamed of being somewhere, someplace else—maybe even like Rory, asleep, safe, full, warm, loved. But most of all, I dreamed of being wanted.

I swore back then that I'd never cause a child to depend on love that I couldn't guarantee. Life so often deals indelible losses through no fault of our own. I didn't want to let a kid down or disappoint them or fail them, or leave them frightened and hopeless.

When I see children like we did at the Magic Castle, I remember all the things I felt at that age—all that raw, directionless emotion—and it's terrifying. I recognize the resentment and confusion and all the boundless hoping and dreaming, when really, the future is nothing but a sparkling, pre-laid path to be painstakingly minded.

I can't be the one to tell a child that her world hinges upon the imagination of Humans and that we barely influence our own destinies. And furthermore, restrict consumption of ice cream and cupcakes. I don't know how you do it, Zell. Motherhood seems insurmountable.

I'm fortunate that Edmund doesn't want to be a parent, either. He doesn't want to dictate anyone's life, forcing costume galas and riding lessons and hunting rifles onto hapless young things. But soon we'll have to answer our subjects' questions. If we don't answer them honestly, won't we borrow trouble down the road?

I think if we just explained ourselves, we could make people see we're being responsible. There are lots of people who know they *do* want to be parents. Like Rory, who's been trying to get pregnant since she woke up. I wish it would happen for her. Maybe the problem stems from an excess of sleep. Maybe it's Henry. Maybe she's trying too hard or not hard enough.

Come to think of it, maybe we can ask Figgy to help. It's the least she can do. Whether or not you believe Bianca's claim that Figgy's addendum of Henry to Rory's Pages wasn't binding, Figgy owes Rory for saddling her with that idiot. I've had my quibbles with Figgy. (Rory and Bianca keep telling me that the birds she sent to help me prepare for Edmund's ball were a lovely gesture. But *they* didn't have to clean up all the bird shit afterward. And don't even get me started on the starlings that attacked Darling and Sweetie at my wedding.)

But I'll forgive and forget for Rory's sake. We need some sort of potion, and Figgy knows how to make one.

Love,
CeCi

Important Fucking Correspondence from Snow B. White
Onyx Manor
West Road, Grimmland

Z,

So, I'm sitting at Shambles with a couple of the dwarves and we're reminiscing over old times in the cabin in the wood, arguing over who folded the best origami napkins and how Ben was constantly nailing "No Soliciting" placards onto the house for my benefit. CeCi stomps in looking purposeful. Max and Tripp finish their martinis and excuse themselves so they can head off to pick out a new end table at Three Bears Antiques.

CeCi barely registers their departure, sliding into a stool on the other side of me and brushing the peanut shells from the table. I pour her a cider from my pitcher and she drinks it down in two big gulps. She shovels a few pretzels into her mouth, drinks half of another glass, and lets go a rather large belch.

"Bianca," she says. "You've taught me something."

"Certainly not table manners." I drop a pile of paper napkins in her lap. "But do tell."

"It's good to be proactive."

"Okay," I say, eyeing her cider. "How many of these did you have before you came over?"

"It's good to be brave, Bianca. To keep moving." She draws a line in the air with her palm. "I worked my whole childhood and, even though I was miserable, I knew my purpose. Now, I'm not miserable. Fine, I'm a little miserable. Because I have no purpose. Yet. I don't know if I'll ever be able to tell anyone how much Cordon Bleu means to me."

Camille Griep

I am momentarily relieved that her behavior seems to be some crisis of gratitude. "It's no big deal. You know, I wanted to explore Outside, anyway."

"I'm serious, Bianca. Your being brave helps me be brave."

"Seriously, stop it with the gushing or I'll cut you off." I slide the already empty pitcher of cider away from her.

"You know how I hate kids?"

"There we go," I say, slapping the table. "That's more like it."

She gives me a shove. "You know what I'm saying, like how I don't want kids?"

"Yes. I am acutely aware."

"You know how Rory really wants kids?"

"Are we playing a game of Twenty Questions We Already Know the Answer To?"

She flaps her hands in frustration. "Come on, Bianca."

"Then yes. I'd have to be deaf not to know both yours and Rory's stance on child—"

"I can help. We can help."

I laugh. "I'm pretty sure that's not how sex works, CeCi."

"Get your mind out of the gutter. We can go to Figgy."

Neither of us is a big Figgy fan, so I am less than enthused. "How's Figgy going to help?"

"Fertility potion," she says, and sweeps the pretzel crumbs into a neat pile. "Figgy saddled Rory with Henry, so she should make things right."

I grit my teeth. I've tried, for Rory's sake, to drop the subject of her revised Pages. Seems to me Fred's banishment more than paid for his mistake, so why did Rory need new Pages at all? She wakes up. The end. No need to intimidate the populace or perpetuate the importance of Fate. Message received: Don't fuck with the Pages.

Figgy seems to have replaced one trial with another—Rory

66

escaped death but now she has to deal with Henry—and you'll never convince me that the change was real or binding. I'm sure it was the result of some quarrel between the Fairy Godmothers (who, incidentally, make me glad I don't have any sisters).

CeCi derails my train of thought. "I know what you're thinking, Bianca. But this time Figgy can give her some actual help."

"You're the one who hates Figgy with, and I quote, 'the fire of one thousand suns.'"

She resumes tearing a paper napkin to bits. "We can take the high road for Rory's sake, can't we? When we go see Figgy, you have to tone it down a little, too."

"If you'll remember, Cecilia, Figgy dismissed us last time because you said if you ever saw one of her birds again you'd 'put them on a rotisserie.'"

She throws the napkin pieces at me. "Well anyway, I'm sure that's all blown over by now. Let's keep it that way."

I think about pressing her, but I decide I'd like to see what happens. "Figgy's expensive," I say. "Do you have enough worms?"

"I'll get them."

"How?"

"Tiaras."

"Just gonna hawk 'em?"

"Why not?"

"Lucinda will have a thousand reasons why not," I say.

She shrugs and shoves another handful of pretzels into her maw. "She promised not to meddle. Signed an agreement, even."

I let the Lucinda issue drop, but I still can't understand why she's picked up Rory's cause so fervently. "So you just woke up and decided that Rory needs to be knocked up?"

"Everyone's attention is elsewhere." Her mouth is still half full of pretzels. I have no idea why this brainstorm has obliterated her etiquette. "We've been wrapped up in sub-terfuge and getting Outside. Not to mention your wedding. Rory's lost in the tumult. Maybe that's why she got so upset with Maro. It's time we made her a priority."

I think Rory gave Maro a wine bath because Maro is a meddlesome bimbo who's bound to cause trouble and, even though Rory doesn't know that's why she doesn't like her, *that's why she doesn't like her.*

Regardless, we set a date to go see the big bird on Friday. As soon as we come to an agreement, CeCi stomps out as baf-flingly as she stomped in. Everyone's going nuts. There must be something in the water.

And speaking of nuts, I'm sure Jason will get used to the country, eventually. It sounded like a good idea to him when you moved, right? I'm assuming you did discuss it together at length like responsible adults before you decided to go, did you not?

Change is hard. He doesn't have William or Edmund around to blow off steam with. I bet there isn't a Shambles within stumbling distance. How long has it been since he's shot magical arrows at something? You'll have to give him some time. He'll see the beauty in it someday, even if the dirt under his nails is looking ugly right now. And if he doesn't come around to loving the place, he'll at least be able to see how happy it makes you. I bet it makes you as happy as getting a letter from your estranged friend who moved to Oz! I got one, so I'm going to go celebrate.

Wish us luck at Figgy's. We'll almost certainly need it.

B

Princess Briar R. Rose
Somnolent Tower Castle
South Road, Grimmland

Dearest Zell,

CeCi, Bianca, and I had a lovely lunch at Gretel's Café today. Hansel traveled Outside recently, scouring Human supermarkets for new ingredients, and so there are quite a few new things on the menu. Gretel has come to favor something called *ketchup*, and while it's delicious, I think maybe not quite so many things should be made with it, pies in particular. It's a very pretty tomato color, and I will admit it goes well with fried potatoes.

Bianca ate quite a lot of it. I told her that she should be careful lest she not fit into her wedding dress and she held up her middle finger at me, like the motor coach men did when we arrived at the Magic Castle. I've gathered that it's a gesture that means that the gesturer does not like what one has said or done and plans to disregard it. Or that the gesturer plans to consume your potatoes as well as hers and ask for another bottle of ketchup. One guess is as likely as the other.

I told CeCi and Bianca about the tea I planned with Maro. CeCi didn't say very much, and Bianca told me to cancel the date. Actually, she commanded it. But I'm finished letting Bianca boss me around. I am going to embrace my own decisions. When I don't like something, they fall in love with that very same thing. When I change my mind, they change theirs back. While amusing for them, I find the exercise completely draining. I'm sure they didn't think I saw them walking away after lunch, heads bent together in secret, not sparing a single thought of how that must have felt to me.

I wonder if you know how lonely it is to have once been a part of a group and then suddenly feel as if you aren't a part of it anymore—as if you've missed out on the joke and it floats around you constantly like a bee ready to sting. I can't say I like the feeling at all. I'm sure they'd tell me it's all in my head or that I've misinterpreted things or that I'm just plain wrong. You may even agree. But that won't make it any better. I feel as if I've been left behind, and yet I'm still standing right here.

If I'm honest, I suppose I've felt that way ever since I woke up.

That's why my new bulldog, Snoozer, is the perfect companion for me—he is a champion sleeper. He's fat and brown and not yet grown into his skin. I'll have the court artist paint a small picture to include in my next post. You'll have to excuse my handwriting; he's chewing on the other end of my quill as I write.

Tonight I'm auditioning cellists for the wedding, and after that I have scheduled relations with Henry. I miss you, Zell, and I hope you're doing all right with all the chaos life is throwing at you. I'm sure Jason will find a way to repair the house and the barn and the well. We're very lucky not to have witches or farmhouses falling out of the sky here in Grimmland. Don't worry, the kids will stop fighting and so will the unicorns. This is your dream and, according to CeCi, dreams never come easily.

Love,
Rory

The Blank Pages of Her Life

From the Desk of Cecilia Cinder Charming
Crystal Palace
North Road, Grimmland

Dear Zell,

Worms are disgusting. In a big pile, they look like raw meat, and they don't smell much better, either. I traded the fisherman's wife an old tiara for two baskets. Edmund won't notice, but Lucinda most definitely will. I'll have to worry about that later.

Figgy's tree looks bigger than ever, if you can believe it. The woodcarver put new stairs in since we'd been there, which was good because things were getting a bit dicey if you ask me. Bianca brought a bottle of ketchup as a gift, a condiment for worms. When I told her she was bizarre, she told me that my trap was flapping and I should shut it.

Figgy has switched her sentinels from those crested blue jays to a bunch of fat robins. Inspection was quicker than usual and we were hustled into her grand living room. She's obviously been doing quite well these past few years.

"Who, who, who comes to visit today?" said Figgy, swiveling her head from her desk to us as she threw out her traditional greeting. She's greyer than she used to be, her plumes a bit shaggy around the edges. But those round, sharp eyes are as clear as ever. "Ah, well. If it isn't my two favorite princesses."

Bianca wheeled around. "Where?"

Figgy burst into laughter as she rose, wrapping us in her wings.

"And Miss Cecilia," Figgy said, composing herself. "What is it that you've brought me?"

"Half is a present and half is a payment for services to be rendered," I said.

"I see," she said, taking a basket on each wing and setting them to the side. "Many thanks—"

"And I brought you some ketchup to try with your meal," Bianca added. Figgy shut one eye as she examined the bottle.

"We're here about Rory. Briar Rose," I said. I didn't want to spend any more time in her warm living room than we had to. A music box tinkled its melody into the room, making things seem even more cloying.

"Briar Rose's Pages are finished," Figgy said, returning to her desk. "What could she possibly need from me?"

Bianca glowered. "She needs your help, Figgy."

"But the birds have told me no such news. She has followed the path, my dear."

I can understand how Figgy was chosen to be the Keeper of the Pages. Solace welcomes new information as it streams through the portals, but Fairy Godmother Figueroa does things strictly by the book. And Grimm help us when there's no book.

"I'm sure you know she wants children," I explained. "But things, they aren't working."

"What things specifically?" asked Figgy.

"Well, I—I'm not sure exactly," I stammered. "But she's not getting pregnant."

"How do you know what sort of assistance she needs, then?"

"I don't. I don't know that." I willed myself to stop blushing.

Bianca rolled her eyes at me. "Are you saying you won't help her?"

Figgy sat back down at her desk, chuckling to herself. "Oh, no, my dears. I didn't quite say that."

"Can't you make a potion? Perhaps a fertility potion or an elixir of romance," I suggested.

"I can indeed. But a potion might not be the solution to her troubles."

"The spell Malice used when she put Rory to sleep—did it damage her, you know, insides?" I asked.

"She has aged, my dears, but not so much so that she is unable to have children. Is this what has you in such a state? I have half a mind to tell the Post to cease delivery of all those fatuous magazines."

Bianca was holding her chin with one hand, and her other arm folded over her chest.

"What?" I growled under my breath. "I can see your clockwork smoking from here."

"Maybe Figgy's trying to tell us something."

"What is it, Figgy? Just tell us." My voice went a little hoarse.

Figgy looked into my eyes. "My dear, it takes two, does it not?"

Bianca began to pace. "I knew it! I heard he's been messing around with at least three of the Waltzing Wandas, and they aren't pregnant, either."

"Who told you that? But they could have—" Figgy looked flustered. "Now girls, you know I never lay blame."

But she had implied it. I wondered if Rory had considered that the problem was Henry's. Knowing her, she'd still find a way to blame herself.

Bianca shrugged. "If he's shooting blanks, then give us something for him instead."

"Is that wise, my dear," said Figgy, "considering his, ah, indiscretions?"

I flopped down in an overstuffed chair. "Shit."

"There, there," said the old owl. She made a slight movement with her head, and two tiny canaries delivered me a handkerchief and a cup of tea. I tried to wave them off. "I don't want any of this, Figgy."

"Come now, we've discussed our differences. You can't continue to harbor ill feelings toward me. The birds and I merely helped you fulfill your Pages."

I couldn't meet Figgy's eyes, lest my surliness betray itself as actual sadness. Maybe we had been unrealistic to think Rory's happiness lay in Henry's attentions or even a child.

"Pages. Horseshit," said Bianca, refolding herself. "Don't get me started."

I picked at the edge of the hanky. "Figgy, how come you're so eager to help people who don't want your help and then can't be bothered to help those who do?"

"Briar Rose is not here seeking my help, is she? I would venture to guess that she doesn't know that you're here at all. Is that true?"

"You aren't being fair." I sniffed. "We're her friends. We can't just let her suffer." Both Bianca and Rory had kept my secret and done everything but take the test for me. Trying to help Rory seems to be the very least I can do.

"Come back in five days. I'll think on it til then." She shooed us out into the branches. It seemed much windier than when we arrived.

I glared at Bianca. "Fat lot of help you were."

"Like you were any better? She said she'd think about it. Stop being so bitchy."

So we came home empty-handed in every way. I don't even feel up to sneaking down to the kitchens to bake. I can't believe I'm so useless that I can't even manage to buy a love potion from a Fairy.

Love,
CeCi

Important Fucking Correspondence from Snow B. White
Onyx Manor
West Road, Grimmland

Z,

Figgy is considering our request. Contrary to what CeCi thinks, all hope is not lost.

I empathize with CeCi's anger, but I can't get it through her thick skull that she's mad at Figgy for the wrong offense. She blames Figgy's birds for Darling and Sweetie's blindness. But CeCi is the one who saddled herself with their care instead of marrying them off to a couple of Edmund's friends. (He has to have at least a couple who aren't picky about feet.)

She made the decision not to send her stepsisters away. And *she* kept Lucinda around for their sake. If she's mad at Figgy for anything, it should be for maiming the twins instead of her father.

I suppose none of you hit the jackpot in the parental division. Not even Rory. Can you imagine what her parents were like? Always doting on her, controlling her, championing her, planning her wedding? Even when they realized Henry was a blustering jerk, they smoothed things over with commentary like "Ahem, is there any more of that wine?" Then they wiped their hands of the entire mess, moved over to the south wing of the palace, and proceeded to order room service for the next five years.

When I find my father, I'm going to tell him that I'm glad my memories of us together, as few as they are, are happy ones. I expect I'll hear from him any day now. He'll tell me where he's been. I'll talk to him about Outside and thank him for all the money and the journals he left for us to use. Without them, I'd never have been able to help CeCi.

Speaking of, we've put off approaching Solace for long enough. We have to go Outside again next week so that CeCi can take the test to finalize her admission to the cooking school. And we still have to buy the rest of her supplies so she can start the week after. This will be a perfect excuse for another bachelorette party. This time, no soufflés. I want to go to a fancy hotel, to a fancy restaurant, to Disneyland!

I wrote you a short poem:

Rapunzel, Rapunzel, let down your hair
And come Outside with three friends fair.
So many fun things to see and do
Alas, you must shovel the unicorn poo.

(Did you see? I can rhyme! I amuse myself.)

B

Princess Briar R. Rose
Somnolent Tower Castle
South Road, Grimmland

Dearest Zell,

When Maro arrived today, she suggested we have tea outdoors on the "pretty green grass." But I told her that here in Grimmland, the weather is perfect and the sky blue and the clouds puffy and the hills purple and the butterflies yellow almost every single day. I may have intimated that she wouldn't be invited to see my tower every single day. And that it was *my* luncheon. (I said that I was trying to be benevolent toward Maro, not that I have perfected such behavior.) She agreed and followed me up all the stairs, her jeweled hand riding on her heaving chest.

Halfway up we met Henry, coming from his chambers. I introduced Maro and, curiously, she bowed instead of curtsied. At first I hoped Henry wasn't looking at her bosom, but I suppose even I was looking at it, as generously as it had been presented. She righted herself and I impulsively invited Henry to join us for tea. He declined, stating he was leaving for a few weeks of hunting and needed to make preparations. However, he did appear to consider it, for which I was quite heartened. I told you we'd eventually make progress.

At the top of the tower, the maids had set out crumpets and scones and fruit and honey. It's a long climb up there, you know, so the tea was a bit tepid. But the complete privacy was splendid—and the view! From the large eastern window, I can see the glittering spires of CeCi's castle to the north and the black columns of Bianca's palace to the west, and the whole town in between. I can see the Wolf Woods and the edge of your castle—or, I suppose, the castle that used to be yours. I can see Figgy's big tree and the large gear on top of Solace's shop and the yellow road that leads to Oz and, eventually, to you. There's so much out there, the Realm ever expanding. And we are so small, aren't we?

Anyway. It was a fine tea. Maro is quite adept at carrying on conversations without input or assistance, and eventually I began to nod off. I excused myself—I'm not used to having to explain how sleepy I get—and she saw herself out. I'm glad I extended an olive branch. I've demonstrated far more maturity than CeCi and Bianca. First they're hot, then they're cold. I'm quite pleased with myself for adjusting my attitude.

One odd thing happened afterward, though. Following my nap, I made my way down to the conference chamber to confirm the musical arrangements with the cellist I've selected for Bianca's wedding. (Can you believe he had the nerve to suggest Pachelbel's monotonous Canon in D? I almost fired him on the spot.)

I was rounding the corner to the courtyard when who should I bump into but Maro, who I thought had left hours earlier. Evidently she'd been so taken with the tea sandwiches that she'd asked for a lesson in the kitchen—in the spirit of CeCi's intrepid pioneering. I reminded her that CeCi's machinations were still secret, and she assured me she hadn't breathed a word. I am a paragon of trust, aren't I? There was a time when I would have gone running to Bianca and CeCi trying to assign Maro nefarious intent.

I hope you enjoy the enclosed portrait of Snoozer. Please send a stuffed unicorn chew toy from the gift shop, if you have one in stock. Oh, and maybe a nice pink unicorn collar? I'll have my barrister forward the appropriate credits.

I'm so sorry to hear about young Bea's continued allergy problems. How fortunate Arthur was spared. (I thought twins shared *everything*!) Being allergic to unicorns while living on a unicorn preserve seems most inconvenient. I ran into Bianca's dwarf friend, the one with chronic rhinitis, at the apothecary yesterday and I'm sending a few of the potions he recommended. Let me know what works best and I'll send another batch. I'm sure Oz has physicians, but after hearing about that whole fake wizard debacle, I'd be careful about who you trust until you get your bearings around there. Also, try bee pollen. Or honey. Or maybe both.

Snoozer needs to perambulate, but I'll write again soon.

Love,
Rory

From the Desk of Cecilia Cinder Charming
Crystal Palace
North Road, Grimmland

Dear Zell,

I don't know why we even went back to Figgy. We should have known that she was going to tell us no. Figgy's the kind of Fairy Godmother who swoops in and claims to save the day, not the kind who grants requests. We'd barely made it past the door when she announced, "I'm dreadfully sorry, girls. But after much consideration I must tell you that I cannot help you."

"That's not true," I said, annoyed I'd gotten my hopes up. "You just won't."

"I've given it a great deal of thought, Cecilia. It's just that there could be too much collateral damage if I interfere. The areas in which I work are grey indeed, but I simply cannot. The possible outcomes are too complex. Lives could be altered in unforeseen ways. Things could go terribly wrong."

"You're completely arbitrary, you know that?" Bianca said. "You were fine with interfering when you repaired her Pages. The least you could do is help her start a family."

"There were greater forces at stake than you could hope to understand, Snow White."

Bianca rolled her eyes. "Oh, quit it, Figgy."

"If I hadn't ended Rory's tale with her rescue by a prince, Malice might have made good on the threat she made at Briar Rose's christening. I saved your friend's life, and this is the thanks I get?"

I could feel the rage creeping hot through my chest. "So giving her a life of miserable futility was better than trying to reason with your sister? If Malice is so big and bad, what's stopping her from setting up another spindle and finishing Rory off? You're covering nonsense with more nonsense."

"You may still be angry with me about your own Pages, Cecilia, but the birds helped you become who you are."

"They also destroyed Darling and Sweetie's lives. There was no justification for you to set loose your winged weapons after my wedding. They didn't deserve to be punished."

"Sometimes my emissaries are a bit overexuberant. If the girls hadn't swatted at them so much—well, what's done is done."

"Why couldn't you have punished Lucinda, instead? Why do you insist on destroying the innocent? The girls. Rory. When does it stop?"

"My actions *were* a punishment for your stepmother, and if you can't see that, then the birds blinded you, too."

"Come on, Bianca. Let's go home."

Figgy's head spun around, as it does when she's spooling herself up. "Not so fast, Cecilia. I'm not even close to finished with you two. As long as we're airing grievances, I'd like to point out that neither of you had been born yet, let alone witnessed the aftermath of the nightmare Rory's paramour, Fred, created. This arrogance and ignorance of yours will bring us all to ruin. What could you possibly hope to accomplish by doing something as dangerous as taking Snow White Outside before she's finished her Pages?"

"Hey, I'm right fucking here," Bianca said. "It was my choice."

"You think I don't know things," the owl continued. "The birds were chattering, of course. It isn't every day three of Grimmland's princesses visit Solace. Where were you off to, I wondered. Neverland? Wonderland? I hear Toyland is quite nice this time of year. But no. You should be ashamed, roping Briar Rose into your nonsense. Think of the memories this must dredge up for her."

"We were perfectly responsible," Bianca said. "And Rory had fun for once. She needs a distraction even more than we do. Which is why we came to you in the first place."

Figgy swept her wings to her side in a flap of annoyance. "The very idea! If you were trapped Outside . . ."

Bianca smiled her not-very-nice smile. "I decide where I go and when. If I go Outside and never come back, it won't make a bit of difference."

A big gust of wind shook the tree house, and Figgy threw her wings wide. "See what you're doing, you—you reckless girl!"

"Oh, come on," Bianca said, unfolding her arms wide. "I'm not a child anymore. You can't expect me to believe that I control the fucking wind. Come on, blow, wind, blow!" Nothing happened. Bianca leaned out the window. "Hey, you blustery bastard, get back here!"

"You girls won't be satisfied until you've completely destroyed our lives." Figgy turned toward the windows, shuddering. "Do you know why there are rules about traveling?"

"Because you are the enemy of fun?" Bianca said, pinching a canary feather from her gown.

"If you became trapped with unfinished Pages the repercussions would be unimaginable. Hasn't Briar Rose served as warning enough?"

"The Fred and Rory story is getting tiresome," I said, "Besides, Fred didn't get trapped Outside; he interfered with her Pages and was banished. It's completely different."

"It is exactly the same outcome, no matter how the Pages are disturbed." Figgy clicked her beak at Bianca. "A great storm, your timeline ripped from the world, every interaction spinning backward, your friends, your family. If your father were here, he would say—"

Bianca was spitting mad. "But my father isn't here, Figgy. I don't need his permission or yours to do anything or to go anywhere. Regardless of your opinion, I *am* an adult." Another big gust rocked the treetop.

"The clock portals regulate the magic of time, time that is *easy to lose track of Outside*. Solace and I agreed her portals would open into a safe place, a place where Humans won't suspect us when we appear, where we can observe them and quickly return. It's just as dangerous for you, Cecilia, as it is for Snow White. If an accident or a disaster or some obstacle shouldn't allow you to return, the magic of the Realm would eventually wear off, and you would never be able to come back."

"You and Solace are pretty cagey about how long *eventually* is," I said.

"Outside," Figgy said stiffly, "is a very complex place."

"Translation: You have no idea," Bianca said. "Typical."

It was Figgy's turn to be ruffled. "Solace ascribes to the dangerous belief that we need to understand how the Humans are evolving. How they think of us. I suppose knowing more about the future of Humans helps us to know how long their imaginations will last, how long we have left—if our Realm will continue to grow or shrink to nothing. But in my opinion, the portals should be shut down entirely. What are we to do with this information once we have it? Needless danger."

Bianca snorted.

"Why can't you girls simply be happy with what *is*?"

"You trap us here and expect us to like it? When there's a gigantic Outside full of shit we don't know anything about— constantly evolving and being created—and we should just sit here and be happy? How does that work?"

"How can we not want more?" I added, more softly.

"Our Realm," said Figgy, "is even bigger than Outside. Explore what's here. Let the birds bring the rest."

"How convenient for you," Bianca said. "Rory remains childless and CeCi is bored silly and I get to marry someone I don't love. Good times."

"We should have known you wouldn't help," I said, for what felt like the nineteenth time.

Figgy froze. "Promise you'll never go Outside again, and I'll help you."

"Go fuck yourself," Bianca spat. Figgy blinked at her sentinels. We needed to get out of there before she sedated us or threw us into the forest like she did the time I threatened to barbecue her guards. I turned for the door.

"Hold it," Bianca snapped. "She owes us a refund."

"How about a nice flying spell?" asked Figgy, slipping a bottle from her apron.

"What the hell are we supposed to do with a flying spell?" Bianca waved the bottle away.

We had somehow lost the upper hand. Figgy gave a slight shake of her head. "A summoning spell, instead? Those are always nice when you need something off a tall shelf—"

I reached out and took the summoning spell with one hand, Bianca's sash with the other, and marched us out the door.

"Way to lose your composure in there," I said. "You were very helpful."

"Like you did any better. Honestly, a summoning spell? You couldn't have held out for something more useful?"

I let go of her once we reached the landing. "You were about two insults away from having us becalmed. You remember how fun that was, right?"

"You can't put that one on me," she said. "That was all you and your little blond temper."

"You know, you aren't a very nice person sometimes."

"Yeah, being called on your shit sucks, doesn't it, Cinderella?"

"Go choke on an apple."

"I would but your fucking worms ate them all."

I fought a panicked giggle. How had we messed things up so badly? "What are we going to do about Rory?"

"Guess she'll have to get knocked up without us."

"You're impossible," I said. We walked the rest of the way, lobbing insults back and forth until we couldn't stop laugh-crying. Bianca asked me in for squab skewers, but as tempting as it was, I suddenly wanted to be home to unravel all of Figgy's threats and insinuations. Why did she offer to help Rory if we agreed to stay? Why is keeping Bianca in line so important? Is my dream really worth all this, if I'm the one responsible?

What do you see in all of this, Zell? What are we missing?

Love,
CeCi

Important Fucking Correspondence from Snow B. White
Onyx Manor
West Road, Grimmland

Z,

Our second trip to Figgy's was such a complete disaster it's barely worth retelling. To sum up, we're all being spied on by birds and CeCi thinks having our principles questioned is permissible because we made it out the door with a summoning potion.

Regardless, we forge ahead with the day of bacheloretting. I discover, upon rescuing CeCi from an intense Q&A with Lucinda, that she's come up with an elaborate story for Solace. She explains it with great big swooping gestures while she, Rory, and I lug our overnight bags to the clock shop, Rory's new dog panting behind us.

"I still don't see why we couldn't use porters," Rory whines.

"Who's going to carry your crap once we're Outside?" I ask. "Making you haul a bag limited the number of slippers you deemed necessary, didn't it?"

CeCi is still going on and on with her confabulated tale. ". . . Then we'll tell her that we left something there. At the Magic Castle. Like my shoe or something, because, you know, that's happened before. Leaving my shoe. Not losing things Outside. If we don't retrieve it, a Human will get suspicious. A Human child, that's better. Because they're curious. And grubby. Remember the one with the popsicle? That will work. And then . . ."

I try to listen as politely as can be expected. But then I can't anymore. "CeCi?"

"And then—"

"CeCi, stop."

"Why?" Her hands are paused in midair so I gently push them to her sides.

"Why don't we try telling Solace the truth?"

"What?"

"Truth. As in facts, events that are actually occurring."

"Thanks, smartass."

"Well?"

She shakes me off. "That's a terrible idea. She'll never let us go."

"How do you know?"

"Fine. I don't know. But I'm not the one who's not allowed to travel."

"She said it was our right, didn't she?" I try to start us walking again by giving CeCi a slight shove.

She refuses to move. "I don't think she said anything about it being *your* right."

"Stop it, you two." Rory drops her bag, takes a seat, and starts patting the dog's head. "We all need each other. CeCi, we'll have to take turns escorting you. Snoozer has obedience classes now and Bianca still has a lot of wedding planning to do."

"This was a dumb idea anyway." CeCi turns and starts walking toward home. "Who knows if I'd even pass the test?"

I call after her. "You'll eat that fucking test for breakfast."

She turns, again, and frowns at me. "You have strange motivational techniques."

"I know." I lead the way to the Clock Shop, feeling somewhat victorious. We've successfully navigated the day's first fight.

Solace is waiting for us at the door. It isn't like she can't tell what we want by looking at us. I see one of Figgy's birds on the windowsill and I give it the middle finger.

Rory says she's going to wait on the lawn until Snoozer

relieves himself. Solace shows CeCi and me to a room behind the counter where the rules plaque sits. Inside the room, it's completely silent.

"Wow," I say, my ears suddenly aching from the quiet.

Solace's face breaks into an ever-so-bucktoothed grin. "You don't think I could stand that noise all of the time, do you?"

"Um," says CeCi, moving a pile of cogs from a dusty chair. "You never know."

"So," says Solace, as we settle into our seats. "Go ahead and ask."

"Ask?" asks CeCi.

"Oh, quit it," I say. "Solace, we need to go Outside again."

"Snow White, what is it that you need from the Humans that is not available to you here?"

I throw CeCi under the proverbial carriage. "It's not for me. It's for her."

"Thanks a lot," CeCi mutters.

Solace folds her paws in her lap. "Well, Cecilia has completed her Pages. She's allowed to travel as long as she has a companion."

"Well, that's just it," I say. "It can't always be Rory—there will be times when she just can't get away. She gets so tired. And she has a new dog. Sometimes I'll have to go."

"I don't understand," says Solace. "*Anyone* else could go."

"No," CeCi says. "It can't be anyone. It's, well, for now, it's a secret."

Solace twitches her nose, perplexed or maybe just vexed. So I jump in. "CeCi thinks if she tells the court, it will go over like a lead balloon. You know, because she used to be a kitchen wench. And now she's supposed to become a queen."

"I wasn't a wench." CeCi shoots me a dirty look. "Solace, I'm in love." This time Solace actually grimaces, and CeCi holds up a hand. "No. Not that way. Not with a person. Of course with Ed. But, I mean, with a vocation. I want to learn to cook—not like Gretel, not with ketchup—well, sometimes with ketchup, but like a real chef at a restaurant Outside."

"Try full sentences," I whisper.

Solace stares at CeCi. "You cannot seek this knowledge anywhere in the Realm of Imagination?"

"No."

"What about Gretel?"

"I was cooking the things she makes when I was ten. No offense or anything. But I want to learn molecular gastronomy. I want to learn the art of French cuisine. I want to make Thai food!"

"How about in Toad Hollow? Or The Land of Sweets? I heard the Muffin Man has pastry classes on Saturdays."

I decide CeCi needs help. "She's talented, Solace. You don't understand. She's a natural. She deserves the chance to grow, to see what she can do."

CeCi takes it from there. "The world of food is expanding as rapidly as the Realm of Imagination. I want to learn from the creators themselves. I want to share it with everyone here. Cooking centers me. It lets me express myself and create something tangible. Solid."

"Sounds very appetizing." I barely stifle a giggle.

"Hm. I see." Solace doesn't sound like she understands, but to her credit, she sounds as if she's trying.

"This trip, I need to take a test and purchase supplies. But that isn't all. See, there's Rory. She's miserable, and Figgy won't help us, and we just thought if we could distract her—" CeCi pauses to take a breath, but her leg has started jimmying despite my periodic attempts to press her knee still.

Solace's eyes narrow at the mention of Figgy. "What do you mean, she won't help?"

CeCi continues like she hasn't heard the question. "Bianca heard about this place where there's a replica of Rory's castle and all kinds of monuments to the Realm, and we thought if we could just spend some time celebrating and exploring, we might all come out better on the other side. We'll look out for one another. I promise."

Solace sighs. "And what happens after?"

"After the test?" CeCi's leg finally quits bouncing.

"Yes."

"Then I'll need to go Outside twice a week for classes. Sometimes Rory will come. Sometimes Bianca. But Edmund can't know for a while. I have to find the right way to tell him."

"I see." Solace looks at her paws, up at us, and down again. "The separation of our worlds is meant to protect people on both sides. Some decisions have lasting consequences."

She doesn't seem to be saying no. I look at CeCi. She's holding her breath.

"If I agree to this, to letting you go Outside on a regular basis, I have additional criteria."

CeCi finally exhales. "Anything."

"Careful with those sorts of promises, Cecilia," says Solace. "They can get you into trouble."

"Yes, of course," CeCi says.

"If I agree to this, you alone would be responsible for Snow White's safety, and you alone would have to unravel your personal timeline to put things right should things go awry. I can't ask any more of Briar Rose. She's been through enough."

"Thank you," CeCi manages, finally taking a deep breath.

"You're asking a great deal of each other," Solace adds.

"I understand," says CeCi. I could hug her, but instead I wink. She has my back, and I have hers. That's how things are supposed to be with best friends. (At least with best friends who stick around.)

"It is easy to lose track of time Outside. Your clock bracelet binds the magic of the portal to you, so guard it well and mind it often."

We nod. I look toward the window, where two of Figgy's sentinels peer inside.

Solace follows my glance, then continues. "In order to conduct your travels in a more private manner, I'd like to place the departure portal somewhere only the three of you know about. It would still route you to the Magic Castle, but you wouldn't start here at the Clock Shop. Think of it as an extension of the portal here."

"Easy," I say. I know just the place for it.

Solace gives me a long look. "Perhaps I should try and stop you, but I think the repercussions of keeping you here would be greater than letting you go. No matter what your business is or becomes on the other side, do not let traveling interfere with completing your Pages. Figueroa may be wrong about some things, but she's not understating—"

"I understand," I interrupt. "I'll be an expert traveler. Just like my father. He'll tell you himself, as soon as he returns."

Solace stares at me in a strange way and says, "You might do well to study your father's things a bit more carefully."

"Thank you, Solace," CeCi says, before I can ask what Solace means. "I'm sure we've already taken enough of your time."

We get to the door of the office when CeCi turns again. "Solace, why are you letting us go? Won't Figgy be angry?"

Solace twitches her nose. "Let me worry about that."

"Haven't you ever heard about looking into the gaping maws of gift horses?" I mutter. Then CeCi and I collect Rory and tell her about the new piece of furniture that will inhabit her long-unused tower starting that evening. Rory, of course, only hears that we've walked the whole way with bags and now have to walk all the way back. At some point, I find myself carrying both my bag and her bag while she carries the dog.

In a few hours we'll leave from Rory's tower. Seems it's a whole new era for the three of us. I do wish you were here.

B

Filling Emptiness
with Words

Princess Briar R. Rose
~~*Somnolent Tower Castle*~~
~~*South Road, Grimmland*~~
Beverly Wilshire Hotel
Los Angeles
Outside

Oh, Zell,

I've just had the most amazing evening. Can you believe I'm writing you from Outside? I hope the Pigeon Post here is reliable. They seem to do all right with Bianca's magazines, but some of these birds look a bit suspect, if you ask me.

I suppose I should slow down and start from the beginning. It has been a whirlwind of a day.

An hour or two after we returned from Solace's clock shop, CeCi and Bianca's contagious excitement swept its way up the stairs, and we found ourselves standing in the tower.

I didn't have any objections to the portal being placed there; in truth I was overwhelmed with elation that their plans included me again.

"No one comes up here, right?" Bianca asked, turning in a circle.

Solace had given us a marking chalk to use on the floor, and I moved it between my clammy hands. I wanted to answer honestly, but I knew mentioning my tea with Maro would upset them and I didn't want to ruin the moment. Besides, not a soul had been up before or since. "No."

I marked a spot on the center of the floor with the chalk, and the three of us moved back against the curved walls. The air shimmered, and soon a grandfather clock, sculpted from jagged pieces of ebony hardwood and bloodred metal, materialized, twice as tall as we are and about a two or three arm spans wide. The numerals on the clock face are written in a strange hand, and instead of the regular tick tock, it makes a low hissing sound. I'm glad it's up in the tower, out of earshot and eyesight—it is more than a bit creepy.

"Did Solace give you the bracelets?" I asked.

Bianca produced them from the pocket of her gown, a set of three twisting bands of the same bloodred metal. The face on each band was decorated with the same slim, silver numerals.

Bianca fumbled with the clasp as she tried to close it around my wrist. "CeCi, you do this. I don't have any nails."

While CeCi lectured Bianca about the filthy habit of nail biting, she took it upon herself to inspect my nails as well, while I stood, still mesmerized by the hideous clock in the middle of the room.

I didn't study the clock long, however, because Bianca began to shake me, asking where the dog had gotten to and what I had done with my overnight bag. "We've got a schedule to keep," she tutted, sounding not very Bianca-like.

Time being of the essence, or so we were informed, we stuck to Bianca's itinerary once we arrived Outside: finance, lodging, sustenance, test, Disneyland, shopping.

First, we stopped at a bank. She'd read in one of her father's journals that carrying around satchels of cash could be dangerous in certain circumstances. So we waited while Bianca exchanged her pile of cash for a thin rectangular card. Whenever the card stops working, one simply brings in another satchel of cash. Or so says the *teller*, evidently named so because they tell one things like "That bag looks vintage," "Good thing you got here when you did, we close at six," and "Sorry this is taking so long, but most people don't really keep their cash in *wads*."

After our errand we got to the best part, checking in to this magnificent hotel called the Beverly Wilshire. It's like a castle yet like a lodge, all filled with Human royalty. Bianca handed the clerk the card from the bank. The clerk gave us three similar cards along with the bank card. These new cards weren't money, though. Even better: They opened up our room.

The room itself is large and white and fluffy and has a balcony. The balcony is quite noisy because of the vehicles and the people and music and air machines known as *helicopters*—but it's amazing nonetheless. And the sunset was full of colors I've never seen before.

Down in the lobby, we met a man whose title was *concierge* (Bianca called him Little Suit, which didn't seem terribly polite, though he seemed to take it in stride), whose sole purpose was to answer our questions. He offered to walk Snoozer for me every few hours and gave us a menu especially for dogs. After he recommended a restaurant for dinner, I asked him to select an appropriate leash for Snoozer to wear. He offered to take Snoozer for the evening, instead, as the restaurant regrettably did not welcome dogs. (Here, pet nursemaids are called *dog sitters*, though I was assured no one would sit on Snoozer.)

The Beverly Wilshire is almost better than home. People wait on you hand and foot, but no one expects you to sign decrees or sit on thrones or hear grievances over chickens or suffer jugglers or listen to halfhearted performances on stringed instruments—though they do have some of those here and there on the lanes as you walk.

We ate dinner at a sumptuous restaurant called Mirabelle. Don't tell DJ, but the wine was much better than at the Swinging Vine, and the food was as amazing as any palace banquet I've ever tasted—dainty course upon dainty course of sparkling green flavors and savory brown sauces. I'd grow as big as a bear if I lived near such a place. No wonder CeCi wants to learn how to make food like that.

The restaurant was quiet, but the street beyond the door was alive with light and sound. We walked a bit because it was warm out and the simple gowns we'd brought were the perfect weight. When we'd had enough walking, we ducked into a bar for a nightcap.

CeCi had consumed a great deal of wine by then, bringing out her loving, gregarious side. She chatted away with some ladies at the next table about what they'd eaten that day and their all-time favorite restaurants.

Bianca tired of all of this once the conversation moved past ketchup. She perched on a stool next to me, tugging on my sleeve, telling me to *just look* at everything—the people, the clothes, the lights, the automobiles. As I looked, an unwelcome and unexpected panic rose up my throat. I stole a glance at my clock bracelet, but we had arrived only a few hours before. I don't know why I couldn't simply enjoy myself. Worry comes so naturally.

CeCi bounced back over to our table. "Come on, Rory. Wake up," she said. "Let's have some fun."

"Would you mind terribly," I asked, "if we went back to the hotel to do so?"

When we got back to the lobby, CeCi ran on ahead to order room service (her new favorite thing) while Bianca and I waited for the concierge to collect Snoozer from the dog sitter's office. I must have dozed off for a few minutes, because when I woke up Bianca was deep in conversation with a woman we'd passed on our way in.

She was dark—skin almost the color of night, with close-cropped hair and a strong face, bare of makeup.

Bianca looked down at Snoozer, then at me. "Good nap?" she asked. "Rory, this is Rachel."

"Lovely to meet you," I said, feeling as if I'd accidentally interrupted. "I assume you've met my dog?"

"I most certainly did. He's quite the charmer." Snoozer grunted and Rachel broke into a grin. It was hard to believe, but she was even more dazzling when she smiled.

Bianca stood and touched my shoulder. "I'll see you in the morning."

"Aren't you coming back to the room?"

"Rachel said she'd show me around. Besides, I'm not that tired," she said.

"I'll have her back before you know it," Rachel said, smiling again. It was hard not to stand there and grin back like a simpleton.

"Sweet dreams," Bianca said.

I meant to lecture Bianca about strangers and getting lost but then found myself falling silent. The way she and Rachel looked at one another was like something from a book. I've only been looked at like that once, a very long time ago—the night I met Fred. I watched them make their way out to the street, chatting about something I couldn't hear or probably even imagine, like the colors of the stars or the pulse of the city beneath us or the many ways a heart feels love.

Sitting there, watching the people glide through the lobby, I let myself think—for just a few moments—about Fred, about what his life might have been here. Did he find his own Rachel? Did he become a poet like he'd always planned? Was he happy? Did he miss me? Would he have left me a clue? It was senseless to dwell on such things. What's done is done.

CeCi looked a bit concerned when I returned without Bianca, but she had ordered champagne and strawberries and proceeded to jump on the bed with Snoozer. I don't know how late they stayed up because I fell asleep soon after. But it was a good night. I'm happy for Bianca. I'm excited for CeCi, too. I hope she didn't drink all the champagne, though. This morning she has to take her test.

Love,
Rory

From the Desk of Cecilia Cinder Charming
~~Crystal Palace~~
~~North Road, Grimmland~~
Beverly Wilshire Hotel
Los Angeles
Outside

Dear Zell,

When Bianca finally got back to the hotel this morning, my first impulse was to kill her, then bring her body home. Instead, I had to concentrate on getting everyone out the door so I could take my test on time.

We were still fighting when we got to the lobby where Rachel was waiting to walk with us.

"Please don't ever do that again," I hissed at Bianca.

"Oh, lighten up. Nothing happened," she said.

"You should get a cell phone," said Rachel. "It's cool you don't have one, but still."

I was irritated that she was with us, even though she was doing us a favor by helping us navigate and making Bianca an all-around more tolerable being. She was so polite and understanding. I didn't want to feel understood. I wanted to burst out of my skin.

"The test you're taking," Rachel said, unleashing a smile that felt like sunshine on a meadow, "is a simple one. It's a test a lot of places use to make sure you have basic reasoning skills. It's nothing to worry about."

She squeezed my arm. I tried to imagine Rachel in the Realm. She would have made a great queen. At the very least, she'd be at the top of everyone's invite list. Kind, calm, self-assured. What I wouldn't give to have her unwavering confidence. What I wouldn't give to feel like the rug wasn't about to be pulled out from under me.

When we got to the door of the testing center, all three wished me luck and told me they'd be waiting. And then it was just me and my so-called reasoning skills.

Darling, Sweetie, and I had that strange tutor from Neverland for a while—a pedantic young woman, Wendy something or other—but I don't remember her being particularly fond of me. Darling was so bright in math and Sweetie excellent in grammar. I preferred stories and daydreaming and getting back to the kitchen where things made sense.

I guess Cordon Bleu deserves to know if I'm smart enough to not cut my arm off, but through the entire test I was worried about failing, because it seems certain I'll screw this all up at some point in this process. On the plus side, if I fail before I begin, I'll never have to tell Edmund.

Bianca says thinking like that means I'm getting in my own way. She's probably right, though I'll never tell her. Grimm, wouldn't she be insufferable then.

Would you like to see how you would have done on some of the questions?

1. Assume the first two statements are true. Is the final statement: (1) true, (2) false, or (3) not certain?

Cats play with yarn. Grandmother knits with yarn. Grandmother has a cat.

The answer is not certain. But why would "not certain" even be an answer on a test in the first place? I could tell them lots of other things I'm uncertain about while I'm at it. I'm uncertain

Camille Griep

whether Rory gives Snoozer too many treats. I'm
uncertain whether we shouldn't use Snoozer's leash
on Bianca instead. I'm uncertain as to why you
abandoned us for unicorns. I'm uncertain if I can
be a chef. I'm uncertain that Edmund will forgive
me if I do become one. See? I could go on and on. I
am certain, however, that I don't wish to answer any
more of these certainty questions.

2. Buttons are sold for 37 cents apiece. What will it
cost to buy 5 buttons?

Thank Grimm Bianca prattled on ad nauseum
about paper money when we were talking to the
bank teller. I don't plan to buy any buttons while
I'm becoming a chef. Maybe button mushrooms . . .
(Come on, you laughed, right?) If I do, I'll be sure to
have $1.85 on my person. Or Bianca's cash card.

3. A train travels 500 feet in 10 seconds. At this same
speed, how many feet will it travel in 60 seconds?

It will travel 3,000 feet. This is just multiplication.
Multiplication will be useful as soon as I get to cater
an event. When I finally tell everyone I'm a real chef,
the whole kingdom will hire me, and I'll charge
three times the going rate for soufflés.

4. Three women open a bakery and agree to divide
the profits equally. Woman A invests $10,000,
Woman B invests $5,000, and Woman C invests
$2,000. If the profits are $15,000, how much less
does Woman A receive than if the profits were
divided proportionally to her investment?

Woman A is an idiot if she puts down twice or five

times as much as her friends and agrees to share the profits equally. I was tempted to refuse to answer this question on the grounds that women aren't actually that stupid.

Regardless, the result is I passed the test. I'm in the program. And now comes the hard part: Being here. Going through with it. Now the only person standing between me and my dream is me. (That, and my tendency to forget the ratios for a basic roux.)

Oh Grimm, what have I set in motion?

I'm posting this as we leave for Disneyland. The concierge called for a car as soon as we returned from the test center. He's watching Snoozer again while we go. It will be a short trip so that we're back in time, but we'll soak in as much as we can, and don't worry, we'll tell you all about it.

Love,
CeCi

Important Fucking Correspondence from Snow B. White
~~Onyx Manor~~
~~West Road, Grimmland~~
Beverly Wilshire Hotel
Los Angeles
Outside

Z,

This is the vacation of my dreams. Who needs sleep? Rory gets enough for all of us. My new friend Rachel and I had an amazing sunrise breakfast at a diner several blocks from the hotel. I would have given anything to stay there all morning, but I had to get back for CeCi's exam. We walked with her to the test center a few blocks away. It took all of a half hour for her to pass. Extraordinarily anticlimactic.

Little Suit offers to take Snoozer off our hands so that we can go to this Disneyland place. When I tell him about our plans to shop afterward, he shakes his head. "Leave a list with me," he says. "I'll have your packages here when you return. The traffic will be too bad if you need to swing by here and still make the Magic Castle by five."

I'm seriously starting to think Human ingenuity is more than a match for magic. CeCi tells me to stop "peppering" him with questions. I tell her to quit it with the food idioms because we get it already: she's Hot-Shit Chef now.

When the car arrives, it takes forever to get to Disneyland— apparently the "traffic" Little Suit referred to. It's like a million Mr. Toads are on the road going to the same place. The number of automobiles in all different shapes and sizes is almost unimaginable. And then there are motorized bicycles driven by what can only be the criminally insane, darting in and out of spaces, trusting bigger motorists won't run them over.

I can't believe I'm saying this, but I love it here. It's so exciting and new and dangerous. I wish I had days and days to explore. All the smells and sights and all the movement and all the life, Zell. It's so different from home.

Turns out we can't just walk right into the theme park. There's a little booth where we buy tickets with the cash card, and those tickets allow us inside. I suppose the reason why they don't let everyone in at once is because it's wall-to-wall people. Imagine, children everywhere—holding hands, holding toys, holding balloons, wearing mouse ears and short pants. (Rory was understandably delighted, but you should have seen CeCi's face. She was terrified, dripping ice cream cones coming at her from every direction.)

When we get through the gates, Rory sees a bunch of horse-drawn buggies and heaves this big sigh as if she's been searching for them for hours. CeCi, however, insists on walking even though it's warm, so that we don't miss anything. We walk past buildings and more carriages and a locomotive of some sort and statues and people in animal suits and ladies dressed like they just came from the Realm. Rory whines that we should have worn our gowns. CeCi interrupts with a tirade about the heat and the impropriety blah blah blah. I tell both of them to shut up.

We're barely paying attention when we come to the end of the walkway and look up. There it is: Rory's castle in miniature. The color is off and they took some liberties with the style, but it certainly isn't mine or yours or CeCi's.

Rory's eyes get big. She takes the wrist of a guy in a prince's costume. "Who's in charge here?" She shakes his hand as much as she's able without his participation.

"Is there a problem, miss?" he asks, trying to step back from her.

"I'd like to know who built this," she says. "There are some unfortunate inaccuracies that I'd like to . . ."

"I'm sorry, miss. I'm not sure how to help you."

CeCi steps in front of Rory, ineffectually fanning herself with her flimsy ticket. "It's the heat. We're going to find her some water. Is it always this hot? Do you know where we can get some water?"

"CeCi, just look!" Rory says, apoplectic. "They made me a *blond*!"

She's pointing and the fake prince is pointing, and I step in, scrambling for an explanation that won't get us booted from the park. "I'm sorry, sir. Our friend is, well, she's manic." (I read in *Cosmo* that manic is when people get uncontrollably excitable about things.)

"Oh, I see," he says with a gracious smile.

"I am *not* a maniac! It's all wrong. Wrong, Bianca! Let me go!"

CeCi and I remove Rory's hand from the poor man's arm. "No one said you were a *maniac*, love," I say, attempting to smile sweetly at the now quite perplexed fake prince. "So stop acting like one. This is an *homage*, if you will. Let's just go and see what's inside."

"Come on, Rory." CeCi flaps her ticket again. "At least it will be cooler in there."

"Sorry about this," I whisper to the prince.

"Happens all the time," he says, graciously. "No worries."

CeCi and I forge ahead, with Rory straggling after. We enter a new Realm, of sorts. One where everything we'd heard about the way Humans had interpreted our stories is correct: It's a complete farce. They see us as inaccurately as we see them.

Ludicrous caricatures of Rory sing and prance around with three Human Fairy Godmothers. A mural depicts her asleep in a big, comfy bed. There's an insinuation that Malice *turned into a dragon* while fighting a very valiant and handsome version of Henry. It's the story exactly as I imagine Henry himself would tell it, had he an ounce of creativity. I might even—on a very good day and with enough bourbon—root for this paragon of princehood, someone who resembles the Fred Rory had all those years ago instead of Henry the Horrible.

CeCi and I are laughing so hard that tears are falling, arguing whether Rory would have indeed selected pink or blue for her pre-sleep birthday party gown, when we emerge from the faux castle to find Rory herself looking uncharacteristically smug.

"Let's see how you like it," she says, grabbing my elbow. She hauls me a short distance to a line that snakes into a building entitled "Snow White's Scary Adventures." My own caricature wears a prim blue bow and a long dress and sings all of the time (what *is* it with all the damned singing, anyway?). We marveled at their interpretation of Valborg as a bent, warty little witch as a disguise of the handsome, statuesque stunner she used to be. I seriously hope the dwarves never get up here to see their namesakes, whose idiosyncrasies are grossly misrepresented. At least at the end of the ride, they're shown vanquishing Valborg with a strategically placed boulder. Everyone cheers at that part. I'll have to put it on the list of execution suggestions.

We decide that we'll continue on, to see if we can see anything else interesting from home. We find women dressed up as Rory and me, and they look almost identical to the pictures inside the attractions. CeCi watches her theme park doppelganger with her fists clenched. We're just leaving when a girl next to us sighs and says, "I just love Cinderella. She's so beautiful. I want her to be my best friend." Before we can stop her, CeCi kneels down and says, "Then you should call her by her real name." Rory and I each grab an arm before she can say anything else.

It's at this point that we stumble into a room and find you! You didn't think you'd get left out, did you? Instead of the solid and ardent Jason, there's a stubbly-chinned adolescent by your side. There are no twins yet and your hair is still enchanted. The little girls who visit can get improbably long braids like yours used to be and sit and chat with you. A lot of little girls. And boys, too. And parents. I feel I should point out that in this room there are no unicorns. Not a single. Rainbow-spewing. Glitter-shitting. One.

You totally should have been here.

They've got tributes to Toad Hollow and Wonderland. They've got Neverland and a whole ride dedicated to Hook. This place is awesomely terrible. It's like the Humans didn't feel like fact-checking the stories they dreamed up in the first place and said, *Fuck it, this is close enough.*

For once and for all, Zell, Figgy is wrong. Humans have built a shrine to Fairy Tales. If anything, they're dreaming more, not less. It's wonderfully freeing, isn't it? Our Realm will never stop expanding. It makes anything possible. Like our lives are wide open for our own dreams.

From what I see, Humans are just like us but with different *kinds* of magic. There are good people like Rachel and bad people like the taxi driver who tried to overcharge us and rich people who live at the Beverly Wilshire and poor buskers on the streets. They all have dreams and desolations, just like we do. How many of them are breaking free from their own expectations?

Here, mirrors aren't magical. Apples are health food. Clocks just tell time, and shoes are made of leather. Hair is for decoration instead of a climbing apparatus, and I didn't see a single spinning wheel anywhere. There's no risk of destroying the city around you just because you don't want to get married.

Here, you have a fucking choice. Try that on for size.

Love (So what. I forgive you a little today),
B

PS. You should have seen Rory when this guy offers her a hot dog. She thinks it's made of real dog until we explain it to her. The look on her face. I'll never laugh that hard again.

PPS. It's so nice to be able to write to you from Outside, even if I have to write this in a taxi. Granted, the pigeons out here are no Cliff, but they'll do for now.

Princess Briar R. Rose
Somnolent Tower Castle
South Road, Grimmland

Dearest Zell,

At first, I suppose I found yesterday's trip to Disneyland quite tiresome. Then I started to see the fun in it. And then it made me tired all over again. I was hungry and I wanted to lie down and I missed Snoozer and then there was all this confusion about dogs in food and all of a sudden it was time to take another very long taxi ride back to the hotel and yet another to the Magic Castle once we'd retrieved CeCi's packages and Snoozer. There are too many motor vehicles here, all confoundedly heading toward the same place.

My clock bracelet read vexingly close to five. Bianca suggested we go through the portal, turn around, and come right back so that she and CeCi could try something called *karaoke*. It sounds like a delicious food, doesn't it? It is actually an activity in which one sings words posted to a magic screen while music is played in the background. At Disneyland we learned Humans are quite convinced that all of us are accomplished singers. I feel a bit of sympathy for their future audiences, as the only way either of them could carry a tune is in a sheaf of sheet music.

"Have you forgotten this morning?" I asked, incredulous. "I don't want to go through that again."

At sunrise, I had woken up to CeCi's incessant pacing, punctuated by the occasional pitching of something into her valise and grumbling under her breath. As soon as she saw my eyes open, she began to blame me for letting Bianca go off with

Rachel in the first place. She reminded me that it would be her sole responsibility if Bianca didn't return, and I reminded her that she was completely mad if she'd vouched for Bianca without considering the ramifications.

We were still fighting when Bianca showed up an hour or so later. She was quite damp from the rain that had been falling, not to mention unassailably elated.

"That was the best night of my life," she said, having flopped onto the couch. "This place is fucking awesome. Let's never leave."

CeCi glared and threw several pillows at her.

"What crawled up your knickers?" Bianca shoved the pillows to the floor.

"You can't just not tell us where you are. Or when you'll be back. What if something happened to you? What if you got caught in the storm?"

"It's just a little rain, worrywart. You sound like Figgy."

"Save it, Bianca. I stood up for you. And get your shit together. My test is in an hour. We have to go."

"Killjoy." Bianca shook her head at me and pried her bag out from underneath Snoozer. She began to hum an off-key version of one of the love songs we'd heard sitting in the hotel lobby the night before.

She was still humming it as we went through the portal home. No one brought up the idea of going back out again, for which I was sincerely grateful. CeCi seemed as drained as I felt, and Bianca looked despondent, glancing back at the hissing portal.

"Did you have a nice time today?" Bianca asked without looking at me.

"Of course, and you?" I patted her arm.

"I can't even tell you."

CeCi rolled her eyes. "I had a good time, too. Thanks for asking!"

"I loved every second of it," Bianca said. She must have been thinking of Rachel, carried in that swell of desire that is so difficult to resist at the beginning of a courtship.

Sometimes I wonder if Bianca knows anything about real love. She certainly doesn't know anything about losing it, though I fear that lesson will be soon in coming.

I made it so many years without allowing myself to think about Fred, about his good intentions. About how all he wanted was to be with me. But since last night, I can hardly think of anything else. I wonder what he would have thought about Disneyland, and Humans, even about Snoozer. I wonder if he regretted trying to save me, or rather regretted the eventual consequences. I hope he wasn't lonely.

I wonder what he thought whenever it started to rain, if storms reminded him of the tempest that came to Grimmland that day. Though I was asleep for much of it, I'm told kings were plucked from their spires and animals from their burrows. Time began to run like paint, and the sky began to bleed into the ground.

I'm told Fred left willingly once he was satisfied that I would live. And so he and I were each given half a life, half a love. The more I know about Outside, the more I think our journeys were probably quite similar—both of us trying to make the best of the story that remained.

I'm sending some posters of Los Angeles for Bea and Arthur. I'm sorry I couldn't find any with unicorns included. Can you believe the clerk laughed at me when I asked? Maybe I'll be more successful next time. After all, I was also told it never even rains in Southern California, and that was clearly false.

Love,
Rory

From the Desk of Cecilia Cinder Charming
Crystal Palace
North Road, Grimmland

Dear Zell,

Of course, as soon as I arrived home, I wished myself anywhere else. I hadn't been in my chambers for five minutes when Lucinda started in about my being gone all day. She wanted to know what kind of ruler left her post for an entire day without notice. The contractors for the nursery had been making too much noise. Darling and Sweetie needed new dresses for the wedding.

"I'm on it, Lucinda."

She glared at me and then her face underwent a series of forced transformations. "You insist on pushing me away. I've told you I'm sorry a hundred times. It's you who can't let the past rest." She feigned a little hiccup.

"I'm not sure how many times we need to discuss this," I said. "You treated me cruelly for my entire childhood. I keep you here to make sure Darling and Sweetie have some stability for their conditions."

Her voice turned sharp. "I pushed you to become your very best. How is it that you caught Edmund's eye if not for my careful rigor?"

"You can't be serious." I dropped my volume in case Darling and Sweetie were listening. "I *caught* Edmund's eye on my own. Or, at worst, by way of Figgy's meddling. Or maybe because he actually found me interesting. Or because I was his best worst option. Take your pick. None of it had anything to do with you."

"He fell in love with you because I raised you to be cooperative." She began to pace the edge of the room, her own voice at full volume. "If you continue to cause a fracas with those two tacky princesses, the delinquent and the antique, you'll jeopardize things for all of us."

"Keeping you here is a kindness. When will you take responsibility for yourself? Your own actions? Your own evil? Look at your children. Look at them!"

"What? They're fragile. Sensitive." We both listened to the girls milling around at the end of the hall. "There's nothing wrong with them."

I couldn't believe that she was altering the narrative of our history so drastically. "You *made* them cut off parts of their feet because you wanted the kingdom so badly. And then—"

"Enough," she said. I found myself wishing I had turned them all out, like you and Bianca told me to before my wedding.

I was thankfully saved from further confrontation when Edmund arrived home. As soon as she heard his footsteps, she turned on her heel and whisked down the corridor, muttering to herself.

Ed looked windblown and ruddy from his ride. I keep expecting to take his beauty for granted and yet sometimes, like today, I look at him and all his purpose and his kindness and how it all unaccountably belongs to me and I almost lose my breath.

"What's going on?" he asked. "Did I hear Lucinda?"

"Just making some decisions about the nursery," I said, baring my teeth in what I hoped was a passable smile.

"Excellent." He kissed my head, his blond stubble rasping my cheek. "I know it's not what you want to be doing, but it will all work itself out. Trust me."

"What do you think? Yellow or green?" I asked, a drapery in each hand.

"I don't want to talk colors. I want to talk about your trip. How did Thing One and Thing Two like Wonderland?"

"Oh, it was fine. Lots of tea, you know."

"Tea, eh? I figured you'd be out at the bars. William says Bianca has quite the nose for bourbon these days. Did you get some sun? You have some new freckles." He tapped my nose.

"It's very sunny there. We played lots of chess with life-sized chess pieces."

He frowned. "Tea and chess? Are you sure you went with Bianca?"

"Well, you know," I said, scrambling to think. "She's mercurial. How about you? I'm not even sure where you're back from."

"Will and I were helping out with a little summit with the Supporters of Robin Hood. We're working on developing a charity system that doesn't involve carriage-jacking and arrows. Robin has good intentions, but questionable methods."

"Wow," I said. "Good luck with that."

He looked back at the mess around us, then dropped his voice to a conspiratorial whisper. "Let's plan what we'll actually do with the room."

"Greenhouse," I said.

"Observatory," he said.

"Secret passageway."

"Swimming pool."

"Sewing room."

Edmund laughed from deep within his chest. "I thought we agreed no working. Only leisure. No gardening. No sewing. No scrubbing."

"Okay." I felt a little tug of disappointment. "Wine cellar?"

"Now you're talking!"

I dropped onto a sheet-covered ottoman. "Edmund?"

"Cecilia?"

"Have you ever had a dream?"

"Almost every night." He stopped to look out the window.

"No. Be serious. A real dream."

"Yes. Sure. When I was younger I had lots. And now, I guess I think I'm living my dreams."

"But what if you weren't?"

"I'd make a change. I'd find a way to go for it. Our lives are long, but, as the old owl says, our ends are uncertain."

"What if your dream was unpopular or unseemly?"

"Well, lucky for me, I'm very seemly." He chuckled for a moment and then looked at me. "What's this all about, CeCi?"

"Nothing. It's just . . . I . . . nothing."

"Are you sure it's nothing?" He moved closer.

"Yes," I said. I faked a sneeze to hide my tears.

I wish I hadn't lied. But I did. After he left, I blew my nose in the green curtain. So I guess the nursery will be yellow.

Love,
CeCi

Important Fucking Correspondence from Snow B. White
Onyx Manor
West Road, Grimmland

Z,

How nice of you to write again! Here I was thinking you actually gave a damn, but instead it was because our intrepid investigator, Rory, has taken to gossiping. Perhaps she should apply for a job at the *Tattler*.

I didn't hide anything from you. I said Rachel was my friend because she is my friend. I suppose I should be flattered that you deemed me worth your petulant lecture, but here's the rest of the story, Ms. In My Business, *nothing happened*. I was honest with her about my situation—that I'm engaged and that I'm from somewhere else—but that I want to know about what life is like in Hollywood or Los Angeles or California and the world.

And I knew, even before I started, she wouldn't laugh at me. Have you ever met anyone like that? Someone you knew wouldn't expect or demand something from you?

When she asked me to go with her for the night, I jumped at the chance.

Picture it, Zell: It's late that night in a beautiful hotel and a beautiful person offers me her hand and I take it and then we walk down Sunset Boulevard past the bars and cafés and restaurants and music shops. We step inside a few, flipping through stacks of music, ordering manhattans. She tells me all about her childhood growing up north of there, a place where it rained almost every day.

She moved to L.A. (short for Los Angeles) to get away from the green and the moss and the wet, and she found this big, warm place where everyone was damaged but moving, impeded but going somewhere. People from, as she calls it, "all walks of life," and from every place with every kind of wish. People who want to make things happen. People who love music, art, food, or just chasing a dream of having a simple life with a family and a dog.

Rachel loves the city like it's a living being. She says it's constantly evolving. I see what she means. It's more than a town with a bakery that adds ketchup. It's a place that changes with its people—a city enriched by all it takes in. I'm not saying I don't have feelings for Rachel, but I do want to learn what she knows.

I assumed my father had regularly traveled Outside to learn about Humans' control over our world. But now, I think he went because it is as beautiful and enigmatic out there as it is in here. I wish he were here to talk to. I wish I could find him. I could use his advice. Maybe just his empathy.

But he isn't here, is he?

As soon as we get back to the Realm, I suggest to William that we have a drink (I turned the closet adjoining our suites into a whiskey bar last month). I decide to clue him in on a few things. Not everything, but a few things.

"It's nice to have you back, buddy," he says, with a nudge of his shoulder.

"It's good to be here," I say. "I think."

"I hear you, B. The call of the road, she's a strong one." He smiles into his glass, probably in a reverie over some past or future adventure.

"Will, if you weren't in line to become a king, what would you do?"

"You know I love kinging, Bianca. Man, if I weren't training to be kinging, I'd probably be plotting someone's overthrow."

I put my hand on his arm to get him to look at me. "But seriously, do you want all this? The trimmings and trappings of royalty?"

"Not all of it. I don't like protests and tariffs and coups. But you know I love the negotiations, the planning, the big picture. This Robin Hood thing I just got back from? It was so rewarding to make progress. To try and find the common ground. Ed is the guy who thought up donation tollbooths for Sherwood Forest Road and how to make them convenient and attractive. I'm the guy who's good at getting Maid Marion and Nottingham to listen to one another instead of screaming their heads off. I like making them see that they really want the same things. And then I also like the part when they break out the bourbon."

"That's altruistic of you," I tease.

"I love the math and the bartering and intrigue. And of course I love the travel and the parties."

"Intrigue, eh?" I push an unbidden, unwelcome image of that silly Maro out of my head. "What about the domestic stuff?"

"I guess I never thought about it. I'm glad to share all of this with you, B. We make a pretty good team, don't we?"

"Yes," I say. "We do." I choose my next words carefully. "But we're not epic lovers for the ages, are we?"

"No." He laughs. "I guess we aren't."

"We're epic pals instead, right?" I laugh, but my cheeks are hurting from forcing them into a grin. He's a handsome man and his dark hair has fallen into his eyes. I know he's beautiful, too. I almost wish I were attracted to him in *that* way. "Do you, you know, miss that? Isn't that something you want? Someday?"

"Truthfully, Bianca, I'd rather be with someone I trust. This life I'm living doesn't leave time for romantic drama. I had a bunch of those relationships when I was younger and I hated the guessing games and the posturing. I don't have to do that with you."

"Yeah," I say. I take a long, burning, preparatory sip. "But isn't that denying some part of yourself?"

"I don't know what you mean."

"Maybe you didn't know what you were getting into when you helped me. That single decision came with a lot more than you bargained for. Gallantly saving the pretty face—"

"I didn't try to rescue you because you were beautiful. I tried to rescue you because you were in trouble. I would have done it for anyone."

"Thanks a lot, jackass."

"You know what I mean. And you don't need other people to tell you what you look like. People trip over themselves in the street staring at you. Don't tell me you're having a crisis of self-esteem."

"I'm just asking if you'll regret not having, you know, True Love or whatever."

"Has Rory been lecturing you again?"

This time I laugh in earnest. "I've just been thinking. What if she's right? What if we're making a hash out of things for no reason?"

"I don't know if everyone wants what Rory wants," he says.

"I don't know if Rory wants what Rory wants," I say.

"I want a partner. I want that partner to be you." He looks at me hard, and for a second I feel like he can see straight through me. "What about you? Does it bother you? I do love you, B. It's just different."

"Of course. I know that." I pause for a second. For all the shit I give CeCi about being truthful with Edmund, I find myself in an uncomfortably similar position. "Enough of this. I want to tell you everything I found out about the theme park. It's this place, right, where these idiot Humans have built a mouse kingdom, and inside . . ."

I don't tell him about Rachel or about CeCi's classes. Maybe these are lies of omission. But I'll probably never see Rachel again and he'll find out about CeCi when everyone else does and he'll laugh that I pulled one over on him.

He wants what I want. A compromise. A partnership. Days spent laughing. Romance is for other people. I lucked out. My prince is my friend. It's the best I could have hoped for, the best I'll ever do.

And on that note, I have a stepmother to execute and a wedding to plan.

Nighty night,
B

Princess Briar R. Rose
Somnolent Tower Castle
South Road, Grimmland

Dearest Zell,

Ever since we returned from our Disneyland trip, something Bianca said has been bothering me. I almost shared it with Maro during our standing tea date yesterday (on the "pretty green grass," of course), but something stopped me.

Shortly after we arrived home, I pressed Bianca about her intentions with Rachel. She told me that she didn't know what she felt.

"If your affections are so arbitrary," I asked her, "then why don't you turn them on William instead?"

She said, "And how's that strategy working out for *you*, Rory?"

Of course I was upset. Bianca knows how hard I've worked on my relationship with Henry. But between her excursions and Henry's hunts, he and I haven't had any time together. What kind of wife does that make me, putting him second over my friendship with Bianca? Even worse, I'm turning into a hypocrite for judging Maro so harshly about her travels.

I wanted to make things right when I heard Henry's party ride in late last night. I sent a note this morning, asking him to my room this evening to share some stories and maybe even some *un*scheduled relations. Oh, Zell, I had such high hopes.

He arrived in full dress. I asked him about the hunting party and he was only too happy to tell me all about the poor jackalopes and snipe they chased and caught and butchered and roasted under a full moon. He told me he had a new favorite hunting dog, and I was excited to tell him I procured a dog, as well. I finally had the chance to introduce him to Snoozer, and Henry laughed with his whole body, saying Snoozer would never be fit to be a hunting dog. I told him that Snoozer wasn't meant to be a hunting dog and then he said that a dog wasn't worth having if it wasn't a hunting dog. In fact he said something quite a lot worse than that, but sometimes people can be mean without intention, so I tried to let it go.

I asked him if he wanted to hear about my trip and first he asked if I'd been gone, because he hadn't noticed, and then he said he would like to hear about it but he needed to be somewhere else. I asked him to stay with me and keep me company instead. And he told me if I needed "a good toss" that he'd be happy to accommodate me, but that he wasn't going to waste a perfectly fine evening indoors. I asked him if he wanted me to accompany him and he told me to stay where I was comfortable. "Sleeping Beauty with her Sleeping Dog." Then he had another good belly laugh.

Sometimes, Zell, I fear that Henry is not a very nice man, not even deep down. Sometimes, I think that it might not even be my fault that he doesn't want to spend time with me. Sometimes I think that there isn't a thing in the world—not a kind word or a deed or a dog or a song or a spell—that would entice him to my side. I must admit that things feel quite hopeless between us. Even when I think I'm doing the right thing it so often turns out to be wrong.

And then I think that sort of cynicism is just Bianca's overly independent influence.

Do you have any advice, Zell? Can't you tell me the trick to putting things back together when they seem most bleak? I suppose you'll tell me to redouble my optimism, like you did after Gothel sent you into the wilderness, so how's this: I'm going to become the woman he wants to spend time with, whatever it takes. I'll stay awake more. I'll attend more functions. I'll go on hunts. I'll wear lower-cut dresses and try to be more engaging. I'll demand to be paid attention to. I'll request flowers and favors. You'll see.

As for your own adventures, I'm so glad the third batch of potions worked for Bea's allergies. Let me see what I can find for Arthur's rash. It's so unfortunate he sat in the poison ivy, but that's the way with boys, or so I hear. Is Jason doing any better adjusting to life in the country? I'm not sure what you mean by "his affinity for the milkmaid." Perhaps you're misunderstanding; doesn't everyone love milkmaids? They're always so cheerful.

Besides, the two of you are perfect together. Whatever the misunderstanding, I'm sure your love will make it work—that's the whole point of love, right?

Kisses,
Rory

From the Desk of Cecilia Cinder Charming
Crystal Palace
North Road, Grimmland

Dear Zell,

I saw something and I can't unsee it. Please write back as soon as you can and tell me what to do.

Earlier this evening, Edmund and I headed to the Swinging Vine to have a glass of wine. Edmund had planned to meet William and the guys at Shambles afterward to challenge Max and Tripp and a few of the other dwarves to a game of billiards.

Once he left, I ordered another drink, hoping to catch up on the latest gossip with DJ before I walked home. I left maybe half an hour later and took the shortcut through the alley.

I was lost in my own thoughts and DJ's story about how Rolf had a confrontation with Thumbelina over a new set of wings he'd crafted for her. (It's hard to take her squeaky voice seriously in the first place and apparently even harder when she's angrily demanding extra sequins.)

The stars were wheeling through the sky, yellow and white, and the crickets were hard at work with their fiddles. It was a soft, warm night with just the right amount of wine and an easy walk ahead.

As I rounded the corner, I heard a thump and a giggle coming from behind the rubbish barrels. I stepped around them to see if everything was all right, and there was Henry pawing all over someone pushed up against the wall. At first I assumed it was Rory because they have those "scheduled relations" nights every once in a while, and she had said something about planning more of them soon. But after I looked away, I realized something about the picture in my mind's eye was wrong. The other person was too tall to be Rory.

I forced myself to look again and, when I did, I recognized the shoes. Wooden shoes. By then, the woman's dress was hiked up around her waist and she was starting to make a lot of noise—the kind most of us keep to ourselves.

My stomach began to churn, wine rising into my throat. All this time, Maro has been luring Rory closer and closer with those absurd tea dates neither of them thinks we know about, all so that she can bag her husband. Sick, sadistic twat. Thank Grimm they didn't see me. I crept backward as quietly as I could and took the swamp lane home. My heart was beating so hard I didn't even notice the mud.

What am I going to do? How can I get rid of Maro without telling Rory what's going on? If I don't tell her and she finds out, she'll never forgive me. If I tell her she'll be crushed and never forgive me for bringing Maro into our lives in the first place. Why did I think it would be a good idea to let someone we didn't know into our circle? Remember when I said no harm could come from making a new friend? What an idiot.

Henry's nameless, faceless conquests are legion. But Rory thinks Maro is her friend. She opened up her home and her—rightfully—judgmental little heart to this ruthless jezebel.

I should have listened to Rory from the beginning, trusted her instincts.

Instead, I've ruined everything.

Love,
CeCi

Painting Her Heart with Dreams

Important Fucking Correspondence from Snow B. White
Onyx Manor
West Road, Grimmland

Z,

Well, here I am thinking my little trip Outside would've at least given everyone a chance to relax, but instead, it succeeded in turning both CeCi and Rory into nagging ninnies.

You'd think everyone would be happy because today is the day we sample wedding cakes at Gretel's. I mean, it's cake, for fuck's sake. Who can be sad about that?

They both arrive, and all that seems to be missing are black veils. They exchange strained pleasantries, and CeCi eases into her chair like it's lined with nails.

I'm positive Rory's pouting has something to do with that gasbag, Henry. So I quiz CeCi, instead. "What's your problem, chef?"

"Nothing. Let's just eat cake like normal princesses." She's that special mix of prickly and peppy that indicates she's keeping a lid on something she shouldn't talk about but wants desperately to share.

"Let's try this again. Good morning, CeCi." I can't help but needle her. The sooner she lets the proverbial cat out of its hypothetical bag, the better for all of us. I whisper, "Your line is: 'How are you,' 'Nice to see you,' 'Fuck you.'"

"Fine. Fuck you, Bianca."

Rory wrings her hands. "Don't start, you two. You can't imagine the terrible night I had last night. I can't handle your bickering on top of everything else."

CeCi looks at Rory, eyes bulging like the Frog Prince's. Her mouth twists, opens, and closes again.

"Out with it," I demand.

"This is the third time we've chosen. I'm just sick of cake, okay?" CeCi starts stabbing the tines of her fork into her napkin.

This takes me somewhat by surprise. CeCi likes cake. Hell, everybody likes cake. As far as I'm concerned, sampling cake is one of the best parts of throwing a wedding. "You can't get sick of cake. It is physically impossible."

She glares at me. "Do you want my help, or not?"

While I mull whether or not I do, in fact, want her help, Gretel blessedly swoops over, arms lined with plates. This distracts us for a while—carrot, dark chocolate, plain white, yellow with colorful speckles, something called red velvet, which I love but Rory calls "vulgar."

"It's cake. It doesn't have a moral compass."

"It's the color of *blood*." Rory looks at me like I've just shat upon the floor.

"I like it. I'm the bride. Haven't you been reading those

magazines I gave you? What the bride wants, the bride gets.
We'll take this red stuff, Gretel."

"What if it gets on your dress?" Rory wrinkles her nose.

"It'll go nicely with the ketchup stains," CeCi says—but
sharply, without laughing.

Their foul moods have officially worn off on me. "Fine. I'll
wear a black dress and it won't matter!"

"Oh, Bianca, be serious," says Rory.

"I am being serious. What about polka dots? Red polka
dots would be fantastic. Hey, Gretel, can you make the frosting polka dot?"

"You're talking about the most important day of your life,
Bianca. Stop treating it like it's a game for your amusement."
Rory's ears are red and I know I've leapt over some invisible,
arbitrary line of offense.

Still, I can't bring myself to care. "It was the most important day of *your* life, Rory," I say. "It will be a fun party, maybe
even a pretty great day, but it won't even land in my top five."

Rory is nearly in tears at this point. "You have *everything*,
Bianca. You get to marry one of your best friends, and he's
handsome and respects you. Your parents have nothing to do
with your wedding. And your evil stepmother is about to be
executed. How can you be so stubborn?" She throws her napkin on the table and bolts out of the café.

CeCi looks at me and says, "Nice work," and follows her
out. I don't go after either of them because our lives seem to
have devolved into a constant stream of someone fleeing from
the room, and the chaos is getting to be a bit fucking much.

Maybe I'll just plan this shindig on my own and let those
two have their nervous breakdowns. I'll keep Rory's cellist,
maybe even her centerpieces. Hell, if there's enough wine,

who'll even notice? I'm pretty sure centerpieces aren't what weddings are supposed to be about. But, then again, what *is* a wedding about?

It's dresses, right? That must be it. Besides, I'm done with existential questions for today. I'm heading to Rumple's this afternoon to pick out new fabrics. Alone. I do love the idea of polka dots, though. Seems much more fun than white. And it is *my* wedding.

Love,
B

PS. About those miniature unicorns: If you send a few more, I can put a whole herd of them on top of my polka dot cake. Or you could set fire to them. That might be good, too.

Princess Briar R. Rose
Somnolent Tower Castle
South Road, Grimmland

Dearest Zell,

I've said it before: CeCi and Bianca have perfect lives and yet they are determined to thumb their noses at their bounty. Why can't they appreciate what they have? If I had the luxury of being friends with Henry, I wouldn't treat our relationship as carelessly as they seem to, dabbling in fibs, white lies, and the art of omission. I certainly wouldn't make a mockery out of my ceremony with red cake. Just think of it, Zell. *Red!*

I walked out of Gretel's in a bit of a snit, and CeCi came running after me. "She didn't mean to upset you, Rory."

"Of course she did," I countered. "She always does."

"You have to let Bianca be Bianca." She took my arm in hers. "I know you want the best for her, but she'll never see things like you do."

"She's wasting her chance at love."

"It's not that simple for her. Or for any of us. In all of our relationships, we're still changing and learning and moving around one another. Bianca's just venting her frustration. Give her time. For some of us it's a process."

The last dam of dignity burst inside me, and I felt warm rage spill through my body. "For some of us," I said, "it never happens. Ever. No matter how hard you hope. No matter how hard you try." I stopped, expecting tears to fall, but, I suppose, admitting my failure was a relief.

I expected—wanted, even—CeCi to argue with me, to reassure me, to tell me that things would be okay and that I should give it some more time and keep my chin up. Instead, she shut her eyes and pulled me into a smothering embrace.

"You're right, and I'm sorry." I didn't want to hug her back. She was supposed to bolster my spirits, even lie to me. Isn't that the job description of a friend—to make the other feel better? She has no problem lying to Edmund, Lucinda, her court—why not me?

"I need to rest," I said through her puffy sleeve.

"You can't sleep your life away," she said, ducking to look into my eyes.

I tried to look away from her, but she reached up and held my chin, checking me over like one checks produce at the market. "You don't understand," I said.

"I do. I do understand. So much more than you know. I understand you're tired and feel like you're empty inside. But you have to find something that fulfills you from within, not from without. We all have to find it. That's what Zell did. It's what we're all trying for. Me. Even Bianca."

But I don't know what any of you expect me to do. Who do you expect me to become? I've been this Rory—the one right here in front of you—for one hundred and twenty years. The rest of you have scampered through the Realm pell mell, wanting this, then wanting that, bending the rules to make your Pages suit the lives you want. When I voiced the same desire, Fred landed us both in a cauldron of misery. Since I woke up, I've strictly adhered to the rules, and still everyone acts like I'm the fly in the ointment.

I know it's not a competition, Zell, but I've had the cruelest fate of all. I missed everything. I missed my whole life. I had a childhood, but not with the three of you. I'm having an adulthood, but not with my childhood friends, not with Fred, not with the family we hoped to have, or the future we imagined. I missed the changes that went on Outside and the changes within the Realm for a century. It's as if everything passed me by, like I'm half in one time and half in another and there's nothing in the here and now.

Bianca and CeCi can preach all day about inner fulfillment, but it's impossible when what I want most is a family. What reason could I possibly have to be satisfied with my life as it stands? Henry hasn't taken the least bit of interest in me since our wedding—it's as if I was just a stepping-stone to greater riches.

I'm not pregnant. I'll never be pregnant. I've been trying since we got married. Scheduled relations almost every week. Last night I overheard Henry's mother talking about a surrogate. CeCi has an entire fancy fake nursery, and I have nothing. *Nothing.*

At least Maro understands me. She stopped by after I got home today to tell me Muffet had begun exterminating the Inn for some dreadful-sounding spiders. I insisted she take our guest quarters straight away and, though she said she couldn't possibly, I finally convinced her. Bianca and CeCi will scold me now that the portal is in the tower, but there's no reason for anyone, let alone Maro, to climb up there—a tedious trek for a (formerly) empty room with a view no better than the ballroom's parapets.

She and I had the most wonderful heart-to-heart. She didn't tell me that I needed to find some way to fulfill myself. She said things like *poor dear* and *there, there*—things friends are supposed to say. Maro agreed Bianca and CeCi should be more understanding. She told me that I should take it easy on myself, that my dreams aren't unreasonable.

I can be a desirable wife and a superlative mother and a good queen. I've come to the conclusion I must be missing something and to find it, I need help. I've been reading too many Outside novels where the protagonists get into trouble trying to fix things on their own. Then I remembered that *we are Fairy Tales*. All I need to do is to rely on the right character in my story: Figgy. She can give me something to set things right. Perhaps I've forgotten or misinterpreted a line in my Pages. Maybe there's a spell or a potion I can take. CeCi and Bianca can do things their way, finding loopholes to suit their needs. I can also work within the rules of the Realm to get what I want.

I'm glad you believe in me, Zell. I believe in you, too. I believe in your dreams and in your love story. That's why I'm quite sure that Arthur didn't mean to shove magic beans up his nose and that it was most certainly an accident when Bea dropped your diamond ring in the manure pile. And, yes, I'm *positive* it's not an omen.

Love,
Rory

Dear Zell,

Bianca's pernicious cake whimsy was the *last* thing I wanted to deal with yesterday morning. I was still trying to process what I'd seen the night before without upsetting Rory. But I needn't have worried, because Bianca handled that all by herself.

Sure, Rory is being a little oversensitive, but every week Bianca changes her wedding plans from top to bottom: the flowers, the colors, the seating charts. The chaos seems to be some sort of bizarre entertainment for her. What's worse, William finds it all amusing in a chummy sort of way. I guess he's the one who has to live with her—and he won't be able to claim he didn't know what he was signing up for.

This morning, I made my way to Rumple's to try on our third set of bridesmaid dresses. Who knows how many iterations we'll have to endure before she finally decides on something. Two weeks ago, they were layer upon layer of silver chiffon. Last week we had bright cobalt pantsuits. Today we were shown zebra-striped ball gowns.

Bianca's fourth seamstress quit last week. I introduced myself to her replacement, a stout woman whose real name I forget but Bianca dubbed Five. Bianca and Five were arguing over an inappropriately placed zebra stripe when Rory bustled in with Snoozer in tow, announcing we needed to hurry up because she had somewhere to be.

"You're the one who's late," Bianca said. "And Snoozer has to try on his doggie tux. Look, I found this adorable matching zebra bow tie!"

Zell, I'm not sure who introduced her to those Human bridal magazines, but they should be drawn and quartered. Valborg might not be the only casualty on Bianca's wedding night; the rest of the guests might die of shock at the fashion alone. But, as Bianca repeats incessantly, what the bride wants, the bride gets.

"I was having breakfast with Maro," Rory said.

Bianca frowned. "I thought Hansel and Gretel decided to close on Tuesdays?"

"We were having breakfast at my palace. She's staying there for a bit."

"Why on Grimm's grave would you—" Bianca broke off to attend my violent coughing fit, caused by the tea I'd inhaled in surprise.

"You never support me," Rory snapped. Bianca let it drop.

Rory took her frustration with Bianca out on Five. She fussed and fidgeted. She frowned and fumed. The neck was too high, too low, too hot, too indecent, too prissy. And then she began to stamp. "Get me out of this infernal creation right now!" Hands full of pins and scissors, Five fell over trying to help Rory extricate herself.

"Take a deep breath," I said. In hindsight, I suppose it was stupid to even bother trying to defuse the situation—like trying to mop up a swamp with a toad.

"You two enjoy yourselves," Rory said. I could count on one hand the number of times I've seen her smirk, but she was smirking, Zell. "I've had my fill of zebra-striped dresses for one lifetime. Besides, we'll no doubt be doing this again next week."

"Where are you going?" Bianca asked, waving the tiny doggy bow tie in her hand. She looked genuinely disappointed as Rory marched toward the door.

"It's none of your business. Either of you. Don't follow me." She clipped Snoozer's rhinestone leash onto his collar and marched out.

Bianca put her hands up in confusion. "What the fucking fuck?"

I shrugged. "Maybe she skipped her morning nap for breakfast with Maro."

Bianca shook her head in disbelief, then tossed a sparkling veil at me. "Breakfast with that woman would make anyone a pain in the ass."

"You have to stop tormenting her." I held my zebra skirt up as evidence. "What's all this about, anyway?"

"Oh, come on, it's my wedding. You can't deny they'll look great with my new red wedding dress!" She held up a short, crimson, fluffy A-line for inspection. "Why can't this be fun for me? When will you two lighten up?"

I flopped down, aiming for the loveseat and landing on an unseen pincushion. "Ouch. Bianca. Stop. Seriously."

Bianca waved Five out of the room. She sat, batting the pincushion to the middle of the couch, and picked up my hand. "Will you please tell me what the hell is going on? And let's skip the part where you do the valiant secret-keeping thing and I beg you to tell me what's wrong and you start crying. Oh, splendid, you're already crying."

I did cry. For a long time. Not just about Rory, but about classes starting next week. How our friendships suddenly seem so tempestuous. How I don't want Edmund's parents to get back and ask questions about the nursery. How I don't want to take care of Darling and Sweetie and fight with Lucinda anymore. How afraid I am to ask for what I want. And, most important, about the secret, the horrible image I carried, the terrible mess of Henry and Maro. I blurted it all out.

Bianca's face began to flush a full range of reds. "Maro? And Henry! Are you sure? It was bad enough when . . . But right under her nose. In her own palace. We told Rory to be nice to her. And now she's staying there? I can't even—" She stood up and began to wander in concentric circles.

"I don't know what to do," I said. "What are we going to do?"

She stopped pacing and glared at me. "Damn it, CeCi. Why did you tell me?"

"You asked what was wrong!"

"I had to ask, didn't I?" She threw her hands up and flopped onto the couch again. "No wonder you're so upset. No one wants to know this."

I felt my stomach turn. "I told Zell, too."

"Oh, great. So now all of us are keeping it from her."

"What now?" I asked.

"We have to tell her."

"If we tell her, she'll know we kept it from her."

Bianca looked at me as if I'd been quacking instead of speaking. "Hello? We *are* keeping it from her."

"Well, you just found out, and she isn't here right this very second."

"Look, it doesn't matter, CeCi. We're screwed either way. The only way out of a situation like this is to not to know about it in the first place."

"No one knows we know but us."

"Ugh, listen to yourself. Maybe you're getting a little too comfortable with half-truths these days. Haven't you had enough subterfuge for one lifetime?"

"Really, Bianca? That's pretty rich for a woman who's planning a fake wedding."

"It's not fake!"

"Is too. It doesn't mean anything."

"It's a partnership that fulfills my Pages."

"But you don't love each other."

Bianca gave me an exasperated smirk. "Not the same way you love Edmund or Zell does Jason but we do love each other. It's just that our love is more of a deep respect than a romance. We don't need the same kind of relationship the rest of you do. That's not a crime."

"It is a crime, Bianca. Against yourself. You clearly need—and want—that kind of relationship. At best, you're cheating yourself. At worst, you're delusional."

"What's that supposed to mean?" She began to stab the pincushion with a pearl-headed pin.

I figured I might as well say it all. "It means you do require companionship, romance, love. You've managed to find some version of it Outside with Rachel. You're denying your true self because you don't think you can have the kind of relationship that you want."

She delivered another withering glare. "Rachel can't become the queen of Onyx Manor, CeCi. You already know that."

"With Rachel, you found someone you wanted to learn about life with. Don't tell me that doesn't mean anything to you. Tell William you're sorry. Tell him you'll still consult on all of his little castle projects. Tell him you'll still have whiskey night. Then go out and find the right person. We'll put you back in your glass box, and whoever it is can come rescue you instead. I'll give Figgy another batch of worms. She'll have to agree. Aren't you the one who always finds the loopholes?"

Bianca gave me her dangerous smile, the one that doesn't quite reach her eyes. "Maybe Rachel *is* the right person, CeCi. But choosing her is, well, it's impossible. And if I try again here in the Realm, what's to say I don't end up with my very own version of Henry? William is the best that I can do here. It doesn't matter who I love out there. It's im-fucking-possible."

"You're lying to yourself," I blurted.

And that's when Bianca slapped me. Hard. "Fix your own mess before you go fixing everyone else's, Cecilia."

I sat there blinking at her. At least I was stunned enough to not say anything I'd want to take back. Maybe I deserved it. The strangest part was, I couldn't figure out whether to keep crying or start laughing.

I'm sorry that I told her about Maro, which means that I'm sorry that I told you, Zell. I didn't mean to put either of you in a bad position; I just didn't want to be the only one. It's such a big secret to carry alone. I didn't mean to be selfish.

What did you mean in your last letter about needing assistance in the kitchen? Don't you have a cook? I didn't realize that your staff couldn't come with you, but if there's a labor shortage in Oz, you'll have to learn quite a few new things. Send me a list of what you want to make and I'll try to help.

Love,
CeCi

Important Fucking Correspondence from Snow B. White
Onyx Manor
West Road, Grimmland

Z,

I've been threatening to slap CeCi for years now, but I don't think I ever meant to do it until it was happening.

There we were, not exactly arguing, but talking about, you know, big shit, and all of a sudden she's calling me a liar and something inside rips open and I slap her.

Maybe she's right. Maybe I'm just as self-deluded as everyone else. But being called a liar hurts. Honesty is the one and only virtue I claim. Sure, maybe I'm even *too* honest about things, like how terrible Gretel's gingerbread tastes and the fact that Puss's boots do have too much fringe, but it's better than the alternative, isn't it? At least you know what you're getting with me. There aren't any two-faced sorts of surprises. My honesty is the one thing that keeps me from becoming like Valborg.

Even though William and I are being honest with one another, CeCi isn't altogether wrong. Our marriage will be an illusion. A deception like Valborg and my father's relationship turned out to be. I never meant for that, I just figure that's how things have to be for us.

I've spent my whole life (since leaving the forest, at any rate) trying to be the antithesis of Valborg. Clearly, I've flat-out failed. I'm a liar and, soon, I'll be a murderer, too.

It's not that I want to save her, but I don't want to be the cause of her suffering. I want to be better than she is. And even though I don't want to kill her, I don't want to think about her anymore, either. I want to start all over again.

I know that's how Rory sees the completion of her Pages, as a new beginning, one she's desperately trying to embrace, but I don't think I'll be able to dismiss my past as easily as she does. She almost never brings up Fred or the way things used to be. She made peace with her Pages, embracing some ideal life she's supposed to eventually have.

But that's not me. I want our lives to be brilliant *right now*, not later, not Ever After. How am I supposed to forget that my wedding will include an execution? No amount of sleep will erase that for me, ever.

But Figgy and the rest of the Council say that's the way it has to be. At least how it happens is still under my control.

First, I considered the whole boulder idea from the theme park—a cake made of stone and frosting strategically placed atop a staircase. But it seems so messy. And I don't want the guests panicking or, Grimm forbid, getting in the way. Plus I'm afraid I'd merely cripple her.

I've considered a poisoned apple. There, you have some real poetic justice on a genuine silver platter. She could go down feeling the same oh-shit feeling I did, when I realized my mistake a few seconds too late. I could watch her eyes get big and her clutch at her throat and cry as she registers her impending doom. But it's a little cliché.

So here's how it will go down: We'll place her in the heated iron shoes as the dancing begins. I'll slip her some herbs, and instead of feeling angry and frightened, she feels the joy of music and movement and rhythm and freedom. And her heart will warm in pace with the shoes on her feet and she'll dance her way to her death, feeling nothing but euphoria. I'll fulfill my Pages and grant her a kindness. I'll be the better woman.

I've tried to explain that I want her death to be merciful a thousand times. But the Council never listens. All they want to know is how I felt then, how I feel now, how I might feel in the future. Tiresome morons. I felt bad. I feel bad. I'll probably continue to feel bad. It is unpleasant, to say the least, when anyone—let alone your stepmother—doesn't just want you gone, but dead.

I missed my own mother so badly after she died. When Valborg came into our lives, I wanted her to love me, to fill in that missing space, more than anything in the world. You understand, don't you? Didn't you find yourself wanting your mother all those long days in the tower? Wasn't there an emptiness where she should have been? A part of you that never belonged because she wasn't there? A part of you that would have traded anything at all to have her back? Wasn't there a sound or a scent or memory that made you think of her and need her with your entire being?

In the absence of my own mother, I wanted a stepmother who was gracious and kind. I wanted someone who would love and cherish her time with me. The truth is, I would have wanted any mother of any sort, as long as she wanted me back. I would have loved her just for loving me in return. Valborg was those things for a while. To my face. Before my father began traveling again.

I loved Valborg for the simple act of being there. I believed the things she said. I took her criticism and her corrections. I listened when she heaped on the rants about my absent father.

But then everything changed with that horrible mirror. She just crawled deeper and deeper inside of herself until she couldn't see anything else.

I want Valborg to see something else about life before she dies. And she will, if I have anything to say about it. She'll feel joy, even if she doesn't mean to. I know my father will approve. He'll tell me I'm doing the right thing.

I know how it is—he's a busy guy. Never in one place too long. It's proving impossible to track him down. But he has to have heard about my wedding. He wouldn't miss it, would he, Zell? Maybe he's keeping quiet so he can surprise me.

William says I should stop caring—as if loving my father were voluntary or something. He loved me unconditionally. That part I remember. I want to thank him. I want to tell him I know he made a mistake marrying Valborg, but that he's my family. My only family. If he doesn't show, I don't know what I'll do.

Maybe I'll come live with you and Jason and the brats and defer this whole mess—you can be my family. See how you like that. I'll have Jason loving the country in no time. With enough bourbon, *anything* is possible.

B

Princess Briar R. Rose
Somnolent Tower Castle
South Road, Grimmland

Dearest Zell,

I should have written off the entire day after the dress fitting went so badly, all the low-cut ruffled, jungle print nonsense and that horrible Five woman sticking me with pins. I should have gone back to bed and tried again the next day. That's what a smart person would have done. Instead, I made my way out of one mess and right into another.

After divesting myself of Bianca's buffoonery, I dropped Snoozer with his nursemaid. I don't know whether Figgy likes dogs or not; however, it was not the day I planned to find out.

Figgy was pleasant at first, niceties and chitchat. And then I said, "I was wondering if you would tell me what a love potion might cost?" She ruffled her feathers and spun her head around as if I'd spilled black tea all over her white chair.

"Whatever do you mean, Briar Rose? I thought I . . . wait, now did Cecilia and Snow send you?"

"Heavens, why would they have sent me?"

"Oh, me and my old age. I simply meant, well, you girls might have discussed it together, as girls do. You know because of those magazines. Never you mind."

I was confused, to be honest, but I went ahead with my request. "I'm simply a woman trying to fulfill the Pages you gave me, Figgy. You said Henry was supposed to be my True Love, and so I foolishly thought you might be able to help me. You may think I'm too naïve to come up with ideas on my own, but I assure you I am self-sufficient." I heard my voice rising, so I wasn't surprised when she called in her little canaries with tea and hankies.

The birds circling my head made me feel as pent up as the little teapot whistling away in Figgy's kitchen. Meanwhile, she wandered the room, muttering, "A love potion? Now, now. Why's that, dear?"

I tried to calm the wavering of my voice. "To make Henry love me."

"How can you be so sure that he doesn't love you now?"

"He doesn't want to spend time with me."

"But he's young and has a great many hobbies. Many young men suffer from such things."

Fred didn't suffer from such things. Perhaps he suffered from the opposite—so much passion that he didn't bother to weigh the consequences of his actions. But that sounds ungracious, doesn't it? Anyway, I tried to be more specific without being indelicate. "Henry doesn't want to, well, you know."

"What, dear?"

"You know! Except for our scheduled relations, he's just not—"

"Oh! Oh, I see. That's enough, dear. I understand perfectly." Figgy flapped her wings upward. "Well, perhaps he drinks a bit too much?"

"I don't think that's it."

"Maybe there's something wrong. With his, well, you know, equipment."

"No. It isn't that, either, Figgy. He simply doesn't seem to enjoy my company. He doesn't seem to want *me*. You know, as a companion. As a lover. As a chess partner. Not at all."

Figgy began to pace faster. "Perhaps you need to give things more time. It's not as if you had a drawn-out courtship. His parents insisted upon an immediate wedding."

"It's been five years, Figgy. He's still not ready to settle down. The only thing I can think to focus his attention is a child. He'll realize that he has the perfect family and he'll settle down. But I can't have his child if he won't sleep with me."

"A child, Briar Rose? I'm not sure that's wise at this juncture. With your relationship so, well, immature?"

"He'll be mature once he has a son to be responsible for."

"How do you know?"

"Because that's the way it works!" I found myself standing and stomping, the canaries fluttering around my head. "Haven't you read any books?"

"My dear, perhaps you've read too many."

"There's no such thing!"

She stopped pacing and unfurled a wing across my shoulders. I wanted to shrug it off, so instead I kept very still. "Now, now, Briar Rose. You've had a very hard time of it. What I am saying is, fiction isn't always reflective of reality. Particularly that brand of Outside nonsense you girls obsess over. Perhaps you've just had a long day. Are you sure you're resting enough?"

"I rest all the damned time. If I rest any more, I might as well go back to sleep. My *dog* sleeps less than I do. I want something different. I want the life I dreamed of before my sixteenth birthday. What Fred did wasn't my fault. It was a silly mistake made by a child in love. You said I had to compensate for his actions. I gave you one hundred years and five more after it. Haven't I paid enough? It's my turn. I want my family and my baby and my Happily Ever After. Where are they, Figgy?"

Unfortunately, the tentative grasp I'd held on my temper now eluded me completely. Figgy started lighting incense and brewing another calming tisane. The canaries settled on the back of my chair and blinked drowsily. I sank down below the birds. My hot tears fell into my hot tea.

"Are you quite finished?" Figgy's voice held an edge that hadn't been there before.

"Why won't you help me?"

"I *cannot* help you. It's a completely different thing."

"But why?"

"As I told your friends, no good could come of this."

"You said that before!" My hands turned cold, and my heart began to pound in my ears. "Why would CeCi and Bianca be consulting with you about my marriage?"

"They came wanting a . . . to help your problems . . . never you mind. This is what comes of you three traipsing around Outside, getting all these ideas."

"This has nothing to do with Outside."

She stood up and fluffed herself again. "So you say. You wouldn't be filled with half these notions if Solace didn't allow your little capers. You read the books and you eat the food and you hear the music, but you don't have any context. I know what you're looking for out there, but he's gone. And he's been gone a long time."

"Don't you think I know that, Figgy? Don't you think I feel that every day? At least Solace isn't trying to hide everything from us. She's the only one who lets us see things as they could be," I said. "You only let us see tiny pieces. I followed your damned rules and still I have nothing. It isn't fair." I drained the rest of my scalding tea and exited without saying good-bye.

Sometimes, if I weren't living it, I'd scarcely believe my life was my own. When I arrived home, there was an urgent note from CeCi asking if I'd accompany her to her first day of cooking classes, as she and Bianca were at a temporary impasse. Though I wanted to inform her that all three of us were at a temporary impasse, I decided to acquiesce.

I felt miserable after that nasty business with Figgy, and I tried to remain civil but cool, so that CeCi would understand where we stood. In truth, Zell, the trip ended up being quite cheering. While there, Snoozer and I met some other pet owners and I discovered a most delicious substance called *coffee*. You have to try it. Its effects are what you might feel if you took ten naps all in a row. Snoozer had to miss his obedience class at Pets & Boots, but if I'm honest, he wasn't destined to be a star pupil anyway.

Love,
Rory

From the Desk of Cecilia Cinder Charming
Crystal Palace
North Road, Grimmland

Dear Zell,

I apologized to Bianca even though she's the one who slapped me, but she still seems to be out of sorts, even refusing to go Outside for my first day of classes. She said she had things to attend to. I told her I wasn't going to beg.

I did, however, beg Rory. She wasn't particularly eager, either, but I gave her the plastic money card and promised to set her (and Snoozer) loose in a place called PetSmart. She was crabby at first, but three steps into the door and she got completely lost in conversation with a man wearing a bow tie leading a rabbit on a leash and a girl with a fat, spotted rodent she kept calling a pig. Humans are baffling, but I'm delighted Rory finally found some companions.

My classes for the next three Outside months are Food Safety, Culinary Foundations, and Intro to Baking and Pastry. Today was Food Safety for an hour, Foundations for an hour, then Baking Lab for two hours.

First, we met the teacher of Food Safety: a tiny woman with a long grey braid, who reminded me a bit of Solace, espousing practicality but with a slightly mischievous bent. She talked about keeping food the correct temperature using *refrigeration*. Instead of cold pantries like we have, Outside has *fridges* cooled by *electricity*. Electricity is not magic like our magic, but it's just as useful. Light and amplification and heating and cooling depend upon it, just like in the Realm. I asked the guy sitting next to me where the electricity came from exactly, but then he asked me what planet I was from and I wasn't quite sure how to answer. "Ours?" I ventured. He asked if I was sure.

She talked about what needs to be cold and what needs to be hot. She talked about cleaning food and storing it. She talked about cleaning our personage, our tools, and our kitchens. She talked about what to cook to what temperature. She talked about when to serve it. She talked about what to do with it after it's been cooked and after it's been served. She talked about freezing and refreezing. She talked and talked and talked. Then we took a quiz. Some of us even passed the quiz. Apparently next week, we learn about illnesses. I can't wait, but a few of my fellow classmates looked a bit queasy at the prospect.

Culinary Foundations is taught by the Food Safety woman's antithesis: a big, thick, olive-skinned man with hands like pork chops—like Hook but, you know, without the *actual* hook. He yells a lot, especially when he calls on people. We were given a tour of the kitchens and then returned to our seats for a long lecture, which I really tried to pay attention to, even though there was so much to look at everywhere and I was tired of sitting. There were so many tools I didn't know the names for hanging in a kitchen twice the size of any I've ever seen. Way better than Disneyland.

I know I'm going to excel in the baking department. Because of all the cookies and scones and bread I made when I was young, it's the thing that's most intuitive. I feel like a fish out of water the rest of the time, but pastry is where I'm at home. I know what dough is supposed to feel like and how long to work it and how to treat batter carefully. Today we made cakes and when I pulled mine out of the oven, I set it in front of the guy next to me and asked him what he thought. He said that I made better cakes than questions, which must be one of those compliments that doesn't sound quite like one. The teacher then told us that the people next to us would be our lab partners going forward.

It's possible that Phil (a princely name at that) and I got off on the wrong foot. I tried to explain to him how delighted I was to make his acquaintance. Then I told him how much I liked his crocodile shoes and he informed me that they were just Crocs, not crocodiles, which will no doubt disappoint Bianca. I told him how much I looked forward to our next class.

"It's not that you aren't a *lot* of fun, my new friend," he said. "But maybe try to keep it all in here." He drew a circle in the air in front of his chest.

"I'm sorry, Phil. It's nerves. I just can't believe I have this chance, and I really want Humans to like me." I clapped my hand over my mouth, realizing my error.

"Don't worry, your secret's safe with me." When I said good-bye, he suggested I attend the next class sober or bring enough to share.

Afterward, I collected Rory, who I found surrounded by a gaggle of pet-toting friends at a café between the school and PetSmart. She was very animated and insisted on my trying *coffee*, which is her new favorite beverage. I thought it tasted a great deal like the bottom of the frog pond. But, as vile as it is, perhaps that's the cure to her sleeping issue—she told me she'd be skipping her afternoon nap.

All in all, it was a good day. A productive day. A day I bested my fears. A day I took one more step.

A day you took one more step toward something, too, I'd imagine. Like cooking. I know you don't eat lettuce, Zell, but salads can be made of other things. I've included some recipes for tomato salad with mozzarella and roasted vegetable salad with onions. Don't be scared. Just cut slowly and keep your fingers out of the way of the knife.

Love,
CeCi

Important Fucking Correspondence from Snow B. White
Onyx Manor
West Road, Grimmland

Z,

For Grimm's sake, Zell, not everyone can be CeCi. How in
the hell did you cut your finger? You bled on my letter. Here's
my advice: Stop ingesting anything that you can't tear or nibble
into small pieces. Eat berries or something.

I should have gone Outside with CeCi, but I told her I
had important things to attend to, and she took Rory instead.
Of course, those important things ended up being a colossal
waste of time, and now I'm in a correspondingly foul mood.
Another bunch of Fairy Godmother bullshit.

Remember all that cryptic crap Solace and Figgy have been
slinging about my dad? All the half sentences and internal mus-
ings and inferences. It got me thinking: They must know something they aren't telling me.

Since Figgy's been of even less help than usual lately, I
decide to start with Solace. She intercepts me at the door.
"How do you always know when we're coming?" I ask, dis-
pensing with formality. "Don't tell me you have one of those
damned mirrors, too."

"I know what you're here for," she says. The clocks in the
shop *bing* and *bong* behind her, and she pulls the door closed
with the paw behind her back.

"I knew you were magical, but not prescient," I say.

Her nose twitches. "I need to speak with Figueroa."

"You can't even tell me where my father is without asking Figgy for permission? What the hell does she have on you broads, anyway?"

"The quarrel between Malice, Figueroa, and me is an old one and a private one. I need you to trust that I think it would be best if I spoke to her first."

"Please, Solace. Just tell me. Don't make me wait like this. Did he go to some new sort of Realm? A place I need to reach him with a fish instead of a bird? I just want to send him a wedding invite. I don't understand why you're making this so hard."

"I can tell you where he went, Snow, but I fear it won't make much sense without Figueroa's explanation of his motivations."

"You're not making any sense."

"Give me one day, Snow. Please."

"Is he safe? Can't you tell me that much?"

Solace loops her long scarf around her neck and locks the shop with a key she fishes from her apron with her paw. I follow her to Figgy's house in silence and watch her walk up the stairs. I hear raised voices but the wind picks up and I can't make out what they're saying. The fat robin sentinels descend to the lowest stair, stating Figgy will not be accepting visitors until the morning. Like I couldn't have figured that out myself.

Still standing at the bottom of Figgy's tree, I decide to swallow my pride (or at least attempt to) and head over to CeCi's to see how her classes went. I'll give the Godmothers their goddamned day and then they're going to answer me.

Before I can even place a foot on the lane, who should happen along but Rory.

"How was CeCi's first day?" I ask, feeling strangely awkward not having spoken to her since the dress fitting. Instead of answering, Rory keeps walking as if she hasn't heard.

"Wait!" I say. Rory (Rory!) holds up her middle finger at me. I trot along behind Snoozer, trying to figure out why she'd be ignoring me.

"Rory. Please? Slow down."

She turns and looks at me, her eyes bluer than I'd seen them in a while. "Do you have something to tell me, Bianca? Something I need to know?"

My heart fills my chest with an uneven rhythm. I can feel my throat flush. Could she have found out about Maro? "No," I say. "What? Maybe. I'm not sure what you mean. Could you be more specific?" Not my most articulate response ever, but I am totally unprepared for a confrontation from the least confrontational among us.

"I gather from Figgy that you and CeCi have been to see her about me, though I have no idea why. Is that where you're coming from just now? Why, Bianca? Why? Why doesn't anyone talk to me? It's always 'tiptoe around Rory' and I'm weary of it. I'm weary of you. I'm weary of CeCi. I'm weary of both of you thinking that you know what's best for me. You don't know what's best for me. You have no idea what it's like to be me." She's yelling at this point, a crescendo of pissed off I've never witnessed from her before.

"Okay," I say. I try to take a few steps closer and put my hands on her shoulders. "You're right. We don't—"

"Stop," she says. "Stop agreeing with me. And stop touching me. What were you doing here, Bianca?"

"I was here for me," I said, another gust of wind tearing across the meadow. "About my father."

"So you say," Rory says.

"I'm not denying we came for you, Rory. We did—a while ago—and I'm sorry," I say. "We didn't do it to hurt you. We just wanted to try to find a way to make you happier. That's all."

"Talk to me! Talk to me next time you want to make me happy. How do you think it made me feel, you two sneaking around behind my back?"

"We . . . I, I didn't think. You know me, I almost never do. I'm sorry. We won't help you, won't go behind your back again."

"I certainly hope not," she says and turns to resume her homeward trajectory.

"Do you forgive us?" I call to her (and the dog's) rear.

She waves, this time with all of her fingers.

Truthfully, Zell—even when Figgy asked us—I didn't understand how Rory would have felt about seeking help on her behalf. In hindsight, I never thought she would see anything but good intentions.

This new anger of Rory's, though, makes the whole Maro situation a lot more urgent. If she's this upset about us going to Figgy to *help* her, I can't even imagine her reaction to us hiding something that will *hurt* her. We have to do something and soon, because she will find out. I've read enough *Cosmo* to know the jilted woman always finds out.

We've all messed up. I declare a truce. A clean slate. A let bygones be by-fucking-gone. Right?

I think I'll go see if William is up for some bourbon.

Zell, I know that I made fun of you and Jason for removing the negative forces from your life and finding a space to clear your heads, but it was a good idea. I look at all the advice flying around here, all the help we try and fail to give one another—I think the biggest Fairy Tale of all is that any of us know what the hell we're doing.

Love,
B

Princess Briar R. Rose
Somnolent Tower Castle
South Road, Grimmland

Dearest Zell,

As the last weeks have rushed past, I feel less and less cross with CeCi and Bianca. I know they meant well. I don't want you to worry about us. There's hardly any time to fight anymore, anyway.

There's so much to do with Maro staying here and trying to explain the subtleties of Bach to Bianca's wedding cellist. And fittings and tastings and obedience classes. And of course trading off with Bianca to accompany CeCi Outside.

Forgiving Figgy has not been as easy. I simply can't believe she won't help me find a way to get closer to Henry. But one morning last week, I began thinking again about my romance novels. The characters always find some magnificent way to use the circumstances around them to their advantage. So I thought I might try to do the same.

Yesterday, it was my turn to go Outside with CeCi, so she and I agreed where and when to meet after she finished class—at six at the Starbucks—and then she said, "Traveling used to make you so nervous. You're as adventurous as Bianca these days."

"I'm nothing at all like Bianca," I said. But even though I was trying to appear indignant, I suppose CeCi's right. And I'd be lying if I didn't feel a tiny bit of pride in her declaration. You *would* be proud of me, Zell. I feel much braver these days. Bravery is exhausting, though, so I do have to drink a good deal of coffee.

"Take it easy on Bianca," CeCi said. "She loves you, you know. We both do."

"I was equally mad at both of you," I said. "But I'm willing to overlook it. Besides, you might think I came out here solely for your benefit, but I have my own business to attend to. Everything isn't always about you, CeCi."

Her eyes went big, and I feared I might have taken things too far when I realized she was trying not to laugh. "I'm sorry. That was a good try, Rory. Really. But mean isn't exactly your core competency."

"I understand you and Bianca were trying to help me," I said. "But I don't want to be anyone's charity case."

CeCi stood there, looking so professional in her chef's coat. She doffed her fluffy little toque and said, "Of course. We are sorry."

Sometimes, though, I just can't relate to CeCi, especially the deeper she gets into this cooking business. If I had her fortune—a man who loved and understood me and wanted to be with me and hoped for my happiness, I wouldn't do anything to jeopardize it. Perhaps I sound jealous, but that's not it at all. A career will never be what I want, just like being a mother will never be what she wants. I don't know why it makes me angry that we don't want the same things.

I headed straight for the coffee shop after I left CeCi. Just as I'd hoped, my new acquaintance Patricia was holding court at one of the sidewalk tables at my favorite Starbucks (yes, there are many, and the beauty of it is, they're all almost exactly the same). She and I met a visit or two ago at the PetSmart next door. Several of us pet owners had continued our conversation over coffee, and she mentioned she was some sort of therapist—that's a Human who helps others with their problems. She carried a satchel practically bursting with files to prove it. She also carried a Pekingese named Jethro. I wasn't sure how Snoozer felt about Jethro, but they seemed content enough to ignore one another.

I asked her if she remembered me and had some time to talk. "This isn't how people normally make appointments." She looked at me from over the rims of her very large sunglasses.

"Well, to whom might I write so that I can make one?"

She laughed and moved her tote bags from the extra chair so I could sit. "What's up?"

"Have you ever had problems attracting the full attention of a man?" I asked. Patricia was shaded by the green umbrella overhead, but with her long black-stockinged legs and red lipstick, I was sure the answer would be no.

She took off her sunglasses. "Are you having man troubles, my dear? You know, that's not my specialty. I consult *about* therapy. You know, for legal cases."

"It's my husband, Henry."

She pursed her lips for a moment, but then smiled, leaning back in her chair. "Okay, Rory. Tell me about Henry."

"I suppose he's rather normal. Though I know that's unkind to say. He's not terribly tall or terribly thin. He likes to hunt and fish and play darts."

"Goodness, are you sure you're from Los Angeles?" She laughed lightly.

"He likes to drink, too," I said. "Is that better?"

"Oh, honey, I'm just joking," she said, petting Jethro's ears absentmindedly. "There's nothing wrong with normal. Tell me about your relationship with him."

"Our courtship was quite rushed, see. He believes that he saved me . . . Maybe I should say, I let him think that, but it isn't quite true. And his parents and my parents thought it would be best for us to marry immediately."

"Were you willing?" She leans forward. "Was it like an arranged marriage? In some places, that's not even legal. What do you mean, *saved you*? Saved you from what?"

"That's just it. He *didn't* save me, he just thinks he did."

She stopped a young servant in a green apron and ordered us two espressos. He began to protest about how it wasn't the way they did things there and he just couldn't, until she slipped him a piece of paper money. The servant dismissed, Patricia continued. "But when you say he thinks he saved you, was it from an accident or is it more of a metaphor—like he saved you from yourself or a bad situation?"

"Neither. But it's closer to the first one, I think. So he deserved to marry me, I guess."

"You aren't property, for Christ's sake."

I brushed some eucalyptus leaves from the edge of the table. "Which one is Christ, again?"

"You're not on drugs, are you? I don't do people who are on drugs. Too complicated."

"You mean potions? No. Never. I haven't had any potions. I've tried to get some to help from someone. I just . . . I can tell this isn't making sense to you."

Patricia took off her sunglasses. "Would it help if I told you it's not even the third strangest thing I've heard today?"

I sat back, relieved. "Maybe it's easier to say I'm from somewhere different and leave it at that. We have different customs. Things we have to do and things that we should do and then things that we can choose to do. The short of it is that we got married quickly and I'm not sure he ended up with what he wanted. I simply want to change that."

"So let me get this straight. You want to change what he wants."

"Exactly."

"That's not a good idea."

"Why not?"

"You can't change what someone wants."

"Why not?"

"Rory." She pointed her sunglasses at me. "What do *you* want?"

"Happily Ever After."

Patricia laughed low and long. "Don't we all, honey."

"You don't have any suggestions?"

"I don't have the kind of silver bullet you're referring to." She zipped Jethro into his tote bag. "The best I can do is take you shopping."

We went to a bunch of shops that sold tight black things, just like Patricia herself wore. We went to a salon specializing in hair. We went to a store that has a whole floor full of items to enhance your facial features. We went to a store that only sold undergarments. It was called Victoria's Secret—a secret, I'd imagine, because you shouldn't tell people that you're going to such a place. I bought red brassieres and lace brassieres and striped pantaloons and perfume and little slippers with feathers on them. I'm sending you a box through the carriage post—a matching unicorn brassiere and pantaloon set. I got them for CeCi and Bianca, too. You are all going to love them.

When Snoozer and I met CeCi at the door of the cooking school, she stared at me for several heartbeats, like she wasn't quite sure who I was. "Rory?" she asked. "Is that you? Or did someone steal your dog?"

"Don't be daft, of course it's me."

She reached up and touched my hair. I'll admit it was a bit crunchy. "What have you done to yourself?"

"What do you think? Do you love it? I had a makeover."

"I'll say."

Hers was not the reaction I'd been hoping for. "You don't like it."

"No. Yes! Yes, I do. It's stunning. You're stunning, just, wow. It's different, that's all."

"See, now Henry won't be able to resist me."

"Oh, Rory. That's not what I meant, either." She twisted her fingers together, wincing.

"I don't understand."

"You're stunning when you're not made over. Henry's a fool if he can't see it. He's a fool to not love you. He's a fool, period."

"That wasn't very nice, CeCi," I said, pulling Snoozer's leash. "I don't say unkind things about Edmund, now do I?"

CeCi fell in behind me. "You're right. I'm sorry. It's only, I—"

I felt very magnanimous with all my new accoutrements. "You're forgiven. Now, it's time to go home and change everything!" I grabbed her arm, and we hailed our taxi to the portal. It was just our luck one stopped immediately.

See, I'm becoming my own woman. I'll let you know how things go as soon as Henry gets back from his hunt. Patricia said it would be a *long shot*. Whatever that means.

Love,
Rory

From the Desk of Cecilia Cinder Charming
Crystal Palace
North Road, Grimmland

Dear Zell,

Lucinda finally counted the tiaras today. I could hear her rummaging through the crown room across the hall. And her subsequent keening.

"CeCi! Alert the guards. Someone has stolen a tiara!"

I came into the room behind her. "No one stole anything."

"It's that new maid. I told you I didn't like the look of her."

"The maid is fine. No one took anything. Leave it alone."

"Then where is it?"

I looked around my room. My room. My sanctuary. I looked at her standing in it. And my stomach began to burn. I could have had her thrown out. I could have had her punished. I could have told her the tiara's value in worms.

"Those tiaras are mine. Not yours. I didn't ask you to inventory them. Furthermore, what I do with them and where I put them is my business. I don't know how many times we have to go over this."

It took her a few seconds too long to put a wounded look on her face. "I'm only trying to help you. I've made my amends and now you're choosing to shut me out."

"You made my life a living hell. And if I didn't know better, I'd say you were still trying."

"That's a bit drastic, don't you think? You're an achiever, thanks to me. And look what you've done. For yourself. For your family."

"None of this was for you. I took your daughters in because you forced them into hysterics over losing a future that was never attainable in the first place."

Lucinda stepped toward me, glowering. "So what, I encouraged them to dream big. They weren't sturdy stock like you. They were delicate. They didn't have any life skills. You just never know how girls will turn out."

"You told them to cut off their feet to fit in a goddamned pair of shoes," I said. "I think it was safe to predict their resulting low self-esteem."

"You and that feckless Snow White run around perpetuating the myth that all stepmothers are like Valborg."

"No. At least Valborg didn't want Bianca to stick around and suffer. At least she tried to make it quick."

"So dramatic. You are certainly entitled to your royal opinion. But you'll always be our Cinderella."

I leaned in very close to her. "Don't ever call me that again."

"Family sticks together," she said. "You'd do well to remember where you came from."

I almost had to laugh. I remember almost every minute of every day. I'm constantly trying to figure out what to keep and what to discard, what is me and what isn't. "You are not my family. The only reason I let you tromp around like you own this castle is because it's easier than fighting you. But I'm tired of the same thing over and over again. Aren't you tired of it? I'm not having this discussion again."

She drew her lips tight. "I'm the only mother you've got."

"You may be right," I said. "But CeCi, Bianca, Zell, Rosemount, DJ, those people are my family."

Her lips spread into a slick smile. "Aha. You didn't say Edmund."

"What do you mean, *aha*? This isn't a test. Edmund's not

family, either. He's something else. Something even better. Something more. Something I wouldn't expect *you* to understand."

She winced, almost imperceptibly, but winced all the same. "About love, you mean? Of course. What could I possibly understand about that?" The dark gleam in her eyes had returned, the one I remembered seeing before I hid in corners as a girl. "Darling and Sweetie's father left me for a chambermaid, and your father left me because we were wallowing in debt. If you want to know, it was a relief when you banished him."

I tried to keep my face still as she studied me. My father was just the latest feature on her revolving carousel of excuses. But I let go of my feelings for him long ago.

"I've always had to rely on myself," she continued. "I've made the best of hard circumstances. What was I supposed to do? Give up? Let my daughters live in garbage or on the street? There was only going to be one queen in the house, if any. How could I know that you would take care of us if you were the chosen one? We weren't your blood. Your father hadn't paid a bill or graced our doorstep in years. I placed my bets. The cards did not fall in my favor."

"But you're not apologizing."

"I can't apologize for a choice I didn't have. Besides, you can't say things didn't work out for the best." She spread her hands wide around her.

"I think we're done here," I said.

"That prince loves you," she said, backing away down the corridor. "You're lucky and you don't even know it. You'll never have to make the choices I did. For your own sake, become whatever he wants."

It's always been easier to think of Lucinda as simply evil, continually wanting the worst outcome for me, a misguided one for the girls. It's even more horrifying to think that she believes she made the right choice. But of course she does.

She turned her back to me, but I could imagine her face. She said, "I don't know what it is that you're up to, disappearing all the time. Even if you don't tell me, I'll find out and ensure it stops. I won't have you throw everything we've got out the window."

I wished I could have thrown the other thirty-seven tiaras out the window. Or her. I don't owe anyone an explanation about my belongings or my time or my marriage. Or anything else, for that matter.

Love,
CeCi

She Sang Songs without End

Important Fucking Correspondence from Snow B. White
Onyx Manor
West Road, Grimmland

Z,

I spend all night in my father's study. I reread every journal. I cross-fucking-reference dates with maps and satchels of money from more lands than I can count.

I finally get to the point I can't concentrate anymore, I'm so tired. I look out the window and the goddamned sun is coming up. In my mind, there's a tiny fear, but I either can't or maybe won't let it grow into an actuality.

I consider going to CeCi or Rory, but instead I head straight to Figgy's. I gave them the time they asked for, and it's time I had some answers, Fairy Godmother sanctioned or not.

When I get there, Figgy sits me down in that damned calming chair with the canaries. "Bianca," she says, expansively. "I suppose we owe you an explanation."

I try to start politely because Rory's always saying how you can get more flies with honey than vinegar, and blah blah blah. I try to be honest about the information I put together in the study the night before.

"Figs, I know my father's been gone awhile, longer than even I care to admit. As far as I can tell, he left for the last time just before I woke up. But there were letters for a long time before that. I always knew he was somewhere, even if I wasn't exactly sure where. So, all I'm asking for is some help narrowing down where he is right now, maybe where he has been over the last couple of years. You know, so I can send him a wedding invitation. See, nothing hard. Nothing scary. Nothing out of control."

"Oh, but it's complicated, my dear," says Figgy.

I wave a tea-toting canary away.

"Complicated how?"

"I was so sure you knew, until Solace came and told me of the real purpose for your ventures Outside."

There it was, that speck of fear again. But this time, it was black and blooming like ink in water. "Real purpose? I thought your birds were omniscient?"

"I thought you'd gone Outside to find your father, dear."

I bop myself on the forehead, and the canaries scatter. "Solace must have given him a dedicated portal. Of course. That must be why there's so much money. But if he's coming back and forth, why—"

"A dedicated portal?" Figgy asks. And all of a sudden I'm more confused than I was when I came in. "For Cecilia's classes?

Oh, heavens, such frivolity. I thought the classes were simply a ruse for you to track him down."

A sickening cold spreads up my limbs. "Track him down? And do what? I love my father, Figgy, whatever mistakes he made. I don't understand . . . If he's Outside, why didn't Solace tell me? How long has he been there?"

"I worried you'd get caught up finding him, take too much time, and be trapped."

"How. Long. Ago. Figgy."

"He wanted to atone for leaving you in Valborg's care. He punished himself for a long time, casting about and cutting ties before he decided to exile himself. He wanted to see you one last time, but he simply couldn't conquer the fear that you wouldn't forgive him."

"Wait. I don't know what you're talking about." I try to get up, but the birds have strategically pinned my shoulders.

"Let me start from the beginning, or at least from after you ate the apple and the dwarves placed you in the glass coffin in the forest. Your father was summoned to Grimmland once Valborg was arrested. He was terribly distraught over what had happened, and he visited the coffin every night. I doubt anyone but Solace and I saw his comings and goings—he only came during our watches."

I couldn't say anything. I opened my mouth but nothing would come out. My father had stayed with me. He was sorry. But then again, he didn't help me, either. He didn't break the glass. He didn't even try to move me somewhere else, as William had so ham-handedly planned to do, to study the situation further. He stood and lamented, and wrung his hands. And to top it all off, he fled.

I want to be anywhere but Figgy's living room. Just when

I think she can't possibly tell me anything more painful, she keeps going.

"When William dropped the coffin and the piece of apple dislodged itself, we Fairy Godmothers saw to your recovery. Your father came one last time, to say farewell. You wouldn't remember, of course. Malice had given you a potion for the pain."

"So he knew I was awake and he *still* left?"

"He rejoiced in your improvement. He said he'd bequeathed you money and maps for every Realm he'd visited, as well as his journals. He thought that was the man you'd wish to know. Not the man he had become. We begged him to stay and make things right, but he felt unworthy."

"But, how long has he been gone?"

"It's been almost two years since you woke up, my dear."

"He exiled himself that day."

"In a manner of speaking, yes." She makes a gesture to the canaries and they began to circle in formation.

Instead of feeling calmer, I feel ripped in two. My beloved father, the coward. I want to find him and hug him and then punch him until he sees stars scouring the sky like Figgy's canaries. And then it comes to me. "The birds! The birds can cross the Realms. Can't the birds find him?"

"Perhaps they might be able to locate him and deliver a letter using trial and error—the mail simply requires time and positive identification. But he no longer possesses enough magic from the Realm for us to track him directly. Certainly not enough to return."

"But he's the only family I have." I hear raindrops pattering on the roof above us. At least the drizzle feels appropriate.

"That's simply not true. You have Cecilia and Briar Rose and William and . . ."

Lightning. "Stop it, Figgy. It's not the same and you know it. Why wouldn't he have waited until we could have had a real conversation? I would have forgiven him."

"He didn't want your forgiveness, my dear. You can't give people what they won't accept."

"So he's never coming back."

"No. I'm afraid not."

Soft thunder rolls outside. "And you and Solace knew the whole time."

"I feared you knowing his whereabouts would cause you to do something futile, at best, and dangerous, at worst. Solace and I had agreed on waiting for the right opportunity to give you the information."

"How about when William knocked the goddamned apple out of my throat? How about right after, when I still could have gone after him? Why wasn't right then the appropriate time? No wonder Rory and CeCi have had it with you."

"I should think," says Figgy, lowering her voice, "your friends have been good examples of what happens when Fairy Tales act rashly."

The wind picks up now so that the rain splatters on the windows. Figgy moves toward the center of the room.

"So let me get this straight. You lie to me to keep me from going Outside to find my father. Meanwhile, you and Solace bicker over when to tell me for such a duration you've now lost track of him."

She folds her wings in on herself as the gusts howl through the chimney. "He is now as Human as any Human."

"Then I'll have to find him myself."

"That sort of hasty thoughtlessness is exactly why we didn't give you the information in the first place!"

"Fat lot of good it did. If you had told me in the first place, he wouldn't be lost."

"He isn't *lost*. He made his own decision, Snow White. Not mine, not yours. The road back for him is forever closed. If you aren't careful, you'll make the same mistake."

"What if it isn't a mistake? What if I want to live Outside? What if I don't want any part of this Realm where you divvy out essential information at your convenience?"

"I cannot stop you. But I can make you wait. You must fulfill your Pages before I allow you to leave permanently."

"I'll go whenever I want." White light splits the room, and we are momentarily deaf from the sound.

"It'll be the end of everything we know."

"How can you be so sure?"

"Look at what you're causing right now." She gestures toward the door, where, through the panes of glass, the boughs are stretched taut. "If you refuse your Pages, the whole book falls apart. You'll destroy Rory and CeCi and William and Edmund and Solace and Hansel and Gretel and me—everyone in our Realm."

"Write me new Pages, then. You did it for Rory. Why not me?"

Hail starts to pelt the roof, violent and distracting. "You don't understand what you're saying." Figgy drew very close. "The destruction *will* happen if you abandon your Pages. You can do whatever you want once you're married and Valborg has been executed—but you cannot change what has already been written. You couldn't be that self-centered."

"I couldn't because I don't know when you're telling the truth. Half the time you deal in destruction and misery and fear and the other half you're doling out fake Happily Ever Afters. Look at what you've done to Rory!"

"Briar Rose lost everything, and she will continue to lose everything. Fred's interference didn't change her fate, it simply prolonged it. His deed was hardly a kindness."

"What are you talking about? She has her *life*. She has her parents. She has us. She has . . . Snoozer."

"Even if she's still alive, she's lost what was real to her," Figgy tuts. "I'm only trying to give her purpose again."

"You're wrong, Figgy. Maybe Rory lost whatever life she had before—but she still has hope. Can't you see her fighting for it? If things are so bleak then why even give her new Pages?"

Figgy blinks. "Because without purpose, there is not even room for hope. If you'd simply stop filling her head with all this dream nonsense and Outside expectations, she might find herself content where she is, instead of measuring herself against you and Cecilia."

"Oh, I get it. It's our fault, then. Fucking great. Fuck this. Fuck you, Figgy."

I stand, upending the chair. Tea, canaries, incense everywhere. The house shakes with the storm. With my footfalls. Candles fall from their holders. It's a miracle I don't burn the whole place down.

So I guess that's it, Zell. I just sit around on my hands for a while so I don't ruin our world. I let my father slip farther and farther away. And Rachel, too. This isn't fair. I don't want to do this anymore. And just as soon as I don't have to, I won't. That's a fucking promise.

B

From the Desk of Cecilia Cinder Charming
Crystal Palace
North Road, Grimmland

Dear Zell,

Edmund has been home the last couple of weeks, organizing groups to salvage the downed limbs from the big storm and donate them to the needy for firewood. Despite how busy he's been, it's become increasingly difficult to get to classes without him asking questions. Today was the worst yet.

It was a simple enough question. "Where are you off to now?"

But maybe his emphasis rested too heavily on *now* or *off* or *you*. Maybe I was just tired of being vague. So I was cruel instead. He put his hand on my shoulder, and I stepped away. "Is there something you need?"

"Am I not allowed to care where you're going, CeCi? You're my wife, in case you've forgotten."

"So what, you need to keep tabs on your property now?"

I could see him weighing whether to try to start over again. "Just stop. I'm sorry I asked." And I'm sorry I answered. But I don't know how to apologize. I just sink deeper and deeper into this chasm, and I let us grow apart.

My classes have been a respite from the drama here in Grimmland. My pastry instructor says I have a knack for understanding texture. I like butchering a lot, too, but my lab partner is much better at it than I am. We've reached a sort of peaceful tolerance, Phil and I. As long as I keep my questions limited to cooking, he doesn't look at me like his eyes are going to pop out anymore. In fact, he laughs a lot now. One day during a break, he made us tinfoil hats to keep us safe from the "Humans." It was a charming gesture. Almost like we're friends.

Speaking of friends, even though Rory, Bianca, and I are bickering more often than not, I am very thankful that Bianca deemed me worthy of becoming her project. She could have devoted her time to fund-raising for your unicorns or making collars for Snoozer and his friends, but instead she devoted her time to launching my cooking career. She can do those other things or not. Hell, I think at this point she's proven she can do almost anything she wants.

Almost, I guess, except find some sort of peace with the news about her father. I can't help but be angry on her behalf. Solace and Figgy always say they have our best interests in mind, but it rarely turns out that way. It seems we constantly end up with more heartbreak than we start with.

Bianca has been so busy convincing everyone else that her father was simply too preoccupied with traveling to RSVP for the wedding that the truth was nearly unbearable. When she did say something to us during the weekly fitting with Five this morning, she more spat than spoke. Then she announced that everyone in the wedding would wear black.

Rory showed up clearly having consumed several coffee beverages, fairly buzzing around the room. When she finally alit, she handed us each boxes of matching unicorn lingerie. Something about someone's secret. I'd be very surprised if a similar shipment does not arrive at your door quite soon. She was still very excited about her makeover and began begging Bianca and me to get our own cosmetic updates.

Surprisingly, Bianca, looking up from the sinister-looking bridal train behind her, agreed. "Sure. Whatever. When are we going?"

"Tomorrow?" Rory suggested.

"Great," said Bianca. Her voice was as flat as a lily pad.

"I have class tomorrow," I said.

"You can meet us afterward." Bianca stood before a three-way mirror, but seemed to be looking everywhere but at the striking figure she made.

"Fun!" squealed Rory, clapping her hands like an over-sugared child. Hansel says there's something called *decaf* we may need to slip Rory's kitchen staff. Phil can help me procure it, I'm sure.

I suspected Bianca was about as interested in a makeover as Rory would be in a bourbon tasting, but I kept my suspicions to myself. Honestly, I kind of wish I could go Outside this once by myself—just to hear myself think—but I can't bear to disappoint either of them. Right now it's hard to say whose emotional crisis is more immediate.

Rory excused herself from our post-fitting lunch, saying she had a big night planned and that she didn't want to ruin anything by eating too many fries. Bianca didn't feel like lunch, either, but I dragged her to Shambles anyway and pushed her onto a bar stool.

I sat down beside her and took her limp hand. "What did William say when you told him about your father?"

I expected her to pull away, but she didn't move. Her voice had lost its flatness, and was heavy with grief instead. "He said he was sorry my father wouldn't be at our wedding. Sorry that he was gone for good. He had no idea my father had visited my little glass box. Then he gave me a hug and offered me a drink."

"Well," I said. "That's something, I guess."

"Maybe. But he doesn't get it. He told me I might have *suspected.*"

I was silent for a beat longer than I should have been.

"You, too? Fantastic, I'm the only idiot in the village. Why didn't *you* say anything, Sherlock? Thanks for leaving me hanging."

I put my remaining hand on top of our clenched ones. "I think we're all pretty scared of talking to you about your father. What happened to you is, at least in part, his fault. And we're angry with him. It would make more sense if you were just a little bit angry with him, as well. Being angry with someone doesn't invalidate all the rest of your feelings for a person. You know that. But you're so defensive."

"Valborg was mostly normal when they met. How could he know she'd resort to homicide as soon as he started traveling again?"

"He should have been there for you. Whether or not she was bad, or good, or murderous. He should have been around more—at least should have spent more days here than gone. He shouldn't have assumed."

"In hindsight, sure. But people need to do what makes them happy. He would have been miserable staying around just to make sure my nursemaids were doing their jobs. He was back and forth my entire childhood—even before my mother died. I think he probably thought Valborg and I would take care of each other. He's a good man, CeCi."

"I'm not saying he isn't," I said, which was a small fib. "But it's like you keep telling me about my own father. He should have protected his child."

"That's different. Your father *knew* what Lucinda was. He *participated* in making you the family's servant."

"The fact remains that your father doesn't want to be found. And even if you could find him Outside—in time, because you *won't* destroy Grimmland, though I can certainly understand the temptation at times—it isn't as if he can come back with you."

"Yeah," she said. She put her face in her hands. "I know."

"On your wedding day, it'll be me and Rory and William standing by you. Same as always. We'll be the ones standing by you afterward. No matter what sort of queen you decide to be, even if it's the queen of your own private rowboat. That's not going to change."

She didn't say much more for the rest of lunch. She didn't finish her cider, just picked it up and plunked it down, making wet rings on the table. She didn't tell me to shut up when I complained my plate of fries was going to require Five to let out my bridesmaid dress. She didn't even laugh when I drew her a sunshine smiley face with a squeeze bottle of ketchup. She shoved the plate back at me and told me she was late. She didn't say for what, and I let her go.

It appeared I was the only one without a mysterious afternoon appointment. I tried staying at Shambles, making idle conversation with a couple of the dwarves coming in for their lunch break from the mine, but I didn't get very far.

"What *do* you mine, anyway?" I asked Tripp, realizing Bianca had never really said.

"Well, darlin'," he said in his rich brogue, "we dig up the luck for all the charms those Humans scarf down at breakfast."

"Don't listen to him," said Max. "We ship our loads of twinkle up to the stars. Damned things would be dull as rock if it weren't for us."

"Helpful, thanks," I said, swallowing the dregs of my cider as they clapped each other on the arms and laughed. "Well, I wouldn't want to keep you from your important tasks."

When I got home, I collapsed on my bed, cursing myself for wondering about stars. I expected Lucinda to descend, barking about something or other, but instead I heard Darling and Sweetie shuffling around my door.

"Can I help you?" It came out sharper than I meant.

"We just were checking to see if you were okay," said Darling, in a voice so low I could barely hear her.

Sweetie felt for the edge of the doorway and poked her head around. "We tried to visit the library, but Edmund seems to be sleeping in there."

"We're not trying to be nosy," Darling added.

"Can we get you some tea?" asked Sweetie. I could hear the clatter of the saucer already in her hand, so I said yes. We drank our tea in silence, but I found myself oddly grateful for their nervous, yet sincere company.

Lucinda had them believing we were all one marital confrontation away from homelessness, so I tried to reassure them—and myself. Honestly I haven't gotten past how painful Edmund's loss of faith in me is. Or how this is all completely my fault. We'll work things out. Or we won't. I have to try and fix this. I'm just not sure how to fix anything anymore.

Have you tried the instructions for the soup I sent you? Really, if you just keep it on a low heat and move the pot holders away from the flame, there's very little chance anything *else* will start on fire.

Love,
CeCi

Princess Briar R. Rose
Somnolent Tower Castle
South Road, Grimmland

Dearest Zell,

I'm sure you know by now that Bianca is inconsolable about her father, though it is certainly understandable in this case. Could he have known how much Bianca would love Outside? Or that she'd become the kind of person who'd spend the rest of her life searching for him? That is one laudable thing about our Bianca, no matter how vexing she can be: She never gives up.

I wish I could claim such tenacity. On my own battlefront, my efforts have once more proven useless. I'm trying to keep myself in good spirits, but it's becoming increasingly difficult.

Last night, I marched into Henry's bedroom with my new hairstyle and makeup and dressed in my new lingerie. I'd envisioned rendering him speechless. He'd drop whatever he was doing and stare, enraptured. Instead, he lowered the scroll he was puzzling over and said, "What are you supposed to be?"

"I'm your fantasy!" I spun around, nearly losing my balance on my new heels. To my credit, his mouth did hang a bit agape. "I'm just trying to become what you want."

He began to laugh, harder than necessary. "Did you happen to bring a sandwich, then?"

I drew a hand across my eyes to catch the welling tears. My fingers came away black and sparkling.

"Come here," he said. I tripped toward him, my heel sticking in the grout between the stones.

"You're a good person, Rosie," he said. "I appreciate the effort."

"But?"

"Hey. Don't cry, babe. I'm sorry that things aren't exactly the way you want them to be with us."

"Not as sorry as I am," I said. I tried to make my way to the door, but I felt warm all of a sudden. And dizzy. I tottered over to a sturdy chair and sat down. "Is it so ridiculous that I need the attention of my husband? I want to start our family, Henry. You can settle down. Stop sowing your oats or whatever you're doing. My father can start including you at court. You won't have go on all those beastly hunts anymore. You can spend more time with my friends—"

"Rosie, wait." He paused, taking a big slug of whatever was in his pewter mug. "I adore you, you know that, right? But we're in two different places right now."

"We're both sitting here in this very room. You aren't making sense."

"Okay. How about this: I don't want to debate social justice with William or design Rodent Roundabouts with Edmund. I *want* to be on hunts. I want to find the next big adventure. Rescue the princess. Slay the dragon. Outwit the ogre. That's who I am. I don't want to be in court, listening to old people debate property lines and knighting bears. I'm still young. So are you. Sort of."

"But everyone grows up eventually, don't they?" I asked.

He shrugged. "We rushed into things, Rosie. We don't have much chemistry. Besides, you must want something other than . . . this." He made a wide sweep of his hands. I looked around his room—a place as foreign to me as someone else's castle.

"I'm not sure what you mean. This"—I mirrored his motion—"is exactly what I want. You are exactly what I want."

"How can that be? I'm not ready for the kind of life you clearly want to live."

"But when will you be ready? Don't you want a baby?"

"Well, I don't *not* want a baby."

"Tell me what you mean." I tried to look him in the eyes, but they were everywhere but on me. It was almost as if he were embarrassed.

"It means that I don't know yet. And I don't want to hurt you any more than I already have. Look, let's just be honest with one another. Lots of Fairy Tale couples make their marriages work for their circumstances. Look at William and Bianca, they—"

"They aren't even married yet!"

"That's not the point. Listen, you don't have to turn yourself into something you're not for my sake," he said, gesturing up and down at my new black lingerie. "Don't get me wrong. You look great. But I know who you are, and it's not . . . whatever this is."

I snuggled up to him like Star did to Sabian in *The Cake and the Damned*. "I can be whoever you want me to be."

He jumped up, moving away from me. "You're creeping me out. Stop."

I felt nauseated. "Why don't you understand I'm willing to wait for you? I'm willing to change for you."

"But *I* don't even know what I want. Can't you understand not knowing? Haven't you ever not known, Rosie?"

"All I know is that I hate it when you call me Rosie." I was overcome by sobs.

"I'll get your nurse," he said and left the room. I spent the night in his bed, covered in the furs of dead animals. I have no idea where he slept. I wish I didn't care.

And now I'm supposed to go Outside with Bianca and CeCi. I can listen to them explain once more how stupid I've been, or I can pretend everything is just fine. There's no preferable option except to go back to bed and pretend last night never happened at all. One thing is certain, Zell: I am a fool.

At least now I know what a long shot is.

Love,
Rory

Important Fucking Correspondence from Snow B. White
Onyx Manor
West Road, Grimmland

Z,

I think and think and think and I decide the only person left who may be able to shed any light on my father's decision is Valborg herself. The guards sedate her, so she was pretty out of it the last time I visited, but I might get lucky. I figure I have to at least try.

She's kept under guard at my father's old hunting retreat just a bit south of Grimmland, near Avalon. A place that's sad and beautiful at the same time. It's usually cool and drizzling, and sometimes fog comes and goes in little puffs. When it's clear, the lake is so still you can see the reflection of the Big Rock Candy Mountains. Waterfowl fly over dead tree trunks in sharp silhouette.

It's bright out when I arrive, but raining at the same time. Almost like the sun is crying. That's how I've felt since I found out about my father. Clear yet bereft, angry but yearning, and all at once.

A guard shows me to a large, wooden door. They tell me no one has come to see Valborg in some time.

"Who was the last to visit?"

"Figueroa. She comes every couple of months." Of course she does. There is nothing that snoopy fowl doesn't meddle in.

Valborg's cavern is huge, hewn from rough grey stone. There are a few muted rugs, a bed, and a couple of chairs, but the otherwise the room is empty. She's dressed in darker grey, as cold as the stone around her, and she's looking out at the sunlit rain without expression.

"The fairest of them all," she says. She sounds like she's been gargling gravel. "You've come for me."

"Valborg."

"Are you here to finally kill me?"

Is she relieved? She can't be. "Haven't they told you about the wedding?"

"They told me. But I was hoping you'd moved up the time-table." Unmistakable disappointment lines her face.

"Figgy says the Pages are pretty specific on the timeline. Can't screw with the Pages, you know."

"So it seems." She doesn't smile. "I do wish someone could make time go faster, though."

"I didn't come to talk about that, anyway," I say, pointing to the chairs.

She turns to face me fully, and I can't stop myself from gasping. She looks a good two decades older than she did the last time I saw her. I wonder if that mirror did more than just *tell* her she was beautiful. Or if the suggestion itself could make up the stark change in her appearance.

"I'll get to it then," I say, not knowing what else to add. "I need to know when you last saw my father."

"It was just after William found you and they arrested me. He came to see me, after all that time and all those letters. He came here." She spreads her hands, then looks at them as if they're revealing this information to her for the first time.

"Did he tell you that he was leaving? Where he was going?"

"As he was preparing to leave on one of his adventures, when you were only eight or nine, he told me I'd been a mistake. I didn't know how to be a mistake. I only knew how to be a woman."

"You don't have to explain anything to me." I turn my back on her. We obviously aren't going to sit down, and I don't want to hear this torrent of berserk.

"This may be my only chance for confession, Snow. Beautiful Snow. The fate that lies before me is a fair one. Never for a moment fool yourself into thinking I had no choice but to hurt you. I didn't care that you had Pages or even what was in them. Not until everything was finished. I alone was responsible. I hurt you because I wanted to, because I could."

"Does *why* matter anymore?"

"Maybe not to you."

I don't have anything to say to this.

She finally sits. "I bought the mirror after your father began to leave us for months at a time. You and I got on well enough then, for strangers. Your father's trips grew longer and longer. On the rare occasions he did return, you were all he cared to see. He was all you cared to see. For a time, I sent you away and told him you were at boarding school or off with your friends. It wasn't until later I sought a more permanent solution."

"Why would you keep us apart?"

"I was lonely and I wanted his attention. I wanted your father to see me and only me, to realize *he'd* made the mistake. The mirror gave me advantages, and I reveled in them."

"But you didn't need them. Even if my father was a jackass."

"The mirror was in my head day and night. It told me that I was not a mistake. It told me that I was beautiful and because I was beautiful, I was worthy. I was wanted. I was necessary. I had a purpose. Can you understand how it healed me? And how it destroyed me?"

"Yes," I whisper. Purpose. Hope. A ladybug crawls across the chest-high balcony wall. Below, a single red rose blooms.

For a brief instant, I understand why CeCi let Lucinda stay. I don't want to feel this way. I don't want to care at all.

"The mirror healed me so fully that it became a second skin. When you awoke and it told me you were once more the fairest, I felt as if that skin was being torn from my body. When you destroyed the mirror, I was able to see myself again. My real self. Not only as a mistake but one who continued to perpetuate mistakes. I hurt you to punish your father for his absence. I hurt the Huntsman to get to you. I hurt you to hurt you. Now you will hurt me."

"Stop with the pronouncements. Do you know where he is? My father. Did he say exactly where he was going?"

"He came to me because you had awakened. He blamed himself. Did you know that?"

She's barely listening to me. I grind my teeth to keep from screaming. "I've heard. I know he's Outside. I just want to know where."

"The blame is mine alone." She looks out into the distance, eyes dull.

I want to shake her, but instead just shake my hands at her. "Blame isn't like a wishbone. It's like the whole fucking chicken—there's more than enough to go around."

A brief smile passes over her face without stopping.

"I'm not talking about blame," I say. "Did you ever travel Outside with him? Do you know where he would have gone?"

"Your father never stayed in one place long."

"Tell me something I don't know."

"If he went anywhere repeatedly, it would have been the place that's a tribute to the Realm called . . ."

"Disneyland?"

"Yes. That. He was going to help them."

"He and Rory, eh?"

"I beg your pardon?"

"Never mind."

"He thought that he could pay tribute to his life here. The Humans thought he was just the sort of creative mind they needed. They were going to send him around their world with his colorful ideas. They thought he was some sort of artist."

"He loved Humans that much?"

"He loved you that much."

"Funny way to show it." I want a drink, though whether it's to dull my senses or smash against the wall, I'm not sure.

"It was a way to maintain a connection with you and still give himself the punishment he thought he deserved."

"But he'll die."

"We'll all die one day, Snow. Some of us simply do it sooner than others."

"I can promise you won't feel any pain. I have a plan."

"Ah, *now* you're willing to talk about that, are you? You can't promise such a thing. No one can. I'm ready. You should be, too."

I take her hands. "We can end with joy. One last dance. It will be painless. What do you say?"

"I gave up my say long ago."

"Whatever. Fuck it." I let go with an involuntary shudder. "If this is how you want it to be. Riddles and vagaries. I'm sorry for how he made you feel. The rest, well . . ."

"That is not your apology to make." She turns away from me, her attention returning to the mist. "It was good of you to come."

I can't see the ladybug anymore. I can't see the rose anymore, either. Everything looks grey. I feel grey.

Isn't it wonderful to get news from me? Don't you miss us? Just another beautiful day, just another perfect once upon a time.

B

From the Desk of Cecilia Cinder Charming
Crystal Palace
North Road, Grimmland

Dear Zell,

No one was very happy when we met at Rory's on make-over morning. We stumbled up the tower steps glowering at our feet until Bianca looked up and threw her arms out to stop us. "Wait a minute. What happened to your new look?" She gave Rory a once-over.

"It wasn't what he wanted."

"No shit." I think Bianca meant to say it to herself in defense of Rory. But it didn't come out that way.

"You're not helping," I said. I took Rory by the shoulders. "What happened?"

"He's repulsed by me." She pulled away and stomped a few more steps past Bianca. "What did you expect?"

"Well, he's repulsive. So everybody wins," Bianca said.

"Still not helping," I sang. Bianca held up her palms and dropped back a step, tripping over Snoozer's leash.

"You're beautiful, Rory," I said. "Outside and inside. So what if Henry wants something else? Maybe it's better that you find something—someone—who makes *you* happy."

Snoozer twisted his leash around Bianca's legs, and she let out a string of curses. "Just give me the damned leash." Rory stopped and shoved the lead into her hand.

"I don't know what will make me happy. I've spent my whole life trying to want *this*. And you're not helping. Either of you."

"Okay," I said. "I'll stop. We'll stop."

At the top of the steps, Snoozer began to growl, hackles raised, and we all slowed. My stomach squirmed but I couldn't see Bianca's face to see if she'd noticed. Rory was too busy being huffy to identify anything out of the ordinary, but I smelled Maro's lavender perfume, though she was nowhere in sight.

I cursed Rory's hospitality. There was no telling how many times Maro had accessed the open room or why. At least we'd hidden the clock bracelets well—until Bianca pulled them from behind the loose brick in the wall.

I tried to make eye contact with Bianca, but she was oblivious. There was no way to turn us around without explaining to Rory.

I set my knives on the tea table and made a quick pass around the small room. Maro was either very well hidden or had very recently vacated the space.

"Chop-chop, Your Royal Chefness," Bianca said, tossing a clock bracelet in my direction. "What's the holdup?" She herded Rory and Snoozer through the portal with a little shove. I took one last look around the room and followed them into the darkened tunnel.

"What were you looking at?" asked Rory.

"I thought I saw a mouse, is all. Oh, my knives! I'll be right back. Wait for me on the other side." I spun and trotted back through the portal.

When I stepped back into the tower, Maro was standing on the other side of the portal, jaw hanging open. She let out a little squeak of surprise; her throat and chest were blotched with a red latticework of guilt.

"I thought I smelled you, Maro. What are you doing up here?"

"CeCi! My goodness, it's been ages!" she said, recovering her composure.

"Not long enough, I'm afraid."

She tittered like a small and stupid bird. "This must be how you get back and forth to your classes, how clever!"

"Were you . . . spying?"

She laughed again, waving her hand dismissively. "I forgot what a ham you are. Didn't Rory mention I'm staying here? You should have seen the tarantulas at the Inn. Poor Muffet! Rory's been such a doll to let me stay. We have tea up here all the time, and the view is just to die for so I thought I'd—"

"Muffet was finished fumigating the Inn weeks ago." I could feel my hatred coming off my skin like sunburn, but she either didn't notice or didn't care.

"What?" asked Maro. "Oh well, maybe I'm confused."

"No," I said. "I'm sure you know exactly what's going on. I'll repeat myself one more time. *Why are you here?*"

"Well, Rory was telling me about the new clock and I just wanted to see it for myself. It's, uh, something. Certainly a work of . . . art." She gestured to the portal. "But I don't want to keep you from your business Outside. Perhaps sometime you'll give me a tour. I've never been, you know."

"You can't be serious," I said. "I wouldn't give you a clock bracelet if . . ."

Henry rounded the corner from the staircase. He froze, taking in the scene: me, Maro, the portal, the rest of the empty room. He closed his eyes and sighed.

"Shit," he said.

"You were this close," I said, pinching my finger and thumb together. I was tempted to push both of them down the steps. "Poor form, Henry, poor form."

"She said she didn't come up here anymore. We thought for a change in scenery we'd—"

"I can't even tell you how much I don't want to hear the end of that sentence." Blood thumped in my ears. I tried to tamp down the anger in my voice. "If you knew anything about her, you'd know this tower is special, private. She only comes up here when it's important."

"I had no idea," Maro said, lying through the giant space in her front teeth.

"Just save it, Maro, your story has changed three times since you started talking. I can't believe the two of you. If you insist on breaking her heart, do it somewhere else."

"You're not going to tell her, are you?" Henry studied the clock, then the floor.

"Who cares?" Maro's voice dropped an octave.

"That's more like it," I said. "Let's see your true colors."

She managed a lopsided sneer, accentuated by her over-rouged lips. "You and Bianca never liked me, anyway."

"It was Rory who knew what you really were. We told her to give you a chance, and look where that got us. Unbelievable. In her own castle!" I shook my head.

"But you aren't going to tell her, right?" Henry asked again. Honestly. I've met pond scum with more integrity.

I walked up to him and shoved my finger in his barrel chest. "No. You are. And you're going to do it soon. I'm not lying to her anymore."

"So what?" Maro crossed her arms and looked at him. "Tell her. Don't tell her. What's the difference?"

"Maro, stop," he said. He looked almost genuinely pained. His face was easier to read than Bianca's *Cosmo*. He evidently had not informed Maro of the balance of monetary power set forth in their pre-marriage bargaining.

I couldn't contain a grin. "Actually, Maro, Henry has quite a bit to lose. Reputation. Money. Title. This castle."

"Whatever do you mean?" asked Maro. "It's already his."

"It's complicated," Henry said, putting his fingers to the bridge of his nose. "My ownership of Rory's, rather, my kingship, my claim . . . There's no heir."

"Oh, it gets better," I said. "Rory's parents wanted to see her get married—a day she'd been waiting for over a hundred long years—but old Henry here's parents got a little greedy, wanting everything to be handed down to the couple immediately. As a compromise, Rory's parents left everything to Henry's heir. They were still overly trusting of the lecherous jerk. But it all worked out in the end, since he's shooting blanks."

Maro paused, seemingly unsure which of us to be angrier with. Then she turned to me. "Don't forget that I can tell everyone about your little cooking excursions. I have leverage, you know."

All of her bluster reminded me of Lucinda. Even I was surprised by the laugh that erupted from my throat. So what if the kingdom thinks I'm common? So what if they talk? I'd rather Edmund knew the truth and have the big, inevitable fight than let this festering ambivalence ruin our relationship. It felt good to throw her words back in her face. "Tell them. Don't tell them. What's the difference?"

"The difference is that everyone will know that you're nothing and you'll always be nothing," Maro said. "Once a filthy little cinder girl, always a filthy little cinder girl."

"Maro," Henry said, looking at the floor. "Don't. Let's go."

"The thing is, Maro, I may be nothing. I may be a tiny, little mention for the *Tattler*," I said, taking a step toward her. "Or even a great big scandal. But you will suffer actual repercussions if you tear Rory's kingdom apart. You'd better clear the hell out of her life. Or next time I'll let Bianca handle you."

Maro let out a *hmph* and began to clomp down the stairs,

Henry blustering after her. I picked up my knives and trotted back through the portal, emerging into blinding sunlight.

"Fuck's sake, CeCi. You're slower than molasses. Some of us have shit to do, you know." Bianca was sprawled out on the grass next to Snoozer.

In my head, I apologized, but all that came out of my mouth was "Rory, did you tell anyone about our new clock? Henry? Or anyone? Maro? Accidentally, even?"

"No. I don't think so. I can't remember. Why?"

"I just . . . I don't know. I guess I was curious. That's all."

Bianca raised her eyebrows at me. I shook my head and mouthed, "Later."

By the time we found a taxi and made it to the school, I was five minutes late for class. We grudgingly agreed on a meeting place for afterward and I left Bianca and Rory rolling their eyes at one another, the dog panting between them.

It was hard to focus during my classes. I answered everything wrong. I wrecked a batch of bread. I scorched the roux.

"There's a special place in hell for people who burn the roux," Phil said to me.

"Says who?" I asked.

"A very wise man," he said.

"Why does everything always go to hell at once?"

He twirled me in a circle and said, "C'est la vie." Then we were reprimanded for unsafe kitchen practices.

Have I told you that Phil has a drawing of a whisk on his forearm? I asked him if he had to wash it off every night, and he asked my favorite question: if I'm "for real." If only I could tell him about the epic irony of his question. I desperately wanted to tell him no, but I focused on looking mildly offended instead.

He explained his *tattoos* were permanent and that I should get one shaped like a question mark on account of my inquisitiveness. He's a charmer, that Phil. I'm going to have to introduce him to Bianca. I think they'll be the best of friends.

Love,
CeCi

Princess Briar R. Rose
Somnolent Tower Castle
South Road, Grimmland

Dearest Zell,

Makeover day started as poorly as I expected. There was incessant bickering, and then CeCi began acting strangely and made us wait while she retrieved her mislaid knives. In between accusations of how *we'd* made *her* late for class, she started badgering me about whether I'd told Maro about the new clock.

I explained that Maro and I met for tea on the lawn and there would be no reason for her to be interested in a new clock or the tower that I could see. Then CeCi started in on the quality of Maro's character. Usually Bianca is the more tiresome of the two on that particular subject, but honestly I've never been gladder to see CeCi disappear though the doors of Cordon Bleu.

After CeCi left us on the sidewalk, I asked Bianca if she might shed some light on the situation. "After all the effort I've made with Maro, why are you two so vile toward her?"

Bianca took my wrist and held it dreadfully tight. "I don't want you around that woman. Ever again. I'm not kidding. Kick her out. Don't contact her. Do you understand me? She's bad news."

"I can make my own decisions, Bianca," I said, correcting my posture a bit.

"Barely," she said. "Look at you and your makeovers. You're practically a poster child for the power of suggestion."

"I was wrong, okay? The makeover didn't work. But you said you wanted to go, so now we're going."

Bianca threw her hip into mine mid stride. "I don't want a fucking makeover, you ninny."

"Then what *do* you want to do?"

"What do you think?"

"Bianca, no. There's not enough time. If your father wanted to be found, wouldn't he have left you some sort of clue? He could be anywhere."

"Rory, this means the whole world to me. Please? Can we just look in one phone book or something?"

"A what?"

"A phone book. Humans use phones, not pigeons. A phone book is . . . never mind. Will you help me?"

I felt as if my heart were strung between two wires. I did want to help, but I also I knew we were going to end up taking frivolous and unnecessary risks. I'd be lying, though, if I said I hadn't considered trying to find some evidence of Fred. "Didn't you say Rachel worked at the library?"

"Oh my God, of course. You brilliant little sleep-aholic, you." She stopped in the middle of the sidewalk and kissed my cheek. The people behind us ran straight into her. She exchanged middle fingers with them.

We began walking, Bianca talking twice as quickly as before, Snoozer trotting along behind us. Bianca stopped abruptly, once again. "Please, Rory, I know it seems like it doesn't make sense, but just don't fight me on this Maro thing. I do have your best interests at heart. I'll explain as soon as I figure out how. Just trust me, okay?"

"Fine," I said. I would be the bigger person, the rational person. Maro had clearly done something unforgivable, though I had no idea why I wasn't privy to the news.

"Thank you." She reached down to scratch Snoozer's ears.

I looked at the city, moving so quickly around us, and considered venturing beyond our well-trod routes. "Do you know where Rachel's library is? Or are you following some sort of bourbon homing beacon?"

Bianca dug through her overflowing satchel until she surfaced with a small card full of dark, neat print. We hailed a cab. "Take us here," she said, handing the driver the card.

It wasn't terribly far, but I think Snoozer appreciated the ride after all of that trotting. Things wouldn't continue to go smoothly, of course. A short woman with big grey hair at the door of the library told us Snoozer couldn't come in at all.

Bianca began to make a scene, but all of a sudden Rachel was there, telling the other woman Snoozer was a "support animal." The frizzy woman demanded to know where his "vest" was and I explained he had one but it was at the tailor's and Bianca rolled her eyes at me and Rachel told her to not worry about it and the frizzy woman finally threw up her hands, asking why she even bothered. I couldn't help but commiserate with her there.

At the ceasing of all that chaos, a private moment seemed to occur. I stepped a few paces away with Snoozer so that Bianca and Rachel could speak. I didn't mean to eavesdrop, Zell, it's just that I couldn't get far enough away *not* to hear.

Rachel seemed both delighted and distraught. "What are you doing here, Bianca?" she asked. "I was afraid I'd never see you again. You said you'd write. But then there was nothing."

"I'm so sorry. The time went so quickly. I didn't mean . . . I'm so happy to see you. But I understand if we can't, well."

"This isn't the place. Do you want to go get a cup of coffee or something?"

"I do. I would, but right now we're here for a reason." Bianca seemed to be fighting to collect herself. "We need your help finding someone."

Rachel spent the next few hours with us in a small room, looking up things on the electronic boxes and in what she told us were Bianca's mythical phone books (which had no narrative to speak of). She was patient for far longer than I would have been in her situation.

"Bianca," she said from behind a teetering stack of reference books, "you know I don't mind helping you. But can you tell me anything else about where you went when you left? I'm trying to understand, but . . ." Rachel trailed off, looking around the room at nothing.

"I want to. And I will, I promise. Just not right now. I don't know how to make it make sense right now. Okay?"

"I'm going to keep doing some digging based on the info you've given me. But Steven White is a fairly common name, and if you're not even sure he's in Los Angeles . . . It would be tough just to narrow down the candidates we'll find here in the metro area."

"We think he might have worked for the theme park. Anything is more than we know now."

"Okay. I'll keep looking. Is there anything, anyone else you want me to look for?"

Bianca looked at me as if I were as transparent as vellum. "Rory? Do you . . ."

Oh, Zell. I wanted so badly to say yes. But instead, I looked at my clock bracelet. "Bianca. We have to go. We'll be late to meet CeCi."

"Do you want me to drive you?" asked Rachel.

Bianca hesitated for a moment and then accepted, much to Snoozer's and, truth be told, my relief. When we arrived, CeCi waved to us from a sidewalk café a few doors down from our rendezvous spot. She was drinking a beer with her lab partner, a handsome, dry-witted fellow called Phil. She finished and piled into Rachel's car where we continued to the Magic Castle.

On the way, everyone seemed lost in her own thoughts. Rachel broke the silence, just as we pulled up to the Magic Castle. "Where are you going now?"

"Home," Bianca answered.

Rachel raised her eyebrows at the Magic Castle. "Home? But the bus station is—"

"I swear I'll explain as soon as I can." Bianca kissed Rachel on her bewildered mouth, and we piled out of the car.

We trudged up the hill toward the portal. "What a day, eh?" Bianca said. She practically sparkled—the way she did when she first met Rachel.

I felt the opposite, bedraggled even. For the first time, returning did not fill me with its usual soft relief. I didn't want to go home at all. I regretted not asking Rachel if she would try to find something about Fred. And it dawned on me I'd never even had my coffee. I circled the tower, looking out the windows, until CeCi and Bianca emerged from the portal.

"Before we go home, we should chat," said CeCi, divesting herself of her chef's coat and hat. "Since Maro is staying here, perhaps we should consider posting a guard downstairs."

"That's perfectly brutal hospitality, CeCi. I couldn't possibly—"

"It's just a precaution," CeCi interrupted.

"I'm sure she wouldn't come up here," I said. But even as I said it, I knew I'd failed to be convincing. "She didn't seem to enjoy the tower at all the time I showed it to her."

"You said no one had been up here!" Bianca said. Snoozer gave a quiet woof, as if in agreement with her.

"Traitor," I said, holding my hand out for his leash.

"Rory, remember you promised me you'd listen." Bianca looked me in the eyes for a long moment. "Until she finds a new place to live, there's a guard at the bottom of these stairs, okay?"

I began to put fuzzy ideas together. Snoozer's bark. CeCi going back through the portal. All this carping about Maro. Something wasn't adding up, but I shoved it all aside. "I said I agreed, Bianca. And in return you'll promise me you won't do anything too risky searching for your father."

"For Grimm's sake," said Bianca. "Don't get all Fairy God-mother on me. I'll finish my Pages."

"Hold on. Your father?" CeCi asked. "Whatever happened to makeover day?"

"Keep up, CeCi. No one wanted a makeover," said Bianca. "And don't you worry, Rory, I won't go anywhere beyond Los Angeles until I go Outside for good."

I was sure I'd misheard.

"Wait, what?" asked CeCi, though her voice had a hard edge to it. One I didn't like. "Say that one more time?" It would have been better to let the comment slide. No good could come of reciprocal hysterics.

"After my wedding, I'm going Outside for good. I'll finish my Pages and then go."

"I can't deal with this right now," said CeCi. She brushed past Bianca and raced down the steps.

"Oh, Poor Princess Put-upon. Don't lose your Crocs on the way down," Bianca called after her. "Never know who might fit into those."

"*Namaste*, bitch."

"Now look who knows Human lingo. Phil give you that one?"

"Yoga, Bianca. You couldn't shut up about it a few weeks ago." CeCi's voice drifted up from the stairwell. "You might want to give it a try. Maybe you'll get flexible enough to pull your head out of your ass."

Bianca stood flipping off the empty stairwell with both hands. If she could have held up her toes, too, I'm sure she would have.

"You can't be serious, Bianca," I said. "After everything we've been through together?"

"I'm going to go find that True Love you've been babbling about unceasingly over the last five years. I finally believe, okay? You were right all along. Grimm's sake, why the face? I thought this would make you happy."

I tried, Zell. I tried to think of something to say as I collected the slack in Snoozer's leash and followed CeCi down the stairs, still reeling.

If things weren't bad enough before, they are now officially out of control.

Love,
Rory

Important Fucking Correspondence from Snow B. White
Onyx Manor
West Road, Grimmland

Z,

Today I made an important decision. I am going to leave the Realm for good after the wedding. I'm going to find my real life. Maybe my father, if I'm lucky. I'm going to see if Rachel is my True Love. I think she might be.

CeCi and Rory didn't take the news very well, both storming off as if I'd taken away their birthdays. I don't know what the problem is. I'll simply live out there instead of in here. And I guess not forever. But how can they not want me to be happy? Do you want me to be happy, Zell?

My wedding is going to be awesome. In two short weeks, I'll walk down the aisle with a man I don't love, flanked by friends who aren't speaking to me, and, afterward, I'll celebrate by killing my stepmother.

I can't imagine why you wouldn't want to come.

B

Dear Zell,

Maybe all this is my fault. If I hadn't wanted to cook, Bianca wouldn't even be entertaining this ridiculous nonsense about Outside. Or maybe this is your fault. You went first. It could also be Figgy's fault for keeping her father's self-imposed exile a secret for so long Bianca can't help but have a disproportionate response.

It isn't as if I can't understand the urge to run away. Outside is such a nice distraction. Right now, Phil seems to be the only objective listener in my life. Don't take that the wrong way. It's different in letters. And it's different talking to someone who loves the same thing you love.

When I started classes, I would have laughed if you'd told me Phil and I would become true friends. Of course there's the everyday chatter. But we got closer when we celebrated winning the class cake competition. And we shared the shame and dark hilarity of the disaster that was geoduck day.

Phil and I have each other's backs. I fixed his bread dough, and he repaired my mis-threaded grinder. He showed me his favorite way to coax the paper jackets off garlic cloves (with a swift whack with the side of a chef's knife). I demonstrated my preferred way to pit avocados (with a swift whack of the same knife).

Over lunch today, Phil took me to meet an old man who hones knives for a living, in hopes that he'd give us a quick lesson while he gave our kits a once-over. The man talked for over an hour about his craft, and we shared an amazing bottle of wine. On our way back, we stopped at a Korean fusion taco truck. It was wonderful, though I haven't eaten Korean or tacos on their own yet. There's just so much to try here, so much to learn.

But crouched on the sidewalk, eating under the sun as our tacos dripped into the gutter, we realized this is the heart of what we were trying to accomplish. We tasted everything with a new appreciation: the meat, the spices, the way they'd cut their vegetables. We knew how it had been done. What we would do differently. Like we had our own alchemical language. I felt empowered and confident. And a little wistful because I'll never be Outside creating with my classmates. Though my classmates will never be able to feel the joy of bringing the gift of something completely new to Grimmland, either.

As angry as I am at Bianca, as selfish as I think she's being, part of me understands why she wants to stay Outside.

Phil asked about my favorite place to eat. I couldn't tell him Gretel's, so I told him Mirabelle because it's the only restaurant I know. I explained I hadn't been in the city very long, and I didn't have much to compare. So he started a list of places we have to explore—cheap dives and fancy bars, family-run places with recipes that will inspire us later on. I feel bad that I don't have as much to contribute to our adventures as he does. But I'm a good explorer now. And I'm an expert at getting a cab. I keep telling him it's magic, but it's just drops of that summoning potion Figgy gave us.

Phil and I have bonded over one more thing: keeping our dreams a secret. See, Phil's partner, Eric, is a nurse. Eric doesn't know about cooking school. Like their parents, they've always fought about money, so Phil still works in the evenings and when he's not in class. They hardly see one another, except for a few hours when they sleep. Phil is planning a big surprise as soon as we graduate. It'll be one of Eric's days off, and he'll serve breakfast in bed: eggs, pastries, jams, bacon, and pancakes. But meanwhile, he acts like he can't cook a damned thing and his whisk tattoo is ironic.

I'd like to say that the secret-keeping is the same for both of us, but that's not true. I'm not lying to protect Edmund. I'm lying to protect myself. I can't pretend I'm being altruistic, or planning anything that will delight Edmund down the line. Even Phil knows that—I can see him weighing whether or not to tell me.

He won't have to anymore. Today, I ran out of excuses.

After I got back from class, I waited in the half-finished nursery until Edmund came home from his weekly game of cups. He returned in generally good spirits, ruddy from the wind and the beer. He paused when he saw me, and I waved him in from the hallway.

"Sit down," I said, gesturing to a yellow divan. "Please."

"Sounds ominous." He flopped instead into an armchair draped in painter's cloth. We've been parrying with small gestures, refusals, deferrals to keep each other at a distance. It's become uncomfortable, at best.

"Edmund, let's not fight."

"I'm not fighting," he said. "I'm sitting, just as you asked."

"I had a bad day," I said.

He patted his knee, half in jest, half in desperate attempt to get back to the time before we'd messed things up so badly. It was tempting. I could have, as had become habit, regaled him with some generic tale of Bianca's whims or Rory's laments. He would have, as had become habit, told me that I was a good friend, and that I needed to relax and take care of myself. Maybe we'd have spent the night together or let the moment pass. We could have kissed chastely, telling ourselves that things were still okay when they clearly weren't. But this time I was brave.

"No, Edmund. I need to tell you something, and I need for you to hear me. I need you not to argue with me or kiss me or placate me. Just promise to listen to me very carefully."

"Okay." He sat back with a good-natured smirk. "I promise."

"I've been lying to you."

He rolled his eyes. "I knew it. You *abhor* yellow, don't you?"

"Don't," I said. "I love you. I love you more than anything, and I never knew I wanted anyone this much or anything this much and this is hard."

"Fine, CeCi. I'm listening."

"I haven't been volunteering to remove oil from ugly ducklings or taking chess lessons. I haven't been bacheloretting in Wonderland or Neverland or Fantasia. I've been taking cooking classes Outside for the last couple of months. I'm going to the Cordon Bleu school in Los Angeles to learn to be a chef."

He blinked, working his way through my confession. "I don't even know how to make sense of any of that. Why, in Grimm's name?"

"Do you remember back when I told you I wanted to cook and you told me that I couldn't because it would embarrass you?"

"Yes, but that's not what I meant—"

"Wait. Listen. You promised." His eyebrows pinched together like they do when he's solving a problem, but he nodded. "When I was young, cooking was the one thing I was good at. Proud of. No matter what horrible things a day might hold, I would be able to make something from nothing. When I myself suddenly became something from nothing, I found I didn't feel like myself without being able to practice my art. Creating food makes me feel powerful, whole, useful.

Not being able to do it made me sad. But I knew it wasn't as simple as declaring my intentions to the palace—we have appearances to keep."

"So your solution was to lie to me?" He leaned forward to put his elbows on his knees.

"I tried to tell you. But you made me feel so ungrateful."

"I was only trying to protect you from, well, everyone. You do understand that, don't you?"

"And I was trying to protect you."

"Nonsense, CeCi. Do you think I care what the staff says or Lucinda says or even my parents say?"

"If you can't tell your parents we don't want a baby, how are you going to tell them that I want to wear an apron instead of a tiara?"

"That's completely different." He put his head in his hands.

"I need your support, Edmund. I want you back in my corner, by my side. Whatever. I hate not sharing this with you."

"I can't even . . ." he started.

"I want to do this as a career. For myself. For the kingdom. At some point, I'll have to tell everyone, and I'll need you to back me up."

"How can I back you up when I can't trust you to clue me in?" He balled his hands into fists. "Damn, CeCi."

"I'm sorry. I just felt like I couldn't. Or I shouldn't."

"Can you imagine how this feels, how I feel to be so unworthy of your secrets? All this time, I've only looked for you on my horizon. I don't even seem to be a part of yours."

I sat down on the arm of the chair. Zell, in all the scenarios I played in my head, in all the reactions I imagined Edmund would have—anger, resentment, disbelief, disdain—hurt was never among them. In all my days, I've never felt guiltier.

"It was never a question of your worth." He looked at me

like I was a stranger. "I was so, so wrong. I was wrong to keep it from you. I assumed your judgment instead of giving you a chance. I was scared, and I didn't think it through."

He didn't reach for me, but he didn't pull away, either. The rift I've caused will take time to heal, if it heals at all. "You're right. We do need to be careful about how we tell my parents."

His concession was a small one, but I grabbed on to it like a drowning woman. "Thank you, Edmund."

"Who else knows?"

"Just Bianca and Rory. Oh, and Maro."

Edmund's face contorted from displeased to dyspeptic. "Maro Green? I'm surprised the whole kingdom doesn't know by now. That woman is trouble."

"So we've discovered." Leave it to Maro to be the topic to temporarily save me from myself.

He looked at me, volume dropping. "Does Rory know yet?"

That's when I realized it was only a matter of time. And that Edmund had had the decency to keep the rumors to himself so that I wouldn't have to decide how to tell her.

That's what kind of friend I should have been to Bianca. And you. And Rory. And Edmund. Things will work out, though, won't they? We can forgive and move on. There's only one final lie to expose. Now to figure out how and when.

I miss you immensely. I'm sorry no one liked your meat loaf. Even though it's supposed to be foolproof, there are a number of surprising ways one can botch things up. I know Bianca keeps telling you that there's no such thing as too much ketchup, but I assure you, there is.

Love,
CeCi

Princess Briar R. Rose
Somnolent Tower Castle
South Road, Grimmland

Dear Zell,

At dinner tonight, I asked the attendant what time it was. Henry said, from the other end of the table, that we should put a clock in the dining room. And I said I'd ask Solace to craft something suitable. And then he said that was fine as long as it wasn't as ugly as the thing in the tower.

I put my fork down. I asked him exactly when he'd been in the tower. And he said, oh, it was a while ago. When he rescued me. Maybe since. He couldn't remember.

I began to feel dizzy. My thoughts swirled, and my blood started to zing through my veins, almost painfully. I felt like I had been pulled out of my own body.

I watched myself get out of my chair and ask him, again, *exactly* when he'd been in *my* tower and why. The red blush on his neck crawled into his ears, and as it did, everything fell into place. Maro here, Maro in my tower, Henry in my tower, Maro happy, Henry happy, Rory deeply unhappy. This must have been the big secret. CeCi knew, Bianca knew, I assume you knew, and not one of you had the decency to tell me.

He said he was sorry. He said it wasn't his fault. Then he said it wasn't me, it was him. And still then he said it *was* me because I was too timid, because I didn't act like I wanted him, because I acted like I wanted him too much. Because he doesn't know me. Because he deserved something, didn't he? What did I want from him, anyway?

I took a walk to clear my head and made a lap around the pond to see if the Frog Prince was playing ball. But he was gone. I sat there for a long time, wondering if the lily pad in the middle of the pond was as lonely as I am. Everyone else has taken charge of her own rowboat, but here I am being pulled along by the current. I'm sleepwalking through my days.

When the Frog Prince re-entered the glade, there was a shining maiden at his side. I told her to be careful she didn't catch the kissing sickness.

I suppose I don't blame you for keeping the secret, Zell. I wouldn't expect you to have written me with the news when you weren't here to verify it. CeCi and Bianca should have told me as soon as they found out instead of creeping on eggshells to avoid Maro. Everything is so much clearer now.

The humorous thing is, Zell, in my grand plot, I wasn't wrong to ask a Fairy Godmother for help. I simply chose the wrong one. After all these years, it's time I paid Malice a visit.

Rory

Her Feet Burned as She Danced

Important Fucking Correspondence from Snow B. White
Onyx Manor
West Road, Grimmland

Z,

You're wrong. I am not going to change my mind. As soon as I said it to Rory, I knew it was what I wanted, what I've always wanted. I can't imagine life any other way anymore. Surely you, of all people, understand. When I picture staying in this stagnant cesspool, I'm flooded with the same sort of misery that CeCi must have felt before she began cooking school. We lacked more than purpose, Zell; we lacked a direction. My direction is Outside.

CeCi might not see the change in herself, but I certainly do. I'm proud to have been a part of her transformation. I wish she'd grant me the same courtesy. I wish Rory would, too, but first she has to stand up for herself—with or without the knowledge of Maro and Henry.

My first order of business is sharing my decision with William. I pour our conversational bourbons and jump right in. "You know how we're getting married next week?"

"Saw something about that on my calendar . . . No joke, I got my big shiny suit and everything." He pumps his fist in mock excitement.

"And you know the conversation we had before about being partners and everything?"

"Of course."

"You're one of my best friends, right?"

"I hope so. Though I might have to reconsider if you don't get to your point soon."

My skin is crawling with nerves. "I need to do something. Something you might not understand. Or like, even."

"Hit me."

"After we get married, I need to leave."

"We talked about this, didn't we? Traveling's no problem. You want to travel. I want to travel. We'll figure it out. For how long?"

"Forever."

"Is this a joke?" He stands up, looking injured. "It's not very funny." His reaction dents my bubble of elation. But I charge ahead.

"I want to go Outside. For good."

He pauses a moment, swallows the rest of his drink, then puts his glass down. "What are you talking about? You can't just renege, B. We had a deal. Plans. Remember? Ruling as a team. Exploring. Together. Separately. No strings. Why now?"

"Well, a lot of reasons. First, there's my father."

He spools up his usual speech, replete with well-timed pacing. "Bianca, he doesn't want to see you. He left. On purpose."

"I know, but it's because he blames himself. I can't live forever knowing that he's dying on the other side with all that guilt."

He practically throws fresh ice into his empty glass. "He *should* be dying with guilt, Bianca. Hell, it's been, what, two years? Who knows? He could be anywhere. Or he could be nowhere. Outside's a dangerous place. He could be sick or even—"

"Don't, Will. Don't say things you can't unsay."

He goes on anyway. "You're always the first one to champion everyone else's injustices. You can hardly stand it when bad things happen to Rory and CeCi. But you can't see the knife poised in front of your own damned heart. Are you broken or something?"

Tears smart in my eyes. "You're supposed to be on my side."

"I am on your side," he says, slumping with his back to the wall. "Or at least I'm trying to be. But you've packed your fucking side into a suitcase bound for a place the rest of us can't go. Are you too obtuse to see that?"

"Obtuse?"

"Stubborn. Inconsistent. Inconsiderate. How am I supposed to feel? I pretend to marry you. Then I lose my friend. I lose my partner. I start over again? Am I not getting the short end of this stick?"

"We have to get married, William. My Pages."

"Fuck your Pages. I thought you were my best friend."

"I am. But I'm not in love with you. You're not in love with me."

"We already discussed this. I don't care about romance. I care about regretting your decision, not being able to come back. I care about you dying out there and me never getting to see you again. Remember when Rapunzel took off? This is a thousand times worse."

He's right, of course. But I have to tell him everything. "I know that you're okay not being in love. But I'm not sure I was being honest when I said I was okay with it."

He pours us both a couple more fingers of whiskey. "So you lied?"

"I didn't lie to you, William. I lied to me. I'm not in love with you. But that doesn't mean I'm not in love."

"Well, why didn't you say so? You're free to love whoever you want. Go, then." He's flustered. I have to stop letting him interrupt me.

"No, William. With someone Outside."

"How is that even possible?" He laughs at himself. "Never mind. Nice work, Bianca. It's not often a guy gets cuckolded before he's even married."

"It's not like that. Nothing worse than the flirting *you* do over at Shambles." I'd elbow him if he'd come near me, but he's wedged himself into a corner, as if I've grown a particularly twisty pair of horns. "She's just different. I want to spend the rest of my life knowing her, getting to know her. No matter how long that may be. And it's not like you'll never see me again."

He takes several moments to collect himself. He drains his glass, fills it, and drains it again.

"Fuck, Bianca. What am I supposed to say? I'm not sure how to be your friend here."

"I'm sorry. I am."

He lets out a long sigh. "I know you are. But still."

"I want to leave everything to you. My castle, the money, the maps. You're going to be a great king. I already know it."

We both cry for a little while, backs to one another. Then we laugh for a long time at each other, with each other, and cry a bit more. I don't want to screw Will over. I think he knows that—at least I hope so.

We'd both regret our original plan if we went through with it. If he ever finds that person, that True Love, for himself, he'll understand. I think maybe he already does, deep down, even though it must feel as if I've hit him in the windpipe. Like we all felt when you left.

But now, it's as if I'm the sky after a rainstorm, you know? Like when all the dust is washed clean. I wouldn't ever want to have a conversation like it again, but I'm glad we had it. I'm making my apologies so that I can start over again. Honestly. Like I always meant to.

I am, Zell, apologizing to you, too. I'm sorry for so very many things. I'm sorry for doubting you and your choice. Can you please forgive me? And support mine in return?

Love,
B

PS. I know your mother-in-law succeeded with the temporary ban, but I'm sure I could pull some strings. We could sneak you into the wedding if we put you inside the cake.

From the Desk of Cecilia Cinder Charming
Crystal Palace
North Road, Grimmland

Dear Zell,

Not ten breaths after Edmund left our chambers this morning, Darling and Sweetie stumbled in, slamming the door behind them. Darling kept her back to the door as Sweetie began to call for me. "CeCi? Quick, help."

I hopped up and out of bed and took her outstretched hand. They still look so young—skin untouched by sun and eyes that healed from the bird attack into a pale, eerie blue. It's been an adjustment, seeing myself as their friend instead of their rival, but every once in a while they surprise me with a gratitude that's almost overwhelming.

Sweetie folded my hands in hers. "We overheard something terrible."

"Horrible," whispered Darling, her back still at the door.

"That Maro woman," Sweetie said. "She's here right now. She told Mother that she has a secret about you."

"Of course Mother took her into her chambers, but our ears are extra good since, well, our eyes, you know," said Darling, head bowed.

"Maro told Mother that you were taking some sort of cooking classes, like a common peasant. She said she trusted that Mother would know what to do with the information." Sweetie was shaking. "Mother's going to tell Edmund that you've been sneaking away, and he'll forbid you from going Outside again. We told him the grooms weren't sure which horse to saddle today and sent him to the barns before she could get to him. But she will find him, eventually. You know she will. Hurry, CeCi, we have to do something before he comes home this evening."

"It's okay," I said, switching our grip so that I was holding both of Sweetie's hands. "He already knows. I told him two nights ago."

"Oh, thank goodness. We were so worried," said Darling, sliding down to the floor.

Sweetie exhaled and tilted her head at me. "Was he very mad at you?"

I pulled her back a few steps to sit on the edge of the bed. "He was angry that I lied to him. As he should have been. But we're talking more, now. We're trying to find a place where we can both be more honest with one another. With the other people in our lives. It's a process, you know. I can't fix what I did overnight. I shouldn't have kept things from him in the first place."

"Is being a chef really what you want to do?" asked Darling.

"Yes," I said. "I know it doesn't make any sense, but yes."

"I think it makes perfect sense," said Darling. "You were brilliant at it. Not that we let you believe it for a minute."

"Oh, just think," said Sweetie. "She might make us those little eggs in a cup like she used to."

Darling hissed. "Hush. She never wants to cook for us again. Remember what Mother said to her? What *we* said?"

"We were perfectly horrid, CeCi. You probably don't even want to eat in the same room as us," Sweetie said, scooting away from me.

"Of course I do. It's different now, right? Maybe we can have a sisters' dinner every once in a while. I know I haven't been around very much. It's nothing to do with you. Maybe you can catch me up on the gossip."

Darling made her way to the bed and sat on the other side of me. "Did you hear about Red Riding Hood?"

"Or the rumor about the shoemaker's elves?" asked Sweetie.

"Sweetie has a crush on the prince with one swan wing."

Sweetie giggled. "So does Darling."

"Oh, my," I said. "I'm further behind than I thought."

They squeezed my hands, and I was overwhelmed by their concern. "Thank you. Thank you for coming to me."

"Of course," said Sweetie. "If this is what you want, we believe in you."

"We'll test all your recipes," said Darling.

"Even the gross ones," said Sweetie.

"We hope you know how much we love you," said Darling. "We don't always know how to tell you, though. We have no right."

"You have every right." I wanted to tell them that we were all just children back then. None of us knew any better. But that's not exactly it, either. A part of them will always remain dependent and brainwashed, and I don't want to exploit them or cultivate their allegiance like Lucinda does. I just want life to be fairer to them than it has been in the past. That can't be too much to hope for, can it?

Then again, things aren't fair. One of my best friends moved to Oz and another is choosing to live the rest of her life as a Human.

Bianca could travel between both worlds. Like I will. She tells me that we'll have a good long life of friendship when I visit her. But I'm afraid it won't be the same. I wish I could change her mind, but each time we come back from Outside, more of her heart seems to remain there.

I complained to Phil that Bianca was thinking of moving to Los Angeles permanently. He told me to quit worrying, and let my friend live her life. I'm not trying to be selfish, but Phil said I needed to try harder.

Since Phil was feeling so sagacious, I also asked him his opinion about Rory and Maro. He asked me what I would want everyone to do if the situation were reversed. Therefore, I've resolved to tell Rory as soon as possible. She wasn't taking visitors when we stopped by on our way to class today. Nor this evening. So I'll try again in the morning. I'll be glad when this vault of secrets is completely empty.

Speaking of empty, noodles always need to be boiled in water. A lot of water. And you have to take them out after forty or so rounds of "Ninety-nine Bottles of Mead on the Wall." I'm sorry your kitchen smells so badly. Perhaps a nice bouquet of flowers or a few bowls of vinegar or baking soda might help absorb the smoke. Let me know how it works.

Love,
CeCi

Princess Briar R. Rose
Somnolent Tower Castle
South Road, Grimmland

Dearest Zell,

CeCi, having evidently taken a lesson in persistence from Bianca, called upon me yesterday evening for the fourth time in two days. I tried to send her away, but she barged right past my nurse. Some guard dog I purchased. Snoozer jumped up and gave her a kiss when she sat down on the chaise.

"Rory, I need to tell you something. I've spent too long trying to figure out how, so I'm just going to come out and say it, okay?"

I stood. I didn't want to hear it. I didn't want to even acknowledge it. "I have things to do, you know." I tried tidying my dressing table, to show her I was serious.

"Please sit down. Please?"

I turned to her. "I already know what you're going to say."

"You do?"

"I do."

"Are you sure?"

"Yes, of course I'm sure, CeCi."

"Sometimes really bad things happen and people aren't sure how to protect their friends and their friends make bad decisions and—"

"I know about Henry and Maro." Saying it made me feel like a candle that'd just been blown out.

"What the hell, Rory? How long have you . . . when? Why haven't you taken my visits?"

"I certainly hope you don't mean to be cross with *me* for putting two and two together."

"No, of course not. It's just, we've been wondering how to tell you, and so . . ."

"And so," I mocked her. "How long have you and Bianca known?"

"Not that long. But longer than we should have. And Bianca hasn't known as long as me, and she wanted to tell you right away. But you were getting so upset about small things, I just couldn't imagine telling you something this painful."

"Small things? Like my life? My dreams of starting a family? My hopes of being loved by a man who wanted Maro all along? Your little revelation could have saved me quite a bit of time and tears, you know."

"That isn't what I meant."

I finally sat down. "CeCi, you've always gotten by relying on people to understand your intentions instead of your actions. It cannot always be that way. It is irrational to think otherwise."

"Fine. Please forgive me, Rory. It's my fault, all of it."

And despite the fact that I probably said something similar in my last letter, Zell, that's not completely true, either. "See, you're doing it again! This isn't all about you. It isn't your fault that Maro is what she is," I said. "Or Henry. But I needed your help more than ever and you kept this from me. You let me make a fool of myself. In front of her. In front of Henry. Why didn't you help me?"

CeCi was sobbing. Snoozer looked back and forth between us, his head cocked.

"Come now," I said. "Things will be better with time. You'll have to give me that time, though. You owe me that much."

She looked up at me, and her tears started again. "I should

be the one comforting you," she said. Maybe she was right. In truth, Zell, I felt nothing at all, just an incredible, yawning emptiness. I told her I was tired.

"Just try to put yourself in our position, Rory. We wanted to protect you. We love you."

I asked her more directly to let me get some rest. Eventually, she departed with minimal fuss.

Perhaps I shouldn't be so hard on her. But I cannot envision our positions being reversed, no matter how hard I try. Our positions simply aren't reversed and that's that.

To make matters worse, CeCi has disrespected fate all along, as has Bianca. Even you, Zell, have chosen a life I can't fathom. None of you have held up your end of the bargain granted to you by your Pages. Meanwhile, I've toed the line and I have nothing to show for it.

The only spark of anger I feel now is directed toward Maro. And, since no one seems to be doing anything about her, I will deal with her myself.

I traded the shoemaker a pair of Louboutins I bought with Patricia for a map to Malice's new lair, and I'll head there as soon as I can, though it's a day's journey by horse and I'll need to leave Snoozer. I don't want you worrying and I especially do not want you discussing this with CeCi and Bianca.

Figgy's new Pages protect me from whatever danger Malice might have once posed. Isn't it you who's always telling me not to dwell on the past? Or perhaps it's CeCi or Bianca. You all know what's best for me, don't you?

I'll make my own decisions from now on.

Rory

Important Fucking Correspondence from Snow B. White
~~*Onyx Manor*~~
~~*West Road, Grimmland*~~
West Hollywood Library
Los Angeles
Outside

Z,

The dwarves insist on throwing their own private bachelorette bash for me. They take over a back room at Shambles, all
cider and ketchup and French fries.

Once I settle in, they tell me how proud they are of me,
and that, even though they have reservations about William,
they know he's no Henry. I don't tell them that I'm planning to
go. I'm not sure how to even start that conversation.

It's odd how formal our relationships have become. It's as
if the Disneyland story were true instead of what actually happened. It wasn't like I was their servant. Not like CeCi was to
her stepsisters, or anything. Our relationship was an exchange.
An economy. A reciprocation.

Or maybe I'm just telling myself that. I needed them desperately, and I ambled right into their house like a stray dog.
I don't know that they so much needed me as made me feel
a part of their routine. I didn't know much about friendship
back then.

The Huntsman warned me Valborg would find me if I wasn't
careful, but I doubted her persistence. The dwarves warned me,
too. I didn't listen the first time when she came peddling the

corset, or the second time with the comb, or the third time with the apple. I understand why the dwarves have never quite trusted my judgment since.

I'm hungover as can be this morning when CeCi collects me bright and early for escort duty. On our way to the portal, she tells me Rory revealed that Tweedle-pea and Tweedle-dumb finally confessed to bumping uglies. She says Rory will eventually forgive us for keeping it from her, but we have to give her all the time she needs to "process the information."

We stop by Rory's chambers on our way to the tower, to politely invite her to join us. Her nurse sends us away, but tells us Rory looks amazing in the lilac bridesmaid dress I finally settled on. That information makes me feel pretty damned hopeful, to tell you the truth. Yeah, I know lilac is a bit tame, but I can be made to see reason. Okay, fine. I chose it because it is Rory's favorite and guilt is a powerful motivation. Zebra stripes don't mean enough to me to break her fragile little heart all over again.

Our detour makes us late, but CeCi uses the last of the summoning potion to get a cab once we arrive in L.A. I see our little chef to her class and then hurry to the library, hoping to find Rachel. I can't wait to tell her about my future, our future. Part of me is nervous because what if she doesn't like my plan? What if I tell her about my dream of being a runaway queen from the Realm of Imagination and she laughs at me?

At the library, the frizzy-haired woman, the one who doesn't like dogs, tells me Rachel isn't there. I ask where to find her, and she laughs at me. Tells me something about public records. Tells me to come back tomorrow. I say some less than polite things to her, and a couple of security men come and deposit me onto the steps, ass first.

Luckily, I found a pigeon. So I'm sending this letter now while I wait for a taxi. The policeman who just drove up must know a better place to catch a cab.

B

From the Desk of Cecilia Cinder Charming
Crystal Palace
North Road, Grimmland

Dear Zell,

I should have known there would come a day when I regretted vouching for Bianca White.

When I stepped came out of class, sweaty and footsore, she was nowhere to be found. Phil had a drink with me at the bar halfway down the block, which is sort of our secondary rendezvous point these days. We sat at a sidewalk table while we waited and watched for her.

I tried to tamp down the little flame of fear that she'd gone home without me. Maybe things hadn't gone well with Rachel or she'd felt ill or something. I wanted to send a pigeon to check, but with Phil there, I decided to wait.

It was nearly dark by the time Phil announced he had to go home. Zell, I've never been so frightened or angry—definitely not both at the same time. My frenzied brain wouldn't even let me choose a first step. I forced myself to breathe while I settled our tab. Perhaps Bianca had gotten carried away with Rachel at the library. Phil agreed to drop me there on his way past.

I asked a lady locking the library doors if Rachel was there. She shook her head and asked me why everyone was looking for Rachel. Then I asked if she'd seen Bianca, and she told me the last time she saw Bianca, she'd called security. I begged her to call Rachel for me because Bianca was missing, and, thank Grimm, she begrudgingly relented.

Rachel's car arrived just as I was sending a pigeon to Solace. I tried to release it discreetly, but I don't know how successful I was. For her part, Rachel hadn't seen Bianca, either, as it had been her day off.

She opened a back door to the library and led me to her office. "I'm going to find Bianca," she said. "But you have to come clean with me. What exactly is the deal with you all?"

"What do you mean?" I asked, unclear as to which of our many idiosyncrasies she wanted me to explain.

She heaved a sigh at me. "You come and you go, I never know when. Bianca shows up and then disappears. I like her. A lot. But I can't have a relationship like this. Where do you all go when you leave here, anyway?"

"I really wish Bianca could tell you all this," I said. "I know she wanted to tell you herself."

"Well, I don't know if I can help you if you can't tell me the truth."

I sat down in a tatty, green chair. "Rachel," I started, "do you believe in magic?"

I had to admit her glare was almost as arresting as her smile. "I don't know," she said. "Do we have time for this screwing around?"

"If you want to know the truth, we do."

You know, for a Human, she took things better than I expected. I told her about the Realm and who we were and how we traveled through a portal to get back and forth from the Magic Castle to avoid suspicion. I explained we came back at first only for my classes, but later because we made friendships we cared deeply about. And then told her it was of the utmost importance that we found Bianca soon, that in half a day, everything we knew would be in grave danger unless we were back home.

"Wow." She slid off her desk and shook her head. "I don't know whether to believe you or not."

"Please try," I said. "I can imagine how this must sound, but without your help, everything and everyone we love will suffer."

Rachel spent all night calling police stations and hospitals, suggesting we continue to wait at the library for Bianca to come back. When she got tired, she slept briefly, and I tried to close my eyes and focus.

I fumbled in my bag for some chewing gum for my rancid breath when my hand bumped the empty bottle of summoning potion. A quick spark of hope burned out. If only I hadn't been so careless using it, I could've somehow used it to find her. A pigeon arrived from Solace with a terse note saying Bianca had not returned and that she'd send more birds to help find her.

By daybreak the next morning, I was so frightened I could barely feel anything but an uncontrollable mounting panic. And as the birds began to chirp, the library windows lit up with blue and red lights and, beyond them, we heard the sound of Bianca's voice.

We burst out of the side door to the curb. I was so relieved. Relieved to see Bianca and relieved that Rachel was handling the constables—policemen—who were in possession of our friend. They explained how they picked her up the day before for disturbing the peace at the library. They held her because she didn't have any identification. The jails were too crowded to hold her any longer, and she'd smartly convinced them to bring her back.

Bianca, on the other hand, didn't look relieved in the least. "Look, I appreciate the ride, sir," she said. I'd never heard her call anyone *sir* before. "But I just need you to . . ."

"I explained it to you, miss," said the taller of the two policemen. "Sometimes we lose things. We're sorry. "

Tears began to well in Bianca's eyes. "You don't understand."

"It's okay, babe," Rachel said, putting her arms around Bianca's shoulders. "What did you lose?"

Bianca extricated herself from Rachel's embrace and grabbed my satchel. "CeCi, I need your summoning potion."

"It's gone, remember? We'll get more when we get home. What's the matter?"

Bianca looked at me and began to cry in earnest, something I've only seen her do a handful of times. She held up a bare wrist. "They took my clock bracelet."

"Who took it? How did they lose it?"

Rachel didn't wait for an answer. She marched us into her office and pushed us into chairs. "Explain."

Bianca had managed to pull herself together. "It was a misunderstanding. I was only looking for you."

"I know. But why didn't you have any ID? Why were you arguing with *the cops*? Why is this bracelet so important to you? You know, I think I've been a pretty good sport about learning that my girlfriend is Snow White, but what the fuck is going on?"

Bianca's face blanched.

"I'm sorry," I said. "I had to."

Bianca began to half sob, half laugh. "You did, did you? Did you tell her who you are?"

"It doesn't matter who we are. She's fine with it." I stood up and walked in little circles, like Darling and Sweetie do when they're fretting. "I needed her help so we could get you home."

"I'll be more *fine with it* if one of you would explain about this damn bracelet you're so worried about," Rachel said.

I held out my wrist. "This is a clock bracelet. It's a sort of timepiece; I think you call them watches."

She picked up my hand and brought it to her closer. "Fine. You lost your watch. It's just a watch."

"Not exactly. The bracelet itself binds us with portal magic. We only use the watch part to count down."

"To what?"

"To the end of one day."

"What happens then?"

"Like I said, if we don't get Bianca home, very, very bad things." I made an exploding motion with my hands. Bianca leaned forward and put her head between her knees.

Rachel sat on her desk, turning her back to us. "Like when it was midnight and your pumpkin disappeared?"

"Sort of," I said. "Except it didn't really happen like that. Never mind. It's the same principle. When our day is up, then poof, the magic disappears."

Rachel nods, but doesn't turn. Bianca lifts her head, takes a deep breath, and stands. "CeCi, can you give Rachel and me a few minutes?"

"Just a few, Bianca. We have to figure this out." I left them and wandered around the library, eventually curling up in a chair in the corner, letting exhaustion overtake me. Part of me wished I could hear their conversation, and part of me was glad for the escape. I wasn't sure I wanted to know what Rachel's capacity for imagination was.

After a bit, I made my way back to the office where I found Bianca and Rachel both in tears, slumped into one another, holding hands.

"I'm sorry to break this up, but can we swing by the police station on the way to the portal?"

Bianca was pale. "If they can't find it, I won't get through."

"CeCi, if staying here messes up Bianca's papers—"

"Pages," Bianca corrected.

"And ruins your kingdom, can't you just give your bracelet to Bianca?"

"No," Bianca said. "If I go through with her bracelet, she'll be stranded here for good. She has a whole life inside. A husband and friends."

"It's an idea," I said, tears starting to smart my nose. The thought of never going home again was petrifying. "I guess it's better than letting Grimmland be torn apart."

"CeCi, I'm so sorry. I never meant—"

"Sh, Bianca. Hysterics don't help us now." I hoped I didn't look as queasy as I felt. "We'll have to see what happens. We can't not try."

The police station ended up being a bust—it was such chaos, it was a wonder they could find anything at all. We hit traffic going back to the portal, and even I began to bite my nails. I wanted to get out and run—at times it would have been faster. Rachel raced to the top of the Magic Castle's long driveway, parking in a line of honking taxis.

"Thank you," I said to her, reaching for a hug.

She grabbed her purse instead. "No. I'm coming with."

"You can't come with," I said, misunderstanding.

Rachel shook her head. "I want to watch you go."

Bianca pursed her lips. "You still don't believe me, do you?"

"I want to," Rachel said, so soft I could barely hear her. "I'm trying."

"Let her come," I said. "We have to hurry."

The portal is usually only visible along the edges, like a trick of the light or a mirage. But when we got there, it was shimmering like a curtain of sequins. A warm wind had picked up, dust devils spinning up a fine grit into our teeth and hair.

My clock bracelet showed two minutes to noon. Bianca kissed Rachel, walked toward the portal, made it halfway inside, and was thrown backward onto the ground.

"Shit." She righted herself and dusted her hands. She'd been agitated but calm until that point. Now, she began to flail at the portal, which, to the casual observer, looked as if she'd gone mental. Thankfully there was a dearth of casual observers.

"Bianca, stop," I said. "We can't freak out. We have to think."

"Does this make you Human now?" Rachel asked.

"Not quite," I said. "She still has magic inside of her. That's why she can still go partway through. The clock bracelet connects her with the other side."

Rachel paused from consoling our hyperventilating friend. "Will the bracelet fit over both of your wrists?"

I inhaled, angry with myself for not thinking of the same thing. "You're brilliant, Rachel. Don't let anyone tell you different." I unhooked my bracelet, handing it to Rachel. Two of Bianca's wrists could have fit into one bracelet, but my wrists are so much bigger. Around both our wrists, the bracelet was at least two fingers from closing.

"I'll cut my wrist," Bianca suggested, wide-eyed.

"Don't be stupid," Rachel said.

The portal began to cloud, bright sparks traced their way through the ether. I stuck my hand in and pulled it back. Something pricked my skin. A large branch erupted from the portal, narrowly missing Rachel. "Rachel, be careful. Step back."

"Just go, CeCi." Bianca hiccupped. "Leave me."

"Oh yeah? And what?" I asked. "I go home and watch our world collapse? Pay the price for your irresponsibility?"

"My irresponsibility? I came up here to help *you*."

"Maybe at first. But now you only want to find out where

your father is, and look where it's gotten us." The sparks were coming thicker and hotter and my patience was shot.

"Okay, fine. You're right. I don't give a shit about you or anyone else. I fell in love for fun." It was Rachel's turn to pale.

"It doesn't matter whose fault it is," I said. "All of ours. None of ours. Look at the portal! The world, your Pages. We have to go back. Now."

"No more fighting." Rachel was pleading. "Do something."

"Take my hand, Bianca." We wouldn't have a home to get to if we didn't get there soon. If only Rory could help us.

I began to scream into the portal. For Rory. For Solace. Hoping our desperation might travel through the pandemonium inside, if our bodies couldn't.

Bianca joined me. "Rory! Snoozer! Please."

The portal shimmered brightly, then faded. Just before it began to shrink, I could have sworn I saw Rory's face. The air began to swirl, and the portal before us grew smaller and smaller.

Then, beyond all hope, we watched as hands groped their way out of the now-smoking air. Rory's arms were marred and scratched from the flotsam and jetsam spinning around inside, but her clock bracelet appeared intact.

"Wait, Rory. Stay there. Don't come any farther," I yelled, yanking Bianca toward me. "Rachel, help me fasten our bracelets together." Two small wrists and one big one. The squeeze hurt, but Rachel managed to force the last hinged clasp closed. The wind roared at the mouth of the portal; thunder and hail pelted our faces. Everything was slippery and cold where it had been burning just a moment before.

"Pull, Rory," I screamed. "Rachel, push!"

The next thing I remember was coming to on the floor of Rory's tower, the walls and the clock itself in pieces all around us.

I am desperately trying to gather my thoughts. And awaiting a summons from Solace, who is no doubt furious. But all I can feel right now is relief.

And gratitude. Rachel. That brave, beautiful woman. How could we possibly thank her? I wonder if she curses the day she ever heard a Fairy Tale or is knee deep in the children's section of the library. I wish we could have spared her seeing all that, learning everything all at once. We owe her everything, at the very least the answers to the rest of her questions.

Love,
CeCi

Princess Briar R. Rose
Somnolent Tower Castle
South Road, Grimmland

Rapunzel,

My first clue something was amiss came when the clouds began to swirl. I'd imagine there were a great many who thought nothing of it, perhaps chalking up the change in atmosphere to an errant fairy or a disgruntled wizard.

It took me a few moments to realize why I was having such terrible déjà vu. And then it came to me. The awful day so long ago. That day, Solace had whisked me—mouth still full of sixteenth birthday party cake—up the stairs to the tower. Fred was calling up to me, even as Figgy's sentinels half-flew, half-dragged him away to learn his sentence. The stone walls seemed to quake each time the thunder roared and the air grew colder and colder.

So when the temperature began to fall just before lunch, I climbed the tower, trying to push the thought out of my mind that Bianca might be responsible for such a breach.

The tower room was littered with small debris. Pebbles and leaves. I slipped on my clock bracelet, and stepped through the clock. At the other end of the tunnel, the portal looked strange. I put my hand above my eyes to shield them from the small twigs and raindrops. When larger branches started to force their way in, I tried to take cover, crawling toward the other end on my stomach. A chair from the tower passed over my head.

A flash of lightning and a thunderbolt sounded, and afterward it was as if someone had drawn a curtain on the sun. The tunnel was black except for a glimmer where the exit to the

Outside should have been. I focused on getting there, slowly but surely.

When I finally did, I couldn't see out clearly. I could hear Bianca and CeCi and I thought Rachel, though that didn't make any sense. I tried to reach through but electric sparks flitted through the air, snapping and cutting my skin.

Just before I drew myself even closer to the ground, wondering whether to turn back or hunker down, I saw CeCi's hand reaching through. I could hear her yelling but it was difficult to make out any words over the roar of wind and thunder.

CeCi screamed for me to wait and then I felt her take my arm and unclasp my bracelet. And then I felt skin on skin on skin. The air began to freeze around us in tiny, razor-sharp crystals. Someone's fingers fumbled and the bracelet tightened down on my wrist, cutting into my skin, now wet with blood.

"Rory, pull!" CeCi shouted. I opened my eyes briefly to see my wrist buried in a pile of three, bound by two interlocking bracelets. I felt an enormous shove from the other side of the portal and heard a sound like the world ripping in half and all of a sudden we were in a pile on the tower floor.

The wind quieted, as did the sky, now visible in the places the tower's ceiling had fallen through. The face of the clock was fogged and cracked, glass tinkling to the floor.

The tower was ruined. The north wall collapsed. The fine furniture in splinters sticking out from what stone remained upright.

"Thank Grimm you came for us," CeCi sobbed.

"Rory," said Bianca, feeling the floor beneath her, as if ensuring it was real. "You came. You saved us, and I'm sorry. I am . . . I'm so sorry."

Bianca and CeCi continued to grovel until the three of us all fell unconscious.

Sometime later my staff retrieved us, and we woke in my quarters.

I ordered tea and scones and listened as they babbled and groveled some more. I let my nurse tend my cuts and scrapes and told her to do the same for my friends and let them stay as long as they wanted and needed in order to get their bearings.

Then I excused myself to get dressed. As tempting as resting might be, I have errands to attend to.

Rory

Important Fucking Correspondence from Snow B. White
Onyx Manor
West Road, Grimmland

Z,

There aren't enough bloody marys in the whole of the Realm to deal with the two surliest bridesmaids ever in the history of pre-wedding brunches.

Ever since our overemotional recovery and Rory's baffling Ice Queen routine, we've avoided discussing the whole portal clusterfuck. So it isn't terribly surprising that we don't have our stories straight when Solace interrupts this morning's event, thumping her back foot on the floor of the open doorway.

"You three obliterated my portal," she says, paws crossed.

CeCi and I begin explaining at the same time. Rory just sits there and picks at her eggs. I mean, Rory saved my ass. Our asses, plural. But she's been completely bizarre ever since she found out about Henry. I know she's pissed at us. For Henry. For ruining her tower. Yes, we're shitty friends. But we still could have used her help with Solace.

"We're sorry," says CeCi. "Things got . . . out of control."

"Did I somehow not make myself clear? I trusted you to treat the situation with gravitas."

"Then you are as gullible as CeCi," Rory says in an unfamiliar drawl. "Good thing our delinquent diva returned in time!"

"I beg your pardon, Briar Rose." Solace drew her ears flat against her head. "I remember a time you also vouched for your friend."

"I never agreed to sacrifice my own timeline," Rory says.

"That's because no one asked you to," CeCi says, her lip half snarl. I wonder momentarily if there's a place I can take these two and exchange them for my old friends, the ones who bickered with me instead of each other.

"You were right, Solace," I say. "It was easy to get distracted—complacent. But thanks to Rory . . ."

"I don't want to hear any more of this. You're welcome. Enough." It's as if someone else has taken over Rory's body. She's even dressed differently, in a simple black gown. No gloves or parasol or purse. No lace. Snoozer wears an unadorned, matte black leather leash.

I know I was pushing things with her before—my cake, my temper, my dresses, my disbelief in True Love. I do know that now. But I miss the romantic, babbling Rory. The Rory who loved us back.

"This is not the day to discuss repercussions." Solace eyes CeCi, then me, then the table of bloody marys. "But there *will* be repercussions."

"Figgy's never going to let us go Outside again, is she?" CeCi sounds like she's making a statement instead of asking a question.

"And what about my tower?" asks Rory, rolling a potato across her plate.

Solace sighs. "It's less of a matter of allowance and more of a matter of physical impossibility. There is a rift in the portal itself. Until it's fixed, no one can go Outside."

My heart skips a beat. "For how long?"

"We'll see. Malice lent me her old spinning wheel to begin making the time threads that will stitch the portal back together. It's a laborious process."

My chest feels constricted. It dawns on me that our mistake

has sealed any tiny chance that I can find my father in time for the wedding. CeCi shakes my shoulder.

"I may require your help once the threads are ready," Solace says before leaving. "For now, attend to matters here. It seems you have plenty."

CeCi and I stare at our plates while Rory finishes her bloody mary, sucking loudly at the bottom of the glass with her straw.

I've always known about cause and effect. But I'm not sure I've ever seen an avalanche like this before. I'll cooperate with Figgy. And Solace. Even Malice, until we fix things. I'll follow the Pages. Every last paragraph. Until I'm free.

Love,
B

From the Desk of Cecilia Cinder Charming
Crystal Palace
North Road, Grimmland

Dear Zell,

Edmund insisted we meet with his parents before Bianca's wedding. Darling talked me through dressing simply yet elegantly. We picked an ice-blue gown, lace ribbon, and pearl jewelry. If I'd only had dark hair, I'd have passed for Rory from far enough away. Meanwhile, Sweetie gave me lessons on calm breathing.

The twins were a constant stream of cheering chatter, all while swearing to keep the conversation secret from Lucinda, who had been curiously quiet with her newly gleaned information, except for the odd, snakelike grin she gives me when we occasionally pass in the halls.

Edmund's parents' chambers are white. And I don't mean the soft sort of neutral kind, but a bright, spotless, blinding sort of white. It feels silly but, as I only met them briefly at our wedding, I don't know them very well at all. They're always visiting the king of this or the queen of that, exchanging skeins of Rumple's golden thread from the north end of Narnia to the south end of Somewhere Out There.

"So, Cecilia," began Edmund's mother, "our son tells us that you've decided to pursue a vocation." The crown sitting on top of her red curls looked like it weighed twenty toads, the silver plating studded with fat rubies.

"Ambitious," his father added, sitting back with his long, snowy beard in his lap. "Don't see that every day."

"Yes, sir," I said. "I've been cooking most of my life and recently began studying at a prestigious school Outside to learn about the ever-expanding realm of food."

"Ambitious but not very progressive," said the queen, frowning.

"Poppycock," the King said. "Now *there's* a Realm I'd like to visit! The Isle of Ice Cream, the Fjords of Filet Mignon, the Bastion of Brulée!"

"Your Highnesses, I want to be clear: I don't wish to return to servanthood. I see myself as an artist. A creator."

"Call me Elvis," said the King with a lazy wave. "Are you doing any of that *avant-garde* sort of food? My latest copy of *Saveur* talks about deconstructed pie. Do you know how to make deconstructed pie? Maybe a nice peanut butter and banana?"

"We've studied some," I said. "I could certainly give it a shot. My emphasis is on pastry."

"Edmund has explained how you plan to balance your occupation with your civic duties, but I'm not sure how you plan to raise children alongside." For the life of me, I could not decipher the queen's facial expression.

Edmund takes my hand. "Well, Mother, see, CeCi and I aren't sure parenthood is . . ."

"I told you, Betty. They're not going to have any grandchildren. You owe me a foot massage. Now we can go on another tour! We'll call it 'Not So Fast: The Return of King Elvis & Queen Betty.' And since we don't have to buy baby toys, we *can* afford the yacht! I'll tell Morrison to put the deal together." Edmund's father, His Highness King Elvis, toddled off, presumably to his chambers to send a pigeon to whoever Morrison is.

Edmund looked so bewildered I almost laughed.

"Is this true?" the queen asked, with a sidelong glance after her husband. We could still hear him humming like he'd won the lottery. Edmund and I shared a long look before turning to her and nodding.

"Well, that certainly simplifies things," she said. "We'll keep our crowns, and you'll become our very first Princess de Cuisine."

"What about William? He still expects to share Kingship with us," said Edmund.

"We'll handle oversight of the seas, since your father can't seem to stand dry land anymore. William can work out the rest with Briar Rose's parents. It doesn't appear Henry will be ripe for kingship any time soon."

"So you don't mind if I cook?" I ask

"Not at all, my dear. It's about time we shake things up around here." She paused, lowering her voice. "Can you teach me how to make baked Alaska? He thinks I can't even make toast. Baked Alaska would really shut him up."

I promised her the recipe, and we both kissed her on the cheek. Then Edmund's mother, adjusting her crown, floated down from her throne and out of the brilliant white room.

This is what I was afraid of the whole time? It seems almost impossible. I told Edmund he had failed to deliver the parents he'd advertised. He claims they must have given up on parenting the day he got married. Lucky us.

Love,
CeCi

Princess Briar R. Rose
Somnolent Tower Castle
South Road, Grimmland

Dear Zell,

I suspect if I'd invited CeCi and Bianca to visit Malice with me, their reactions would have been similar to yours. Besides, were I in their shoes, I would stay as far away from Fairy Godmothers as possible for a time. Though in truth, Solace wasn't nearly as angry as I thought she'd be.

As for me, I left for Malice's sea cave the afternoon of that awful brunch so that I could arrive the following morning. I traveled light, asking the Huntsman Bianca pardoned to act as my escort.

I was exceedingly amused to find Malice's damp, black lair unguarded, or perhaps protected through invisible means. I couldn't tell if she was surprised to see me, but she certainly wasn't prepared for such early company. She must have been breakfasting, for she was wearing only a light robe. I crossed the room to sit down at her table.

"And to what do I owe this . . . this visit?" she asked. Her mottled, scaly fingers tightened around a mug of what appeared to be a thick tea. "You've caught me quite unaware, Briar Rose. I haven't even had time to dress."

I suppose some amount of fear would have been natural, seeing the fish-headed woman for the first time since my childhood, but my rage toward Maro was so fierce that all trepidation had been displaced. "Malice." I nodded. "I need your help."

She folded her napkin in her lap. I watched her rainbow-colored throat gills opening and closing. "Your parents, your friends, they are not aware that you are here?"

"I'm not in danger, am I?"

"Quite to the contrary. Had anyone else tried to get through my door, they would have been assaulted by charms of all kinds. But there are those who I feel are owed remittance, such as yourself, and may enter unmolested." She flicked her wrist. "It's a small cosmic bargain."

"I'm not here to strike back at you, Malice. I do need your help."

"It's been some time since anyone in your circles has needed *my* help."

"This is beyond Figgy and Solace."

"Don't be fooled, Briar Rose. Very little is beyond my sisters within white or black magic. If we're being honest, I am indeed more amenable to the greyer side of things."

"Is that why you did what you did to me? Was I a grey side of things?"

"No. Not in the slightest. I was a young sorceress who had trouble being accepted into an established circle. You were, as they say, collateral damage in my rise to power. The threat I made when you were a child turned out to be the first step in a cascade of terrible choices that could not be stilled. I was what I was, and my sisters were what they were. No more, no less."

"Well, that sounds . . . convenient." I traced the grain of the wooden table with my fingers.

"I was trying to find a way to remedy things when Fred stole your Pages from Figgy. And in just a few short moments, my threat became the least of anyone's worries. Even if I had wanted to craft time, as Solace does, or channel the Fates, like Figueroa, one act of darkness begets another. And so it was for you and me. Solace slowed time to minimize the damage of the storm—a small piece of the same magic she used during your recent portal debacle. And while she did that, I gave you and your palace a sleeping potion. Either way, I am still your transgressor."

I had never thought of things that way before. It seemed unfathomable that the Fairy Godmothers once felt as backed into their corners as we have all of our lives.

She continued. "It is a pity we've not had this conversation sooner. I can see in your eyes that you are about to make a similar decision, and I am, regrettably, in no position to refuse you."

My words came out braver than I suddenly felt. "You have no right to judge me."

Malice lowered her head, and the fins on her forearms twitched. "I am the Fairy Godmother of Sorrow, and I will grant whatever you wish. Tell me what it is."

"I need the same sleeping potion you gave me on my sixteenth birthday."

"For whom?"

"For one who desires intrigue."

"Has she wronged you so deeply?"

I picked my head up and looked fully into Malice's wizened face. "She's taken my life away."

"Are you quite sure?"

"As sure as the first time my life was taken from me," I said. She closed her eyes as if my words had weight. "I am sure this time, as well."

"Why not kill her outright, then?"

"Because I want her to wake up and feel loss. I want her to yearn for a life and a love she can no longer have."

"That is a heavy burden, Briar Rose. One that you might not even wish on your worst enemy."

"I have borne that same burden of sleep. It is certainly survivable. Maro Green *is* my worst enemy. She keeps saying how fascinating my life sounds. She can have it."

"There's a chance you'd be killing her, regardless." Malice slid her golden chair back from the table and rose. "If the length of Human imagination is shorter than one hundred years—"

"You all keep saying that. I've been Outside. You fairies should try it. It would certainly change your perspective."

Malice glided smoothly to my side, holding a glowing green vial. I reached for it, and she placed her hand on mine. "For what it is worth, Briar Rose, I am sorry. I am sorry for both of us."

"Well," I said. I looked at my hands, at the table's centerpiece strewn with simple fruits.

"You can return this to me at any time and I shall destroy it."

"I'm quite sure I won't be doing that."

As I headed toward the door, Malice gave me one final warning: "Briar Rose, it is possible that you'll incur more victims than you've planned."

I suppose she means I'll be punishing Henry, as well. Which is sort of the whole idea. What a sad and strange sorceress Malice is, presiding over all that grey area. There sure seems to be a lot of it in this life.

I appreciate her excess caution, as rich as I find it, but my mind is made up.

Rory

Important Fucking Correspondence from Snow B. White
Onyx Manor
West Road, Grimmland

Z,

The morning of the wedding is a blur. CeCi and Rory pull on their admittedly gorgeous lilac dresses and fuss with my hair and makeup. I catch CeCi pouting, and Rory still isn't saying much to either of us.

"I thought all your problems were over, CeCi. What's the matter now?" I ask.

"Well, how am I supposed to feel, Bianca? There's kind of a lot going on."

"For example?"

"Fine, Bridezilla, I don't want to say good-bye to you. Happy?"

"Oh, CeCi. Let's worry about later later. I won't be leaving until the portal is fixed, anyway."

"Maybe we should leave it broken," she sniffs.

"That's a stupid thing to say. Have you been drinking tea with Figgy or something?"

"I'm going to miss you. Is that so wrong?" I roll my eyes at her, but she still isn't finished. "Everyone leaves," she says. I fight the urge to slap her again.

Rory gives CeCi a wounded look. She's been so quiet lately, it's refreshing to see her react to something—anything. "Not *everyone* leaves, Cecilia."

CeCi blinks at her. "Oh, Rory. You know that's not what I meant."

I interrupt. "This is *my* wedding day. For crying out loud, CeCi, it's not fucking always about you." I'm not being terribly fair. All three of us have been inexcusably self-absorbed lately.

CeCi wraps her arms around herself as if she's been hit in the stomach by a flying carpet. She drops down on the chaise, a puddle of lavender. "Why does everyone keep saying that? Am I really that selfish?"

"Right this second, you are. What are you doing? Get up." I should apologize, but I can't for some reason. "You can't quit in the middle of bridal cosmetology. Wedding bells. 'Get me to the church on time.' Vamoose. Chop-chop."

Rory shakes her head at CeCi and assumes the task of adjusting of my headpiece—an infernal creation that seems to need a magical sort of glue to adhere to my head. I try to stay still as I pour champagne for each of us, but I'm likely making Rory's job even more difficult.

"Let's celebrate today, ladies. Okay? Let's be together right now, just us, and, for once, not worry about tomorrow." They lift their glasses and we toast to conquering my monster veil. "To the first day of the rest of our lives."

Out in the hall, guests finish their chicken or trout or lamb and polish off their luncheon wine. (Can you believe Humans don't feed their guests until after the ceremony? Cruel and unusual.) I step out into the hallway to signal the cellist to start warming up. DJ is heading down the hall with a martini in his hand and gives me the thumbs up.

"Just a few more minutes," I tell him. I'm glad he agreed to walk me down the aisle. For my something borrowed, he lends me his favorite CD, *Best Ibiza Anthems . . . Ever.* Yes, it's funny. Particularly because the only place in Grimmland with a CD player is the Swinging Vine.

"Oooh, look, a shiny Frisbee!" I say.

He wags a finger at me. "Don't you dare, sister."

"Where the hell is Ibiza?" I ask.

He shrugs. "Someplace where they dance a whole lot." He spins three times and lands with jazz hands.

"You *have* to tell me so that I never accidentally end up there."

He grins and puts a hand on my wrist. "There'd better not be any scratches on this when I get it back, either."

Rory gifts me something blue. It's a necklace—an improbably blue stone in a silver setting she tells me is from a place called Tiffany & Co. in a city called New York. Patricia helped her get it. I hug her as tight as I can, and she manages to smile at me and nod her approval before starting to cry, first polite tears of joys and then what I can only assume are sobs of a more convoluted set of emotions. I whisper to her that when she's ready, I need her to put the rings into the pockets of Snoozer's tuxedo vest.

CeCi gives me something old—though not that old. It's the clock bracelet from our first trip Outside together, when we went from Solace's shop. She had Solace deactivate it, and she had it set with a few jewels from each of our jewelry collections. And I'm wearing the beautiful new unicorn-horn earrings you sent. I can imagine you performing the ritual request for a piece of horn, carefully gathering it so the animal wasn't harmed. I know you're probably dying not being here. And we miss you just as much.

DJ is knocking. So it's time I wrap this up. I can't help but be excited. Here comes the rest of my life.

Love,
B

From the Desk of Cecilia Cinder Charming
Crystal Palace
North Road, Grimmland

Dear Zell,

I wish you could have seen Bianca in her wedding gown. Her polka dots were small and white. You couldn't even see them until you got close. Even Rory thought her dress was marvelous.

Bianca was radiant, so happy that I hoped for a tiny moment she might have changed her mind about leaving. But when I saw William's resigned face at the end of the aisle, I knew that he was getting ready to let Bianca go just like we were. It was heartbreaking and endearing all at the same time. Our near miss with the portal only seems to have solidified her decision. I think if it weren't for the destruction of the Realm, she would have stayed with Rachel until the end of time without a second thought for her old life.

Even though I have been feeling sorry for myself, Bianca's right: It's *not* about me. I'll only lose Bianca if I allow myself to. Our friendship—just like our friendships with you, Zell—will become different animals than they are now. It's not the end of anything as long as we treat it like another beginning.

Bianca's shindig easily doubled the attendance of any of our own weddings. And it was fun. There was dancing and drinking and toasting and nonsense. At some point, we all went out and smoked cigars with the groomsmen. I found myself lost in the breadth of the evening, blissfully ignoring the changes to our lives up ahead. Bianca asked us, and we obliged, forgetting—mostly—just for one night.

The vows were standard and short. Toasts were made afterward when the cake was cut. And while I won't recite them for you, they were everything you might imagine. Love and possibility and friendship and celebration.

William, Rory, Bianca, and I joined the Council in an adjoining room, where Valborg sat at a long table in a grey shift, drinking wine from a large cup. Bianca had spiked her drink with euphorics. When the old woman stood, a strange smile played across her eyes and lips. She held her arms out.

"Come, my dear," she said. "Let this mistake be over." I thought it sort of trivialized the situation, and I looked at Rory, who tacitly confirmed my puzzlement. Bianca didn't seem to take offense, only embraced her—perhaps they had some sort of understanding. Perhaps there are many things I think I know that I don't actually know.

The Council asked Bianca to repeat some standard sentencing language and then she stepped back. A small quartet filled the room. The lead Councilor looked at his paperwork askance. "Is this right?"

"Give her the shoes and let her dance," Bianca said.

The Councilor opened his mouth but then closed it again. It was the smart thing to do. Valborg was already swaying back and forth, even without music, and the attendants had trouble getting her still enough to put on the shoes at all. But by that time, we were moving backward toward the door.

As soon as the Councilor nodded, we made our exit—Rory and I holding Bianca's hands and William following behind, holding her shoulders. Over the swelling string music, all we heard was laughter, great peals of it, and then it faded as we re-entered the noise of the big reception hall. Bianca stopped and took a deep breath.

"Are you okay?" William asked.

Bianca nodded, though she was fighting back tears, and biting her lip.

"Come now," Rory said, taking her by the elbow. "You wouldn't want to ruin that perfect makeup, now would you?"

Edmund was on the other side of the room, scanning the crowd. I raised a hand and waved.

Bianca pushed the small of my back. "I'm fine. Go."

I looked at Rory. "I've got this," she said.

Bianca nodded. "I'm good. I promise. Nothing a little champagne won't fix. William, would you?"

"I'd like some unicorn cake," said Rory.

Bianca's lips split into a wide grin. "Let's go." I watched them retreat arm in arm, feeling calmer than I had in a long while.

When I crossed the room, I saw Darling and Sweetie against the wall chatting with the prince with one swan wing. They had some suspect-looking oysters in their palms, and I collected them on my way past. "Don't eat those, okay? Stick to the crudités." They nodded and giggled, and the Swan Prince gave me a light nod. I hoped he knew they'd be a handful.

Lucinda had her back to me, busy hissing into Edmund's ear. His face was all concentrated mock earnestness. "And here's our girl now!" he said, beaming.

"Ta-da!" I said, pirouetting in my lilac petticoats for good measure.

Lucinda looked at me like Snoozer looks at Rory when he gets caught chewing her slippers. "I tried to tell her. Disgrace over our house."

Edmund clapped Lucinda on the back. "Nonsense, Lucinda. I couldn't be prouder."

"What?" she asked with a cough. Oyster shells clattered on the plate in the hand not clutching her throat. "You know? You've known about this, this . . . outrage?"

"She cooked for you, didn't she?"

"Well, yes, but . . . That's different. She was a servant."

"Your servant? I thought you said she was a member of your family."

"Of course. She was my daughter. Cooking was simply a chore that she managed. A chore no longer befitting of her status. Queens do not . . . cook!"

"Then you'll be exceedingly relieved to learn I won't be becoming a queen anytime soon," I said.

Her eyes widened. She looked like she was about to collapse. "Our fortunes are cast to the streets, then. Just as I'd feared."

"Nonsense," said Edmund. "Nothing changes at all. My folks keep their crowns. CeCi becomes a chef. You do . . . whatever it is you do."

"Cooking makes me happy, Lucinda," I said. "You should try it. Making yourself happy. Maybe you'd be less of a meddling swine." I heard Darling and Sweetie giggle. But they were too far away to hear me insult their mother. They were merely flirting. My heart swelled for them. "Hear your joyful daughters? You should get to know them. You should get to know me. You should get to know you. We're free to live our dreams now. Why wouldn't we?"

"A toast!" Edmund waved a waiter over with a tray of glasses. "To my brilliant wife and her big dream."

"To dreaming dreams together," I added. I whispered in Edmund's ear, "Tonight you are my hero."

Bianca swirled drunkenly into our circle. "What are we toasting? I toast it! To you! To me! Hooray!" She took Lucinda's full glass from her and spun away again, like a cottonwood seed in the breeze.

Love,
CeCi

Princess Briar R. Rose
Somnolent Tower Castle
South Road, Grimmland

Dearest Zell,

I missed you the most at the wedding. Everything was as beautiful as you might have expected. Snoozer did an absolutely perfect job as the ring bearer. He didn't even try to chew Bianca's shoes. My centerpieces were well received. Many people commented that they'd never seen such unique sculptures before.

The second worst part of the evening was having to be civil to Henry. But most of the time I was with Bianca and CeCi, anyway. I was still having that out-of-body feeling. I watched our friends talking to me, and I watched myself struggling to participate in the conversation. I tried hard to put aside Bianca's decision to leave the Realm, as she requested, but I suppose I never quite shook it.

I won't deny I was surprised to see Maro at the reception. She was most definitely not invited, but it isn't as if decorum stops a woman like her from doing whatever she pleases. I avoided her and it felt good for a while, knowing that I had the perfect revenge, the upper hand, and she would remain completely unaware until it was too late.

Unfortunately, I didn't manage to avoid her all evening. Accordingly, the worst part of the party occurred when she cornered me near the cake display, mouth full of red velvet and frosting.

"I have nothing to say to you," I said, trying to fight a wave of people descending on the groom's cake.

She dabbed the corner of her mouth. "Henry tells me that you're aware of our situation."

I stared at her. "Situation? Is that what they're calling it these days?"

"He tells me that you could make life very difficult for us. That the contract between your family included certain provisos."

I nodded. My parents had been eager to see Figgy's new Pages fulfilled, yet they had protected me, too. "Actions have consequences, Maro. Betrayal is an action."

"He also tells me that his fortunes change when he has an heir."

"Then it's a good thing he doesn't."

She sidled even closer to me. "Ah, but there's where you're wrong."

I would have moved if I could have. "I'm not sure I follow."

"Henry has an heir." She put her hand on her middle and smiled. "It'll all work out fine. I am your surrogate."

"You fabricating cow," I said quietly. But somewhere deep down I knew she wasn't lying.

Rapunzel, I wanted to kill her. I wanted to grind her into the stones, throw her into the cake, rip her teeth from her skull, slap her into next week. I scanned the room for Henry. He was there, but wasn't watching us. I wanted to rip his heart out, so that he could feel like I felt. Torn apart and mortified.

But Bianca *had* seen us. She made a sharp beeline toward us from the champagne table, snapping at guards on the way, her face dark.

I threw the second drink of my life in Maro's face and began swinging wildly, hoping to connect with any part of her body, but Bianca—so tall in her wedding shoes—hauled me backward, demanding the guards remove Maro and Henry and anyone who'd been talking to them. She was whispering in my ear, telling me to breathe. She said if I didn't, I'd "give that bitch power" over me. I didn't have the energy to tell her that Maro did have power over me, no matter how hard I tried to get the upper hand.

It'll never get better, will it? Oh, Zell, what will I do? I can't give her the sleeping potion if she's pregnant. Or can I? The child means nothing to me. What if she's lying about the child? If I take the risk, what kind of monster do I become? Is that what Malice meant?

Sometimes, when I look around, it becomes completely clear that there's nothing and no one left for me in this life. How silly I was to have once thought any differently.

Rory

Important Fucking Correspondence from Snow B. White
Onyx Manor
West Road, Grimmland

Z,

It's early, but I can't sleep. Part of the problem is that I'm violently ill. I had some champagne, of course, but not as much as you think. Seems the royal caterers messed something up, and I'm told the majority of wedding guests have come down with food poisoning. The captain of William's guard said the oysters were to blame. So you can still be upset that you weren't there, but not upset that you missed the food. Maybe I should've had CeCi cater the stupid thing after all.

But that isn't the only reason for the insomnia. I can't stop this infernal thinking about everything in front of me and everything behind me. I'm excited but honestly, Zell, just a little disappointed. There's this small part of me that hoped my father would show up yesterday. That he'd find a way to surprise me. A part that believed that with enough Human ingenuity, he'd have figured out how to be there for me, how to make amends for leaving me.

But this is the end of surprises. I have completed my Pages, delivered at the end of the wedding by Figgy's canaries in a roll tied with a red ribbon. I go forward from here my own woman on my own journey, singing my own song and dancing my own dance.

Speaking of dancing, I suppose Valborg's farewell went smoothly enough. I'm glad she died laughing. I'm glad I was surrounded by friends—family. It's almost like it was a dream. One I both do and don't want to remember.

After our guests went home, William and I spent the night with a bottle of bourbon at the beach, watching for shooting stars and renaming constellations. Well, at least until I got sick.

This morning, William (who, luckily, eschews oysters) springs into action, transforming our bar into a tactical den for my relocation. He says if I'm going to go, I might as well do it correctly, so I have the things I need to avoid homesickness and so that everyone can visit me as often as they'd like. He's chosen ten strong birds expressly for letter-carrying and has started the search for a large guard dog to send with me.

Once I feel well enough to get up, an unexpected thing happens. He sits me down with a glass of ginger beer and says, "B, I've been thinking. Would you like me to come with you?"

I start bawling. And laughing, between great big gulps of air. "Fuck yeah, Will. That'd be awesome," I manage. "But this, here, is what *you* want. And even though I'll miss the shit out of you, I couldn't ask that much. We'd get old and resent each other. You can't be a king up there. They don't have those anymore. I mean, they do, but they aren't the same."

"But I want you to know that I would."

Will's a good man, Zell. And I tell him so. "Your friendship is the best gift a princess could have."

"I love you, Bianca. Not in the way you probably need, but in the best way I can."

I know he's trying to make this easier for me, but it's the opposite. "I know. Me, too."

"We'll visit all the time."

I pat his hand. "No, you won't. But you'll visit enough."

"Okay," he says. "I expect to be shown the best bourbon Outside has to offer."

"Of course," I sniff. "Nothing less."

"Let's get to work, then."

And so we do. We set dates and make lists. We arrange trunks for donation and for storage. We plan what we'll do when he comes to visit. We take a break so that I can throw up again. It's a grand time.

Not two hours later, the pigeons deliver an envelope on unfamiliar stationery. I had forgotten the letter I sent to Odette a couple of months ago. I open her reply with Will's pocketknife.

Bianca darling,

I'm so sorry for the late reply. I spent a month at our summer home in Neverland, and we were invaded by pirates! Can you imagine? Oh, they were nice enough, though, and once we sorted out that we both knew Smee, we invited them to stay on. (Besides, they brought some killer rum.)

Goodness, it's been ages since we last saw you. I hope this arrives in time to congratulate you on your marriage. I so wish we could have come, but the timing was just no good. I'm shipping you a couple of swan-down pillows with the next Fed-Ox shipment.

I suppose the last time we caught up was at Puss's animal welfare ball. Is it true that Rapunzel and Jason set off to live on a farm? Too much. Did you hear about the debacle when the Emperor of Toyland came to visit? He marched through the streets stark naked, claiming to be wearing the latest in fashion. Let me tell you, the stationery store almost sold out of paper with all the sympathy cards sent to the Empress.

As to the matter at hand, however, I am deeply sorry to hear about the arrival of Maro Green in your fair kingdom. That woman is nothing but a barnacle, and it is the fault of our bumbling royal guard she escaped at all.

It started simply enough. My cousin Albert's father insisted his son stop faffing about and get married—to anyone at all. But Albert, the cad, insisted he wouldn't marry anyone but a real princess.

His first mistake was making his quest public. What followed was a parade of princess impersonators of which I've never seen the like.

Maro was certainly the most convincing of the impostors. She had the palace staff falling all over themselves. She claimed to have felt a pebble in her mattress, and Albert was completely snowed by her sensitivity, which he swore was a virtue only the royal can possess. All the constant partying had become a bit much for me, and by the time Maro came about, I had begun the process of drying out for a bit, but my few interactions with her led me to believe that she was at best unpolished and at worst, a regular strumpet.

I assure you she felt something hard in her bed, but it wasn't a pebble. (Albert was rabid about her cleavage, which I'm sure you've been more than privy to.)

Maro insisted on being married right away, and Albert was in no position to deny her. It was the queen who finally discovered her ruse. When Maro demanded the pebble she'd found in her bed be displayed at the Royal Museum, the queen was livid and demanded to know Maro's lineage. No princess, Ms. Green is simply the daughter of tulip growers from the north with big dreams. Her deception, though shocking, was not the worst of her offenses. When exposed, she absconded with the royal jewels! Most of them were recovered from pawn shops between here and Toad Hollow.

If you need me to send someone to pick her up, just send word and I can arrange it. She'll be welcome in Cell 1B of the Swan Lake

Municipal Jail. King Ludwig paid off the Tattler lest thieves began to think they were an easy mark, so please be discreet.

A word of advice: Do keep her away from men with wandering eyes. She seems to rather enjoy activities of the carnal variety, regardless of prior claim.

Toodles,
Odette

I can't wait to tell Rory she was right from the start. After their confrontation last night, she'll no doubt be ecstatic to learn we'll be sending Maro back where she belongs, just as soon as the constable recovers from his oyster consumption.

I leap to my feet, swaying like an inebriated privateer, but I bargain with my stomach that if it will stay calm, I will give it as much ginger beer as it can hold when we return.

When I arrive, though, Rory's nursemaid tells me she's out. I hang around for a while, pitching a frayed pair of slippers for Snoozer until he gets tired and falls asleep with his head in my lap. She rarely leaves Snoozer behind, but then again, it's been a long time since she's been herself. Perhaps she went to the alchemist for some stomach potions. I don't know if she had any oysters before I pulled her off Maro.

I'd like to know how the conniving little troll got into my wedding in the first place. I'd also like to know what exactly made Rory throw another drink in her face. It was undoubtedly deserved, but still.

I give up waiting for Rory and head to CeCi's to see if she's heard from our wayward friend. CeCi is playing nursemaid to Lucinda, who apparently ate enough oysters for six people. Serves her right, the great, greedy snag.

CeCi hasn't heard from Rory, either. She didn't see her after the sentencing, too busy enjoying Edmund's deflation of Lucinda's big news bubble. As I had hoped, she's delighted to hear about Maro's feloniousness.

I feel so productive and energetic—the walking made me feel so much better—I decide to go home and fill the rows of empty trunks William procured for me. Helpful, supportive William. Damn, Zell, I am gonna miss him.

But I can't wait to build a place of my own and share it with all of you. Just wait. It'll be better than we can even imagine.

Love,
B

From the Desk of Cecilia Cinder Charming
Crystal Palace
North Road, Grimmland

Dear Zell,

Honestly, if I had seen where the oysters had been stored—in the sun, for Grimm's sake!—I'd have taken them off the buffet table myself. I don't know how many Spew-cinda ate, but enough to make her miserable the night of the wedding, yesterday, and today.

And she isn't the only victim. Yesterday morning, a courier brought me a note from Hansel and Gretel. They're both sick, as well, and there's a gaggle of tourists in from Neverland who're scheduled to lunch at their café today. They'd been wondering how they'd ever manage, when word made it to them, somehow, that I could help.

So, I signed on for my very first restaurant gig.

This morning (after turning over my nursing duties to Darling and Sweetie), I started with bread and soup. I proofed the yeast and mixed sixteen loaves of whole-wheat dough in the big mixer. Then I set them to rise while I chopped a mirepoix for some beer cheese chowder, ensuring I didn't burn the roux. I prepped my *mise en place* for the luncheon sandwiches and made sure the tables were set correctly. I squeezed lemonade and set the iced tea in the sun to steep. I wish Phil could have been there to see it. DJ stopped by with air kisses and white wine spritzers. Evidently, my trial run was big news around town, particularly as word of my extracurriculars circulated through the wedding guests in record time.

In the afternoon, orders flew out and compliments flooded back in. Bianca came. And Darling and Sweetie, though they didn't stay long before returning home to check on their mother. Plates were licked clean, and I began to see the bottom of the soup pot with each ladle. The dining room finally went quiet and I set to returning everything to its original state. The pots hung gleaming from the racks and the spoons nestled in the drawers.

I have long fantasized about having a restaurant of my own. Every day would be this day. I would create. I would teach. I would lay exhausted in my triumph. I would feed my friends, my family, my village, my Realm. I would give them the gifts of my two hands.

I was just about to turn off the lights when Edmund arrived at the back door with roses and a bottle of champagne. "I'm so proud of you," he said.

I kissed him. "I almost can't wait to see what the future brings."

"I'm more interested in the next hour or three," he said, winking. We took the long way home. It felt like the night we got married. Everything was light, like I was dancing through clouds.

My feet are tired and my back is sore, but if my dream can make me feel this happy—even for a few minutes a day—it's worth it. I want to do this for the rest of my life. I'll let DJ manage the wine list. I'll hire Rory to make weird centerpieces. Darling and Sweetie can greet customers. Snoozer can help with cleanup. Just kidding. Food Safety deems that sort of thing a health violation.

See what you've done, Zell? You've inspired us all to dream. I'll never be able to thank you enough.

Love,
CeCi

PS. Did you hear about Maro? Bianca is falling on that news like hellfire. Just wait until we tell Rory.

Princess Briar R. Rose
Somnolent Tower Castle
South Road, Grimmland

Zell, CeCi, & Bianca,

First, please understand that I love you. I know that in the light of tomorrow, what I've done will not seem prudent. You will not understand fully. You will be angry with me, with my choice, but it is the only one I have left.

You see, at first, I blamed Maro for taking something away from me. But it turns out, I never had any of it to begin with.

I never had the kind of relationship with Henry that allowed us to be anything—not friends, not lovers, not confidants, not companions. We couldn't even chat politely. He went looking to fulfill his needs elsewhere.

This is not to say I'm without blame, either. I'm quite sure I've been in love with Fred all this time, and Henry would never have been equal. All those subconscious expectations weren't quite fair.

This can't be completely Maro's fault, either. She shares the blame, but her unchecked desire, her desperation must stem from some other, older wound we likely cannot fathom. I regret that I did not trust myself and, eventually, you—my friends.

CeCi, I regret that you blame yourself for Maro's introduction into our lives. Please don't. This kindling would have come to a fire no matter the order of events. She was not Henry's first indiscretion. I suspected, of course, but it was easier when those others were just flings, nameless, passing ships. This time it involves love and a relationship and complexity. Most importantly, a child.

I didn't like who I was when I was plotting Maro's demise. I felt powerful, but not in a way that made me feel anything but black and crusted inside. When I went to seek Malice's help, I felt fierce, but not happy.

And now that I've felt the extremes of both emotions, I think I'd trade strong for happy almost any day. I bet the three of you would tell me, once again, to try to find a balance, but I'm just too tired. I can't do this anymore.

There are some final items I need your assistance with:

- CeCi and Bianca, it is imperative that you make up. Not just obligatory civility, but forgiving those past slights I'll bet neither of you even remember. Face life together, not separately. Stand by each other no matter where your journeys take you. Find a way to have a new friendship, as we've done with Zell.

- One of you has to take Snoozer. He eats promptly at the nine in the morning and prefers his rib-eyes medium rare.

- CeCi, I hope you'll name something after me at the Unicorn Café. Please do not put ketchup in it.

- Bianca, follow your heart. If you want Outside and your father and Rachel, that's what you should do. I know you think I don't believe in you. I do. More than any Fairy Tale could believe in another unwritten story.

- Zell, you're stronger than you think you are. If your dream doesn't make you happy, find another. Things don't always work out like we plan. And be there for CeCi and Bianca. They'll need you soon.

- Tell Maro that I forgive her.

- Even if you can't manage the previous request, as I know it will be difficult, please do not punish the child. The baby bears no fault.

Please don't be sad. Just because we won't see each other again doesn't mean that I'm gone. In a hundred years, I'll try again, fully rested and restored, shored up by the lessons I've learned from all of you. I'll know how to ask for what I want and how to walk away. But I can't face another day right now. Not even another hour.

I cannot put you all through this any longer, either. I know what you tried to do for me all this time. I know you love me, and I'm trying to spare you, though I'm sure it won't feel that way at first.

I'll miss you all. You've been the bright lights of this part of my life. But I need to turn them off for a bit, battle away this despair, and rest.

Love always,
Rory

PS. You'll find me by the swamp. It was always one of my favorite places. I'd prefer to rest in my own room this time, if you'll make the arrangements. I expect the tower (and the portal) to be in perfect repair by the time I wake up.

She Lost Herself in Starlight

From the Desk of Cecilia Cinder Charming
Crystal Palace
North Road, Grimmland

Dear Zell,

Surely this is some sort of horrible, tasteless joke. A prank by thoughtless children. Kidnappers. Sprites. Pirates. Rory wouldn't leave us. Not like this. Would she? Did we really not see this coming? We were just at the wedding, and she wasn't fine yet, but she was closer than she had been in a while. Or maybe I've been blind all along.

We'll figure this out. Malice will undo it. Or we'll take her Outside. The doctors there can save her, I'm sure of it. Solace can help me get her there, slow time or something. Or Figgy can rewrite things again.

All morning, Edmund kept telling me to slow down and talk to him, but there isn't any time. I have to get back to

Rory's. Her parents aren't accepting visitors, but maybe I can slip through the kitchens.

Come back as soon as you can. Rory will need all of our help once she wakes up. I've sent a note to the Council on your behalf. I'll send an express pigeon when I get a reply.

CeCi

Important Fucking Correspondence from Snow B. White
Onyx Manor
West Road, Grimmland

Z,

I'm swearing these oaths to you as my witness.

I swear I won't go Outside. I'll stay here. I'll wear a crown and wave a scepter. I'll be the queenliest queen ever. I'll never leave my goddamned castle. I'll sleep on my fucking throne.

I'll stop swearing. I'll stop drinking. I'll be nicer. I won't make fun of unicorn figurines. I'll wear whatever dress Rory says I should. Even pink ones. And purple ones. At the same time. I'll read *The Cake and the Damned* every night. I'll preach True Love. We can have a cellist every day. Following us around. In a cart. And we'll beat him if he plays Pachelbel.

I won't eat ketchup ever again. I won't sign anyone up for classes. I won't order oysters. I won't rock the boat. I won't petition the Council. I'll keep my opinions to myself. In fact, I won't even have opinions anymore.

This can't be happening. Can't we go back to the wedding? I'll throw Maro into the cake myself. I'll stay by Rory's side all night. I'll make sure it doesn't happen. We'll figure it out. Won't we?

Won't we, Zell? Please, for Grimm's sake, answer me.

B

From the Desk of Cecilia Cinder Charming
Crystal Palace
North Road, Grimmland

Dear Zell,

William has agreed to sedate Bianca for a bit. I've never seen her like this before. Right now, she's babbling all sorts of nonsense, saying she's sorry, that she wants to be a queen, saying she won't leave. It's almost as if she believes some magical combination of words will undo what's happened, or wake us all up from this abysmal dream.

Under the circumstances, your mother-in-law was amenable to my proposal for a temporary rescinding of your ban. You'll find it detailed on the pink page at the back of this letter. Let me know when you'll be arriving, and I'll meet you at the Clock Shop. I believe the nearest portal is at the Wizard's old shop in Oz, though I'm unsure who's running it these days. Most likely the Tin Man, but it doesn't really matter. I know it will take you some time to get there, but please hurry.

As much as I refused to believe the news about Rory at first, the same sorrow has been replaced with a searing sort of anger. Anger at myself. Anger at Henry and Maro. Anger at the Godmothers. Anger at Rory herself.

How could she have been so terribly shortsighted? Didn't she know things would change for the better? If she just could have waited one more day, we could have told her about Maro and Swan Lake and the missing jewels and how Maro'd be in prison soon. Rory could have started over. Not with Henry, just again.

Bianca was still in no state to accompany me this morning, reportedly having broken every piece of unanchored glass in her chambers. I slipped out of the kitchens without Edmund or the girls fussing over me. I had a few things to say to our Fairy Godmonsters, and I didn't want any valiance or pity.

Malice met me at her door and I went straight for her throat. Unfortunately, Figgy and Solace were there, too. I yelled and thrashed, but they held me back, murmuring soothing words. I told them I'd had enough of their comfort. I wanted our friend back. I wanted revenge.

"Let go of me. Do something. Don't tell me that you can't do anything. Solace, take us back in time. We can rescue her."

"Time can slow or quicken, Cecilia. But we cannot turn it back completely," said Solace.

"What good is being Fairy Godmother of Time, then?" I screamed. "What good are you?"

"Indeed, what good are any of us?" asked Malice, looking sunken and dull, her scales as tattered as Figgy's feathers. The three sisters exchanged dark glares.

"Then let me take her Outside," I said. "They can help her there. I'm sure of it."

"I'm sorry," said Figgy, not sounding as sorry as she should have. "But Outside isn't an option."

My heart skipped a slow beat. I did this. We did this. They'd warned us, and we'd gone anyway. I had somehow forgotten, in all the chaos, the highs and lows, the wedding, and the café, and Rory, what we had wrought. "Still?" I asked.

"I used a fair bit of my power minimizing the damage from the storm that started," Solace said, cringing. "I wish there were another way."

"You said I could help. Tell me what to do. Can't these two help you repair the portal?"

"Time is not our specialty," said Figgy.

"Oh, quit the sanctimonious bullshit, Figgy." I shook my head. "Just admit you won't help because you want to say *I told you so.*"

"We thought we had a solution that would involve the three of you. But now—" Malice started.

"You could have prevented all this." A new wave of anger hit my chest. "You gave her the weapon. Why?"

"I did not have the power to refuse her request."

"Twice. Twice in her life you've put her to sleep! How is it even possible? How can you look yourself in the eye? I should declare war on you. Make your life a living hell."

"Do you think I wanted to be painted a monster? Briar Rose slept through her first life, true. But it was the only way I could avoid killing her outright."

"I don't understand," I said. All this time, we'd believed Malice to be a shadowy villain with a chip on her shoulder. Her motivations weren't something any of us knew much about.

"I had to renege on a threat I'd made in anger. The threat I'd made because my pride demanded that I be as important as my sisters. Would that I knew how little being important would matter to me later in life. I *don't* look myself in the eye, Cecilia. My life is already a living hell, locked away here so I can minimize the damage I cause. Do you think it's any kind of life? Bring on your war. I welcome it."

"A war with us will not heal your pain," said Solace. "Besides, if Malice hadn't put Briar Rose to sleep the first time, she wouldn't have been in your lives at all."

"We're in mourning, too, Cecilia," said Figgy.

"You have no right." I let myself drop onto a wobbling stool. "No right at all. You just stood by and watched. Grimm help all three of you when Bianca gets herself under control."

"I know you don't want to hear such things," Figgy began, "but Briar Rose made this decision for herself. We did not make it for her. Nor did you or Bianca or Henry or even Maro."

"Don't say her name in the same breath as Rory's. If you want to do anything to honor Rory you'll get rid of her right now. Harlot. Thief. Send her to jail, back to her home. Anywhere."

"That is not our purview, Cecilia," said Solace.

"Trying to hurt Maro is what got us to here in the first place," Malice said, her voice low.

I lost steam. "The lot of you. I don't know why I even bothered. I thought you were supposed to know things."

Figgy shook her head. "There are many things we are able to see and twice as many we cannot even begin to guess at. This is one of the latter."

"Briar Rose sought temporary solutions to long-term problems," said Malice. "Time cannot heal everything. Sometimes, it just causes you to live with a wound for longer." She and Solace both shot scowls at Figgy.

"I did what I thought was best for her," said Figgy. "After her first sleep, I thought she might thrive amidst the Pages of a romantic sort of Fairy Tale. How can you say it's not better than the alternative? She'd always had Pages before. How could she be expected to live without them? How was I to know she'd one day turn inward?"

"Ridiculous," said Malice. "Had you not forced my hand in the first place by publicly mocking my exclusion, demanding to know what I was going to do about it . . . You were and always will be drunk with power."

Figgy ruffled her feathers. "I was testing you. And you took the bait."

"You two and your pride," said Solace. "If either of you had tried to be gracious to each other instead of acting like children, we wouldn't be having this conversation."

"We *were* children," Malice said, turning away. "Besides, *I* saved Rory by putting her to sleep."

"*I* saved her by slowing the storm," said Solace.

"*I* saved her by writing new Pages," said Figgy.

"All of you saved her. None of you saved her." I was shaking, marveling at how quickly it seemed we had all moved from grief to blame. "I didn't save her, either."

"Cecilia—"

"The only way this works is if you're together," I said. "Look at the mess you made trying to prove each other wrong."

"Over a hundred years we've been fighting," said Malice.

"I wasn't wrong," said Figgy.

"Nonsense," said Solace.

"Answer me one question, Figgy," I said. "Was Henry necessary to Rory's Pages?"

Figgy's gaze fell to the floor, her wings wrapped loosely around her body. "Don't you think I've been trying to find a solution to the Henry problem this whole time? Of all the eligible men who could have landed on her doorstep when she awoke, it had to be him."

Solace threw a beseeching gesture at Figgy. "Will you never cease your meddling, Figueroa?"

"Once it became clear that he had a wandering sort of eye, I gave him a potion, you know, to ensure there wouldn't be any lasting consequences."

"You what?" Malice drew herself out of her chair to her terrifyingly full height.

"It was supposed to last longer, you see. There must have been a mistake, old bottle of feverfew, maybe. It wore off. Or perhaps Maro found a way to counteract it. I'm still not sure."

I didn't think it was possible to be any angrier at Figgy than I already was. "That's why you wouldn't help us. You had already interfered. And worst of all, you let her think it was her fault she couldn't have a baby."

"I was protecting her. All you were doing was confusing her with all that Human nonsense. Therapists and coffee and makeovers."

"You tried to make us think we'd made some sort of mistake going Outside. You even told us you'd help if we stopped traveling!"

"I still maintain I was in the right." Figgy stamped the cold floor, but it was a hollow gesture.

I thought of how confident Rory had become Outside, and I almost felt sorry for Figgy. "Hide out in your tree all you want, but studying Humans—getting to know them—enriches our lives, helps us to understand what we are, successes, failures, mistakes, love, hate, sex, war. We're more than stories, more than characters, more than a set of Pages. Rory was—is—more than those things."

"Don't you think I know that?" Figgy asked.

"Obviously you don't think any of us are more than ink and paper." I dissolved into tears again.

This time it was Malice who handed me a steaming mug, and I took it, gratefully. When I came to, I was at home. Darling and Sweetie were stationed in high-backed chairs at the foot of my bed.

"I think I heard her wake up," whispered Darling.

"Get the tea," said Sweetie. "And a cold compress."

"What time is it?" I asked. My eyes were gritty, as if I'd trekked through a dust storm, and my throat felt as if I'd swallowed a farrier's rasp.

Sweetie felt her way to the head of the bed and patted the

cloth to my forehead. "It's evening, now. And you're safe. Solace brought you. Are you hungry, thirsty?"

And then I remembered, again—the memory a visceral convulsion that rolled up my body from my toes to my throat. Rory was gone. Rory would always be gone. It felt as painful as it did when I first read her letter. And from somewhere, the desiccated well of tears deep within found a new source of water.

How many days will I wake up and learn it all over? How many nights will I dream of us together and whole and happy and wake up to a reality that's as broken as Valborg's old mirror? How will we ever be okay again?

"I just want her back," I told Sweetie. "I want things to go back to the way they used to be."

"We can't go back," she said, sweeping the hair from my eyes. "The only way out is through."

Darling joined us, and the three of us held hands and cried for a very long time.

Love,
CeCi

Important Fucking Correspondence from Snow B. White
Onyx Manor
West Road, Grimmland

Z,

I apologize for this pathetic scrawl. They're keeping me on a lot of potions lately. One minute I'm a raging storm and the next I feel like I'm floating away on a nice fluffy cloud. I'm told I caused quite a scene after I opened Rory's letter. I can't remember doing it, but it seems a lot of things are broken that, sadly, can't be magicked back together.

I remember before the letter, when I was happy. Drunk and toasting William with impossibly thin champagne glasses. On the beach racing the tide in our formal wear, collapsing in giggles, and doing it all over again.

And then there's now. I feel almost nothing at all—a fucking giant, gaping, soul-sucking emptiness. I can't remember anything in between.

This morning, William creeps in with Snoozer on his ridiculous rhinestone leash. I don't know whether to be cheered up or more miserable than I was when I awoke. I order him a rare filet mignon from the kitchen. He doesn't eat it. The dog may be many things, but he's not stupid. I asked William to retrieve some of Rory's old slippers so that Snoozer won't feel so alone. As if that will help. I am the embodiment of uselessness.

There's an expression Outside when something unexpected happens. They say "the rug's been pulled out from under you." That's the exact fucking feeling. I can't even process what I want for breakfast, let alone navigate a whole day, a whole week, a whole lifetime without Rory. I know that I meant to leave, but that was when I knew she'd be here living her life, she and CeCi visiting me all the time. I didn't mean for everything to end. Now nothing makes sense.

CeCi says she went to see the Godmothers, but they weren't particularly helpful. She's angry and wants me to be angry, too—angry at Maro, at Malice, at Rory even. I just can't. And I don't feel like trying to feel, either.

William keeps asking me to talk to him. I'm just not sure what to say except for "How can this be happening?" which is getting repetitive, even to me. It's the only question that matters, and one I don't know the answer to.

I can't think. I can't move. I can't get out of bed. I'm pretty sure this is all my fault, and I have no idea how to undo it. You know how much Rory and I pushed one another. If I had only known that it wasn't making us both stronger. I don't know, Zell. I want to think I'd have done things better. Differently, at least.

Rory wrote in her letter that I should follow through with my plan to go Outside. CeCi and William say I should be ready for when the portal is fixed—but how can I? How can I pretend everything doesn't look completely different than it did yesterday?

William puts things in trunks, and I take them out. Because of the broken portal, I can't even write Rachel to tell her what happened. Even if I could, how would I explain why we haven't been back and that I might need her more than ever now that I can't have her at all? Thinking about her makes everything even worse. So I try not to. I try to act normal when there is no normal.

Maybe the best I can hope for is some new version of normal. A normal where the hurt doesn't ever go completely away, but where each day doesn't stab quite as deeply as the one before.

B

Dear Zell,

I sent Edmund to Rory's parents today with some brown sugar and cream scones and some coffee I'd bought for Rory's next birthday. He said they still haven't decided whether or not to go back to sleep themselves. They'd like to be there when she wakes up again, but they're worried that there may not be a next time. And they have lives they're in the middle of living. Their guilt, their anger, that's hard to imagine. They see what Henry is, and they know they were blind. They only wanted the best for Rory. We all did.

I understand how conflicted they feel. Sometimes I think it's the Fates telling me to give everything up. That it's my fault. Perhaps if I quietly took the throne bedecked in a cape of diamonds, everything would return to its place. If I just tried to want a child because Rory wanted one, things might make sense again. I cringe every time I walk past our faux nursery. And yet, I know none of that would bring her back. It would simply make the remainder of my own life a prolonged tribute instead of a celebration of her memory.

And there's so much to celebrate. So much to share with one another. Stories untold. Gifts undiscovered. For instance, did you know Rory became infinitely more supportive of my culinary training when she discovered ice cream came in more flavors than vanilla and chocolate? We were Outside after class one day, and we stopped at a place advertising thirty-one flavors. She insisted on counting them, but of course stopped once she found the coffee flavor. I watched her eat a three-scoop cone in the sun without getting a drop of it on her white dress. Afterward she moved in on my ice cream—some sort of dressed-up chocolate—and after I got it all over myself, I let her have the rest.

It's a silly memory, but it's one of my favorites, her lecturing me on how queenly queens should practice eating drippy things before trying it in public.

Do you remember at my wedding when she accidentally drank way too much champagne and started hiccupping during her toast? None of us even knew she physically could swear. "And my friends—hic—mean the whole—hic—world to me and so—hic—here's to you—hic—I . . . damn it—hic—Bianca, stop—hic—you're making it worse—hic—shit." I couldn't stop laughing. Not even later that night when Edmund and I were back home alone trying to do serious things.

When something's impossibly hard, I hear her voice, that infectious optimism that pervaded everything she said and did. It used to frustrate me sometimes. I used to see it as an inability to confront reality, but I understand now that it was her only way to cope. She thought if she just believed hard enough she could make it so. When she lost that ability, right at the end, it was like she became an altogether different person. Empty. Somebody else's Rory.

Wouldn't we be better friends to one another, better lovers, better people if we all believed the best of ourselves, our friends, the future—at least every once in a while?

Love,
CeCi

Important Fucking Correspondence from Snow B. White
Onyx Manor
West Road, Grimmland

Z,

You'll never guess who slithers into Onyx Manor today. Says she has some things to say to me. I tell my maid to send her away, but Maro goes where Maro wants to go, and so she barges in, stamping her inane clogs up and down my hallway and smoothing down her clinging gown.

I don't feel like waiting for her to put herself together. "Spit it out or get lost," I say. "You're lucky we've all been too busy mourning our best friend to have you taken back to jail where you belong."

She takes about two steps onto the balcony where I'm sitting. "I didn't mean for this to happen," she says. She looks wrong somehow, dark bags under her eyes.

"But it did happen, didn't it? So it doesn't matter what you meant." I deeply regret having already broken all the projectiles in my chambers, though I do briefly consider repurposing a newly placed pot of geraniums.

"I just want to explain myself. You owe me that."

"I don't owe you shit, you backstabbing tramp." She winces, and I feel a surge of satisfaction that I've wounded her with words. (Screw sticks and stones. Words *can* hurt if one simply tries hard enough.) I should take the high road or strive for some modicum of tact, but, for the first time in days, I feel something instead of nothing. It's raw-edged rage and it burns my throat and I'll take it. "Rory trusted you and you let her. You moved in on her husband right under her nose. How did you *think* this would all turn out? That she'd just welcome you into her husband's bed? Where were you born, in a goddamned brothel?"

"I didn't mean it to happen . . . not at first. It all happened so quickly." She's fidgety and paces across the room. "They clearly weren't happy together."

"What do you know about it?"

She puts her hand on her hip. "I know more about it than you, Bianca. Actually, I know both sides of the story, and I think if you'd just hear—"

I almost want to laugh. "You are a piece of work, you know that? Do you honestly think I give a flying monkey's ass what Henry's side of the story is? Especially now that she's gone?"

"If I had known that she would, well—" She stops herself from finishing.

"You what? Wouldn't have slept with her husband? Wouldn't have threatened her with your pregnancy at *my* wedding? Wouldn't have taken away everything she wanted for her own?"

"That's not fair. It's not like I set out to do all that. I did want to be a comfort to her. And then later to him. And then, it got complicated."

"Understatement of the decade. Grimm's sake, Maro, this isn't the way you show you care about other people. It's no wonder you don't have any friends."

She begins to twist her hands together, a forced sort of modesty. "I've moved around so much, it's hard for me to bond with people."

I'm further annoyed by the fact she hasn't yet realized I'm immune to her bullshit. "And ex-lovers? Have a lot of those?"

She gives up on the façade. Her face falls, and she looks a good ten years older. "You've already called me a whore, why even ask?" Her voice ices over. She's done being the supplicant. "You've made up your mind. Judge and jury. Coming here was a waste of time."

"I won't argue with you there."

"Well, at least *I* tried."

I allow myself to smile. "Maro, do you know my very favorite saying of Rory's? I want you to remember this: 'The common denominator in all of your failed relationships is you.' "

Her breath catches. "I deserve happiness just like all of you."

"Not at the expense of other people. Figure that the fuck out before you bring that poor kid into the world."

She places her hands on her stomach. "So you're never going to forgive me?"

Damn Rory. Damn her forgiveness. I try telling Maro what Rory wrote to us, but at that moment, the words stick in my throat as if they're made of chalk. The more she talks, the more I hate her. "I don't want anything more to do with you. You're a thief, an impostor, and a liar."

"How *did* you find out about Swan Lake?"

"Odette and I attended summer camp together. I wrote her about you way back when you first started hanging around. We'd planned to send you back with the constable as soon as he recovered from the oyster debacle. I don't know what to do with you now."

"Is it even your call to make?"

I rise from my seat and spread my hands wide. "I'll ask Odette to send someone to come get you. Should give you a day or two to get your shit together. That's the best I can do."

"They'll send me to prison." She tosses her sausage curls behind her shoulders. "Besides, I was Albert's wife! That jewelry was rightfully mine."

"I don't care what you did or whether you're guilty or where they put you once you get back there. I don't care what happens to you as long as you're not here."

"You're a heartless bitch, Bianca White."

"Takes one to know one," I say. "Can you find your way out, or do you need to hump a guard first?"

She turns, shoulders heaving. I don't feel guilty for hurting her feelings, but I do feel guilty for ignoring Rory's instructions. "Maro. Wait."

She stops, but she doesn't turn.

"It'll be a long time before I stop holding you responsible for this, whether it's *my place* or not." I take a deep breath. "But you should know that Rory forgave you. And she told us to tell you she did."

Maro opens her fists and closes them again, and her head dips almost imperceptibly. She's sobbing loudly when she walks out of my life, for what I fervently hope is forever.

I feel better for having said my piece, lighter for having said Rory's. When my pulse slows a bit, I put Snoozer on his leash. We walk to the Swinging Vine to see DJ. He puts on Rory's favorite disco CD, then pours us two giant glasses of champagne and a beer for Snoozer. No one finishes. Rory's absence is as palpable as the day she left.

I hear you'll be attending the wake. I know Rory would have been glad.

B

From the Desk of Cecilia Cinder Charming
Crystal Palace
North Road, Grimmland

Dear Zell,

I realize it's only been a matter of months you've been gone, but it feels like a lifetime has passed. Hell, it feels like a lifetime since last week. And in light of everything that's happened, I hope you'll understand why your arrival was a bit, well, complicated. For both Bianca and me.

I didn't pay enough attention. We talk a lot about blindness—my sisters, Jason, even—but I was the blind one this time. I was wrapped up in secrets, even when I was trying to help, and I didn't see Rory suffering.

Bianca did. And because she did, this entire situation has been particularly hard on her because neither you nor I listened.

Imagine the elation of her wedding and her big plans followed by this total devastation—she had a long way to fall. It's not that I don't hurt as much or you don't hurt as much, it's just a matter of being broadsided. I doubt anyone was quite as unprepared for Rory's decision as Bianca.

She also feels a lot of guilt. We all do. While you're right, in the end it was Rory's decision—her own fault, even—Bianca's too raw to hear that right now. She may be for a while.

And, honestly, I don't know what in the hell you were thinking, offering to take Snoozer.

It's tantamount to pouring salt in a wound. What do you know about this part of our lives—this part of Rory's life? You exited stage right and expected us to live on the scraps of paper you deigned to send our direction. And now you come in and try to mop things up?

I'm not making excuses for Bianca, but I am telling you that I think her umbrage is valid. Step back for a moment, Zell. *This crisis—losing our friend—this is what it takes for you to be there for us.* Not my birthday. Not Bianca's wedding. Not as Rory begged for your help with Maro. Not even as Bianca prepared to leave the Realm for Outside.

I know you feel some amount of mea culpa, and I'm not trying to throw this back in your face. But for Grimm's sake, Zell. You've made it so much harder than it needed to be. We thought we understood what was important. Bianca feels like she overestimated her importance in your life, and worse than being hurt, she's embarrassed.

She'll come around. Her pride always heals quickly. She's angry because she loves you and she wants you to love her back.

I'm angry because I love you and I want you to trust us. I know you were only trying to tell us that we'd done as much as we could. But when you said we "hadn't let Rory be her own person," and that's part of the reason you didn't tell us you were leaving, I felt like you'd dismissed our friendship. I hope you didn't mean that. You couldn't have. You know full well we didn't set out to change Rory. We only wanted to protect her.

I'm sorry I made you feel as if you couldn't trust me, or that I wanted you to be anything other than who you are. I love who you are: yesterday, today, and tomorrow. I hope you love me as I am and as the person I eventually become.

I'm sorry things have been going so badly at the preserve. I'm sorry none of us came out to help you. We had no idea things were falling apart from the tiny bits of your life you shared in your letters. I can understand your need to hold things back. But it isn't fair for you to turn around and be angry that we aren't empathetic to your plight when we don't even understand what your plight is.

I do care, Zell. I wish you could have stayed longer. We both made mistakes. We both failed to tell one another we were hurting. We both let the other believe in some version of us that doesn't exist. I let you think I couldn't live without one particular version of you. You let me believe you could live without any version of me. Let's start over again. Let me know how to help you.

Love,
CeCi

Important Fucking Correspondence from Snow B. White
Onyx Manor
West Road, Grimmland

Z,

I'm sure CeCi has already apologized and explained and placated and smoothed over as is her core competency. I'm not going to pretend that's my gig.

So, first, I'm going to tell you I love you.

Second, I'm going to ask who the fuck you think you are. Do you even know what Snoozer eats? Do you know which pair of slippers are his favorite to chew on in the morning? What about at night? Are you going to brush his slobbery doggy teeth and wash his muddy paws and take him out to piss at three in the morning? Well, I don't give a fuck. I love that spoiled, shedding, farting ball of drool. You can't have him.

But, third, I shouldn't have blown up at you at the wake.

Fourth, I really shouldn't have thrown shrimp at you.

Fifth, and final, for what it's worth, I'm sorry. I'm scared to move forward with our lives without her, and I panicked at seeing you, at seeing how different our lives have become.

And Zell, I think you panicked, too. I don't know all the details of what's going on with you and Jason, but it certainly isn't CeCi's fault. You wanted to be your own person, and you weren't sure you could do that around us? Well, thanks a lot, Zell.

I know what it's like to look around and want to cast blame, but you can't do that here. We love you. We've always loved you. And we're not going to stop loving you just because you're being a jerk. If that were the case, I would have been cast out of this particular circle of friends a long time ago.

Look, friends influence friends. That's the whole point. We grow when we listen to each other. We give gifts of ourselves. Sometimes these are intangibles like hope or assertiveness. Sometimes it's ketchup and house music. At the end of our lives we're made up of those bits and pieces of the people who came into our lives.

I'm also intimately familiar with trying to save face. When you left, you had to act like you had shit under control. Clearly you didn't. Your marriage was on the rocks, your finances an afterthought, your children in no way prepared for country life. I get it. It didn't work like you thought it would. I'm sorry we put you on a pedestal. That's the only thing we could do, because you blocked us out.

CeCi and you were closest. That was never a secret. So whatever identity crisis you're in the middle of, you have to fix it and, ideally, let us help. Be honest with us—but especially her. I can see through your bullshit, Zell, and I still love you. But CeCi? She'd believe you if you told her you lit the night sky yourself. So play fair.

Do you want us to help you put things together again? Fine. I hope you know we'll help you through whatever comes next. As friends, we have to promise to listen to one another knowing that the frame of reference is love, whether the advice is right or wrong, whether you heed said advice or tell us to shove it up our asses.

What *are* you going to do? Will you stay in Oz? Drop a house on Dorothy the wayward gift-shop girl? Saddle up your unicorns and ride on to the next hitching post?

I know you feel like you've reached an impasse, a point where you and Jason can't do anything but make each other unhappier. Maybe time heals that and maybe not. I know your heart's probably smashed in a million pieces. But I don't want to let anything else spin out of control while we all stare at our feet and let you "process your grief" or some banal bullshit.

I'll be there. Actually, physically there. You just tell me when. I mean it. Snoozer and I will come to you.

I have to start doing something with myself anyway. Maybe there's no place like home, but sometimes it's the wrong place to be. Everywhere it seems I'm underfoot. In Will's map room, at the café, at Shambles. I'm there but I'm not. I'm living in the present, but in the past, at the same time.

I miss her so fucking much. That incessant sparkle, the way she always jumped at loud noises, how she was always studying everything like it might have a secret compartment. I miss her stupid colloquialisms and ridiculous lacy collars and her prissy beaded slippers. I miss the way she dreamed of precious things and trusted us—even me—with them. I'd give anything to have five more minutes with her, even if she was dozing off. I'd tell her that she couldn't go. That we need her. That I'm sorry I took her constant presence in my life for granted.

So let's not take anything for granted anymore, okay?

Love,
B

From the Desk of Cecilia Cinder Charming
Crystal Palace
North Road, Grimmland

Dear Zell,

Bianca told me Maro stopped by a couple of days ago, so I was not surprised when Henry arrived in our throne room this morning. In fact, I had been expecting him.

I didn't have to ask Edmund to accompany me, he was simply at my side. It was reassuring, to say the least, but I had the sudden, horrid realization that I'd never even asked how he was doing. He and Rory weren't best friends, but I know he's likely mourning, too. Mourning her. Mourning how our lives have been upended.

Grief is a selfish thing. When I look up from my own misery, I can see how much Rory's absence affects everything and everyone around us, even indirectly. It's like a strange ache that no one quite knows how to admit, how to heal.

And until Bianca told me of Maro's visit, I hadn't spared Henry's frame of mind much thought, either. He wasn't invited to attend her wake at the Swinging Vine. Nor the ceremony at the frog pond. Or the dedication in the tower before they started to rebuild the outer walls. No one had seen him out in weeks.

And it was no wonder. He looked terrible. He had bags under his eyes, and a three-day beard. Part of me wanted to punish him further. Ensure he felt as desolate as she had in the end. Trade his life for hers.

"Well, what can we do for you?" I asked, trying to look imposing. After all the months in the kitchens, my cold, unused throne made me feel like a child playing dress-up, a princess playing queen.

"I want to start by saying Rory loved you very much," he said, hands to his heart.

I wanted to start by throwing up on him. "How dare you tell me anything at all about her."

"Grimm's sake, CeCi. We've all known each other for a long time. Don't treat me like an outsider. It's not like I didn't lose her, too."

I imagined the red mark my hand would leave if I slapped him. "Are you kidding me? You never wanted her in the first place."

"That's not true. It isn't that simple. At first I did. I tried to explain to her that I didn't want her to be . . . that maybe we just wanted different things. We weren't compatible. It doesn't mean that I wanted this. It doesn't mean that I'm not hurting here."

"Oh, you're hurting, are you? Do stay and tell us all about it. Unless you have to hurry off and boink someone else. We wouldn't want to keep you."

His eyes hardened. "Fine. I'm a bad guy. Blame me. Whatever you need to do. But seriously, CeCi, can you call off your dogs? Maro says someone turned her in to the Swan Lake authorities for stolen jewels."

"Maro got herself into that mess all by herself. Bianca simply asked a friend about how she came to be in Grimmland. It's not our fault the reply included a warrant."

"Rory's parents have kicked Maro and me out of the castle. And my parents won't receive us because they've heard she's a criminal."

"I'm sorry to hear that, Henry."

"I've lost *everything*, CeCi. There's nowhere for me to go." Henry ran his hands through his greasy hair. Ed got up and mercifully poured us all a whiskey.

"How will you feel if your daughter meets a man like you? You're lucky Rory's father hasn't asked Hook to give you a long walk off a short plank. All she wanted from you was your attention and your honesty."

"I know," he said. "I get it."

"The only one who's lost everything here is Rory. We still have lives to live. We owe it to her to live them well."

"I fucked up, CeCi. Okay? Are you happy?"

"Of course I'm not happy. More misery doesn't fix this. Which is why I think you need a new start. Don't you think Rory's family has been through enough? Without seeing the cause of their daughter's catastrophic decision waltzing around with the baby she so desperately wanted?"

"This is my home," he said, quietly. "I don't want to be an exile like Fred. Like your father."

I was momentarily dizzy. "Excuse me?"

He drained his whiskey. "No, really, Cecilia. Is there any scenario in which a bad man can make things right? Or do you just write them all off? Pack them somewhere you can forget about them."

Ed made a move forward, but I stopped him. "Henry, if you stay, your child will grow up with whispers and glances from a kingdom that has twice had a rightful queen yanked from their hearts. Why not start over again somewhere new?"

He throws his hands up. "Running away makes me a better man?"

"Being a better man makes you a better man, you idiot. Having empathy, investing in your relationships, putting other people first will make you a better man."

"CeCi, I can't be any sorrier."

"You did this to yourself, Henry. This was Rory's home first. A home you laid claim to with your puffed-up stories.

Next time around she'll be woken up by someone who deserves her. And, if not, she'll go find that person."

"You kind of sounded like her just then." I couldn't place the look on his face—a strange mix of wistful and desperate.

My voice caught. "I hope I can carry half the optimism in my heart that she did."

"I hope so, too," he said. He lifted the empty glass toward Edmund. "Thanks for the whiskey."

Then came the hardest part, as all the rage and pain flooded back in. I should have offered him the deal the minute he walked in. I suppose a part of me wanted to see whether he'd say anything redeeming, whether Rory had been right to hold out hope. Regardless, Bianca and I promised each other, for Rory's sake. "Did you come here to ask for our help?"

"Maybe. I don't know anymore, CeCi. I can see myself out."

"If you decide you've come to ask for our assistance, we have an offer for you. Bianca and I have contacted Odette. No one will come to arrest Maro, if you accept our terms."

"You've just explained how little you think of us." He shook his head, bewildered. "Why would you help?"

"It's not for you, Henry. It's for all the kids who grew up missing their mothers. Me, Bianca, Zell. It's for all the children whose fathers became ghosts; that's all of us, too. It's so little Henry or little Maro can have you both in a place you can all be happy. It's so another princess doesn't grow up wondering what love is supposed to be, what family is supposed to be."

There were tears in his eyes. "I'm not sure I follow." For a couple of heartbeats, I had to remind myself how much I hated him. What he had taken away from us.

I sat back in my throne. "Bianca's father's hunting lodge near Avalon was refashioned as a jail for Valborg. The property now sits empty. King Ludwig has agreed that Maro can serve house arrest for the jewels she took from Swan Lake. Meanwhile, you can hunt every day, should you wish. This will allow you to have a life with Maro away from both of your pasts."

"That would be . . . perfect. Thank you, CeCi. Thank Bianca for me."

"It's what Rory would have wanted. But should Maro return to a life of crime or you return to a life of excess, we can and will rescind the arrangement."

"Yes. Of course. I understand. Thank you. I'll repay you both somehow."

"Please don't. Just do one thing for us: Live honestly, okay? We've all jeopardized too much because of lies."

Ed squeezed my hand and stood to take Henry's elbow. He gave him the map and keys, and with a shake of hands, it was done.

I think—I hope—Rory would be more than proud. Of all of us.

Love,
CeCi

She Found Herself in Sunset

.

Important Fucking Correspondence from Snow B. White
~~*Onyx Manor*~~
~~*West Road, Grimmland*~~
Rapunzel's Unicorn Preserve & Petting Zoo
Post Box 4242
East of Oz

CeCi,

    This place is fucking awesome. The grass is an obnoxious green. The lake is so clear you can see to the bottom—all the fish and rocks and plants. Sitting behind everything are cute little hills covered in shaggy pines. It looks like a painting. Hell, it probably was a painting once upon a time. The trip from the portal into Oz is long, but the scenery totally makes up for it.

    I've also found it's pretty hard to be unhappy around a bunch of unicorns. They're always frolicking and sparkling and begging for apples. (Although you have to be careful. They're a little like Snoozer—they'll eat damned near anything.) Visitors file in and out all day long from sunrise to twilight to visit them, to rub their noses or make a wish or to push a finger pad to the end of a sharp horn. Even though they're warned, there are always long lines for a bandage.

Snoozer is having a blast. He's pretty hot on rolling around in and/or eating unicorn poop. He also loves playing with the kids, chasing squirrels, napping under the trees.

Zell puts on a brave face, but she's pretty scared to go this alone. After all this time (and all my excellent lectures!) she's still having trouble believing in herself. But I know she'll be okay.

Jason's been living in the barn. He plans to move back to Grimmland soon. Since Zell and the kids will be back and forth, his mother will have to permanently rescind her asinine ban. They aren't calling it quits, exactly, just taking some time to figure out what they both need. What they both want from life. And how to be honest with each other about it.

Three months ago, I would have told you such an exercise was pathetically futile, but I'm not so sure anymore. I think everyone should try anything they can to be happy, to stay as far away as possible from the ends of their ever-fraying ropes.

"I never thought it would be like this," Zell says. And of course she didn't. None of us do. We all stumble around, trying to land in a place that makes us happy. When she first left, I blamed her for running away, but she wasn't. She was taking the first step. I only just understood how many steps come afterward.

We've been misinformed by the ones who came before—inside the Realm and out. There is no perfect contentment. Happily Ever After isn't an ending, it's the journey we take from here.

Zell's staying, and I understand why. She says if she comes back to Grimmland, she'll blame Jason for her failure and it will guarantee their dissolution. I think Zell feels trapped by the walls of a castle after all those years imprisoned in the same grey stone. I'm sure Jason is trying to understand, but how could he? His greatest trauma was wandering blind through a place not unlike here, wild and windy and full of trees, until he found Zell again.

They've each discovered their strongest selves, but maybe those strongest selves have grown to need different things. He hates the memories of the forest. She craves the turretless sky. Life is too short to live resenting the person who's supposed to be your best friend.

If I've learned anything about the past year it's that maybe none of us were listening to one another. Maybe we weren't even listening to ourselves. I'm listening now. I hear you, CeCi. I hear Zell.

I hear Rachel, too. I started a letter to send once the portal is repaired, but I can't seem to get it right. I can't figure out how to tell her about Rory and explain how I can't possibly leave anymore. I wish I could have one last date, thank her for everything she did for us. But saying good-bye to her forever over dinner would be impossible. It's hard enough to do in writing.

Speaking of dinner, your instructions have done nada for Zell's cooking. Perhaps you can host a hands-on culinary camp for single princesses. (I'm sure the Rhumba-ing Raynas would sign up in a heartbeat.) Thank Grimm I brought a valise full of ketchup. Even Snoozer won't eat Zell's meals.

Regardless, you should visit. You'd like it here. It would be good for Zell. Arthur and Bea have gotten so big. And most of the time, they aren't very sticky at all. Besides, you can get them spun up on sugar, then leave.

Rory would have liked it here. I hope she can visit the twins' grandchildren someday. Hell, the unicorns might be running a preserve for Fairy Tales by then.

See you next week.

Love,
B

From the Desk of Cecilia Cinder Charming
Crystal Palace
North Road, Grimmland

Dear Bianca,

I hope you're continuing to have fun at the preserve, and I hope you've picked out some nice unicorn stationery for your letter to Rachel. One word of advice, though: Don't rush into any decisions. Rory's absence has colored everything in a strange way.

I've said this before, but staying in Grimmland won't change what happened. It doesn't bring Rory back. And someday when that knife edge of pain we're feeling starts to dull, your heart will be filled with something else. A yearning, a regret—even that resentment you were talking about with Jason and Zell in your last letter.

I bet Zell herself would tell you—even as her marriage falls apart—that it was worth it to try. Think it through, Bianca, before you let your dream go. We're all still here, standing behind you, believing in you.

As for my own dream, I've skipped so many classes I'm sure I wouldn't be able to graduate with my class, even if the portal were working. I've started to miss Outside, though. I wonder how Phil is doing, whether he's eaten at the teriyaki gyro truck or tried the mystical cronut. Whether he's made Eric the surprise breakfast of a lifetime. I can't imagine how much you must miss Rachel.

So I decided to stop wishing and start doing. As the first order of business, I headed to the Clock Shop to see how I could help speed things up.

Solace was all gentle smiles and murmured greetings, at first. A small pack of villagers were making a trek to Neverland, so I waited until they'd finished, looking into the yawning torsos of the clocks around the room.

"Cecilia. You've finally come." Solace spoke from a darkened hallway.

"About the portal we injured," I said. "You said you might be able to use our help."

"Oh, the timing of everything," she said, coming closer, though not quite looking at me. "I've been meaning to discuss it with you, but it never seemed to be the right moment."

"Rory's . . . decision . . . it caught us all off guard. I'm sorry for that day—"

She waved me off, guiding me to her quiet office and gesturing for me to sit. "To build the portal in Briar Rose's tower, I used a small piece of the main portal here in my shop."

I felt my stomach sink. "And that piece is gone."

"Quite," said Solace. "Actually, the damage started earlier than you think. The piece of the original clock began to smolder when Bianca was separated from her bracelet. By the time Rory pulled the three of you through, the piece had been incinerated completely."

"The prickles," I said, looking at my hand. "It was fire."

"As it stands, neither of the portals is functional. No one can go Outside. Not even the birds." She gestured to her front window, where a field of pigeons sat idly pecking at the ground. "Something must be done. And, as such, Malice, Figgy, and I have come up with a compromise."

And that's when she dragged me to Figgy's, where I was assigned a brand new set of Pages. The owl assured me that, unlike Rory's second set of Pages—filled with nonbinding embellishments—mine are very much real.

Love,
CeCi

Important Fucking Correspondence from Snow B. White
Onyx Manor
West Road, Grimmland

Z,

It's my first week back, but my new husband cannot wait to lecture me about moving forward, keeping up my momentum. He says I owe it to Rory to follow through.

Is that true, Zell? I don't know what I owe anyone anymore. I used to know, but I've lost track. I feel like I'm moving at a gallop and then, all of a sudden, the horse throws me and I can't get out of the fucking mud. It's like everything is slow and cold and wrong. And yet, it's less wrong than yesterday. And even that makes me feel guilty. I have to figure out a way to remember and keep living at the same time. Some way to let her know we never forgot her but still went on. Is that even realistic?

William reinstalls his tactical logistics chalkboard this morning. He sets arbitrary dates and tasks and checkboxes, dragging my moving trunks back in from wherever the servants had stashed them.

"So, what," I say. "You're kicking me out now?"

"You have to start living again. Your own dream, B. Go find your destiny. It's still out there. It didn't change just because Rory left. Go visit your friends in the Realm. Go watch the cows jump over the moon. Heckle Humpty. Whatever. But don't sit here and brood."

"Fuck off." I stick up my middle finger.

He mirrors the gesture. "Same to you, I'm sure," he says.

I pitch a loose throw pillow at him.

"Fine. Get pissed off. At least it's something besides this incessant *malaise*."

"Don't judge me. I'm in pain, damn you."

He takes me by the shoulders, and his face falls into seriousness. "I know. I do. But you don't honor her memory by refusing to go on."

I can't argue with him. He's right, and it's all I can do to not start crying.

He points to the window. "Time is moving out there—fast. And without you."

"Gee, thanks, pal. You sure know how to make a girl feel better."

"You know I'm right. Hate me, scream at me, throw things at me—just do something. Anything." He turns and storms out the door. I don't even have a chance to argue.

So I go to see CeCi. I find her in the kitchens, instructing some of the younger village girls about quick breads. She looks good; the hard edges she had when I left for the preserve are gone. She seems a little tired, but her hair is shiny and her eyes are bright. She chatters away with her back to me about the Unicorn Café and its grand opening and everything she needs to do. Then she turns around and says, "Oh no, Bianca. Just look at you."

First, she dismisses the wide-eyed girls and orders the servants to leave. She wraps her arms around my shoulders and slides onto the bench beside me, pushing a plate of warm scones in front of me.

"When's the last time you slept? Ate?" She plunks a crock of fresh butter down next to the plate. We eat scones and stop to cry and then eat some more. By the time the cooks come in to start dinner service, we've almost emptied the little pot of strawberry preserves and are packing away the last of the scones.

"I think I'm going to go," I say between mouthfuls.

"I know," she says. "I'm glad."

"You do?" I plop a spoonful of jam onto my scone. "You are?"

"I can't see you like this. This isn't you. I'll miss you, but we'll always have each other, won't we?"

And it dawns on me, a wave of calm. "I'll be immortal because you'll always remember."

"More like infamous," she says. "Imagine the stories I'll make up about you once you're gone: *The Almost True Story of Snow White and the Poisonous Oyster Wedding!*"

I feel almost like a fog is clearing. Giddiness bubbles up, and I fight the urge to tamp it down, to tell it to come later. But sure enough, the dread comes. "What if there's nothing out there for me anymore? I haven't been able to write to Rachel. It's been weeks now. She'll have given up on me."

CeCi stands up. "Nothing has changed, Bianca. You can't go for any reason other than because you can't imagine living another life. Maybe she's in it, maybe she isn't, but you have to make the decision because *you* want to go."

"But the portal's still broken. I can't do anything, anyway."

"Actually . . . you can. I need your help, and I've been waiting for you to be ready."

"Okay."

"If you really want to stay, I won't make you help me. I can find someone else who wants to go Outside. Or wait until someone gets banished and make them assist—"

"I hate it when you do that." I pound the butter knife on the table. "Please just explain yourself."

"Repairing the portal so far has been a lot like a mending project, except we're re-creating a tunnel made of both worlds. We've already cleared the debris and restored most of the tunnel to its original state. Solace has bound the tunnel together with strings of time magic. It's a beautiful spell—the shimmering edges we see when we're Outside are actually the places where all the strings are tied together."

"Yeah, yeah. Neato. Can we get to the part where I help?"

"Fine. To finish, we need to place one last piece of stone in the middle of the clock face. It anchors the hands of the clock itself. The catch is, it needs to be a shared piece of stone."

I am sure I've misheard. "You need me to get you a fucking rock? You're stitching with threads of time, but you can't bend over and pick one up?"

"It's a little more complicated than that. We'll find a stone at the end of the tunnel, one on the border of Outside and the Realm, then we'll split it with Solace's time string. We place one piece in the portal clock and mount the other in your clock bracelet. When you go Outside, you'll bury the bracelet wherever you deem the new portal to be safe. The binding magic will stay with the stone.

"The stone never ages and never loses its magic unless the portal is harmed. So unless another three idiots force their way through, that stone you drop will keep the portal anchored at the Magic Castle, the cooking school, Disneyland—wherever you want to place it."

"What happened to the old stone?"

CeCi throws her hands up. "Poof."

"So you're telling me when we wrecked the portal, someone at the Magic Castle watched a rock go up in flames?" I ask.

"Pretty much."

"Why can't you bury the stone yourself?"

"The person who goes through has to abandon the magic that brought them through the portal. Besides, you're our foremost expert at separating oneself from one's bracelet."

I try to say something, but nothing comes out. Permanence didn't scare me before, but now it is sobering.

CeCi puts a hand on mine. "You don't have to if you're not ready."

"I didn't say that. I want to go. More than anything. I'm just a little—"

"Scared? Of course you are. But I'll be there to help. It's all in my new Pages." She fishes a couple of crumpled sheets from the pocket of her apron. "This time, all three Fairy Godmothers wrote it together. Read it."

Once upon a time, there was a princess who yearned to cook. She was so enamored of learning, she went Outside, where the Masters of the realm of food plied their trade.

Returning, she and her friends caused a rip in the fabric between worlds. Tasked with repairing the tear, the princess carefully stitched the pieces together and, with help, anchored each side.

In return, The Fairy Godmother of Time asked that the princess continue to bring knowledge from the other world; The Fairy Godmother of Sorrow asked that the princess help someone in need each time she traveled; The Fairy Godmother of Fate asked that she adhere to these new Pages, as a good-faith gesture, so that future Pages may include the hopes and dreams of the characters within them.

"What kind of knowledge?" I ask, passing the Pages back to her.

"Like how to travel without getting stuck. How to get an ID. How to hail a taxi. Who to trust. That kind of stuff."

"How did you convince Figgy?"

"Solace managed to change her mind, arguing that a lack of knowledge is what damaged the portal in the first place. Said that Rory taught us all that our lives have to be bigger, even in the confines of our Pages. Malice said we owed it to Rory to help others. I agreed to test their compromise. Living fully within my destiny."

"So when are these Pages complete?"

"This is my Ever After. There *is* no end."

"And you're okay?"

"That's just it, Bianca. *We changed everything.* This time my Pages include my own dreams, not someone else's. Maybe this means that the daughters of our Realm will finally get to be who they want to be."

I think maybe she's right. But don't tell her. She'd really be insufferable then.

Love,
B

From the Desk of Cecilia Cinder Charming
Crystal Palace
North Road, Grimmland

Dear Zell,

How are you holding up? I suppose you're missing Bianca by now—the way the sky misses a tornado, I'm sure. How did her good-bye dinner go? Did your roast turn out okay? She probably put loads of ketchup on it, so I guess it doesn't matter.

It shouldn't take but a few more days for the portal to be ready to anchor, and then Bianca will leave. The glass in the clock at Solace's shop is whole again, though the clock face itself remains dark and still. It's strange, and a little frightening, to work in the tunnel. But Solace insisted that Figgy start allowing travelers to be responsible for their own mistakes. And this time, I have Pages that I can't wait to start.

Especially because there's so much more to do than repair the portal. I worked all day prepping for our grand opening this coming weekend. Edmund and I painted the sign, and we put a bunch of your unicorn figurines on top. There's more interior work to be done tomorrow and then food prep on Friday. I can't believe it's really happening. I can't believe the place is all mine.

I had a dream last night. The colors of the dream were so vibrant, I could hardly breathe. I was dining in a beachfront restaurant in Los Angeles, and the waves were the most beautiful cerulean blue. They swelled and grew, coming nearer and nearer until they were cresting over the roof, crashing down against the windows.

I was sure we were about to float away.

There was an old man in a crimson jacket sitting beside me, and I asked him to tell me what it all meant, if the whole tableau was Rory's doing. If the waves were good or bad omens. But he wouldn't say a word.

It seemed so important when I woke up, but now it seems inconsequential—the opposite of real life.

When I finally woke up—throat parched and feet aching— I realized that I'd become the woman I wanted to be. Princess de Cuisine. Partner. Friend. It was genuine, heart-squeezing, grin-splitting elation. Thank you. I couldn't have done it alone.

Love,
CeCi

The Journey Continues Ever After

Important Fucking Correspondence from Snow B. White
Onyx Manor
West Road, Grimmland

Z,

Opening day at the Unicorn Café.

Edmund built CeCi a soft-grey building on the north edge of the square. It has high ceilings and windows that stretch from the floor to the top of the wall and look out on the wolf woods and the big blue sky. There are tables on the patio with umbrellas just like at Starbucks except that they're yellow instead of green.

The lunch menu has six different kinds of salad. Goat cheese and candied nuts and vinaigrettes and fruit. There are soups and sandwiches and rolled pastries with greens and bacon. The dinner is even better, everything decorated with tiny sprigs of dill and flowers. Oh, and I can't forget the signature dessert, Gâteau Briar Rose, a chocolate cake served with a very large cup of coffee.

Hansel and Gretel are there to congratulate CeCi. Figgy and Solace arrive with a note from Malice and a lush bouquet of sea flowers. There is brandy from Toad Hollow and balloons from the Wizard (who everyone thought was on the lam). A woozy flamingo delivers a card from the Queen of Hearts.

And at the head of all of this wonderment is CeCi. CeCi in a yellow party dress, crinoline veritably exploding from underneath her chef's jacket. Her stepsisters greet people at the door, using their deft hands to deliver menus to people patiently waiting in line. While William and I wait, they tell us all about their new favorite hobby, knitting, and how excited they are to have jobs as hostesses. I introduce them to Snoozer, and they tell me how soft his ears are.

Snoozer's wedding tux has been donned for the occasion. Ladies feed him the ends of their steaks, and men scratch his chin. He's a restaurant celebrity, but ends up falling asleep halfway through dinner service.

There are no fires, no complaints, and there is enough wine to make a long night feel like a luxury instead of a chore. CeCi did it. And she'll keep on doing it.

When everyone finally files out, William, Edmund, CeCi, and I all share a glass of champagne in the middle of a pile of dishes. DJ shows up with a second bottle and we drink it, too. CeCi's almost falling asleep on her feet, but she exudes happiness. It's as content as I've seen her since before.

There was a quiet moment when we all must have been thinking about Rory. She's the one element that would've made the day perfect, but we all managed to get through it without breaking down. It's time for all of us to move ahead. I'm proud of CeCi for taking the lead. Soon it will be my turn.

Love,
B

From the Desk of Cecilia Cinder Charming
Crystal Palace
North Road, Grimmland

Dear Zell,

The opening was successful beyond my wildest dreams. Darling and Sweetie had come home much earlier, but they were still up when we got home, giggling in the company of the winsome Swan Prince, who waved his good arm at me as I passed their chambers. I love seeing them so happy.

Edmund halted in front of the closed door of our useless nursery.

"I know it's been a long day." He gave me a reassuring sort of kiss.

I leaned into him. "I'm ready for bed."

"Just one more thing." He gestured at the door.

"I really don't want to talk about the nursery right now." I felt the tenuous grip I had on wakefulness slipping away like the tail of a cloud.

"I have a quick surprise for you." He opened the door, and inside was no longer a half-finished nursery. It was a library. In one corner, a small wine cabinet and a whole section of cookbooks— books he'd procured with the help of the Pigeon Post from every corner of the Realm and even a few from Outside. Edmund tells me that the room is his way of telling me that he trusts me, he believes in me, and he wants me to be happy. "I did it for us. I'm proud of what we are, who we are."

I let the tears fall freely. "I am, too. I'm sorry I didn't believe enough at first."

"Forward, CeCi, forward."

"Forward, Edmund."

We shared a couple of glasses of champagne as I studied my new books, my treasures. He'd hung a painting of Rory, Bianca, you, and me posed in the meadow right before my wedding. On the large desk, I found his blueprints for the Unicorn Café.

"I have some news myself, CeCi. I'm thinking of returning to university to study architecture," he said. "Just a regular Wonderland U, but still. There's no reason not to. William's doing the kinging for Grimmland, since Rory's folks went back to sleep. And my parents left to sail around Narnia in their new yacht. Will says as soon as I come back, I can be Grimmland's Chief Engineer. Since we're living our dreams, I just thought . . ."

I interrupted him with a kiss. I couldn't be prouder.

I ran to get Darling and Sweetie and the Swan Prince, and all five of us ran our hands down the spines of the new books and bookmarked our favorite recipes and smelled the paper and the leather. I sent the three of them back to bed with more champagne and wishes for sweet dreams. I took Edmund back to our chambers and tried to tell him how much it all meant to me.

I wish I could show Rory, but it's a bittersweet wish this time. I have to apologize to Malice because she was right—carrying a wound doesn't heal it. I have a business to run and menus to plan. I need to hire servers and prep cooks and a dishwasher since Bianca's taking Snoozer with her. (Just kidding. I haven't really been letting him wash the dishes.) I have to take some more classes and make plans to visit Phil and Bianca and Rachel.

I'm so happy to hear how much the twins loved their birthday cake. Just think when they get older the stories we'll be able to tell them about all the dreams we saw come true. We'll say, "Once upon a time there were four friends who rewrote their Pages . . ."

Love,
CeCi

Z,

William says, "Let's go drink wine." This should tip me off because we don't ever go drink wine, but all the same, my surprise party is, in fact, a surprise.

There's house music blasting from the Swinging Vine, but the place seems darker than usual and pretty empty for a Friday. I stomp my way up to the bar, complaining about the music, about the fireflies, about Will interrupting my packing, when DJ pops up from behind the bar and yells, "She's here!"

All of a sudden the floor is completely full. I see the Dancing Princesses and Puss and Hansel and Gretel. Odette shows up with rum, and Alice brings the Cheshire Cat, and even King Peter from Narnia shows up to say farewell. Everyone is excited for me and more than a little wistful. Even the dwarves. I don't know what William has told them to make them so accepting. I expected to be met at the portal with pitchforks. Instead, they all demand individual weekly letters. I'm going to have to get one of those computers or my hand is going to fall off.

DJ unveils a karaoke system, and we all sing until we're hoarse. Songs of the Realm. Songs we know by heart from his CD collection. Who knew Goldi had such a great voice? I make up in gusto what I lack in talent. We're falling over each other giggling, grabbing for the microphone. I'm made to promise I'll send new karaoke discs once a month.

I get pretty drunk. I make a speech about friendship and taking care of one another. Edmund says, "I'll miss you, Thing One." And we all think of Thing Two, and so I start crying about Rory. But it's okay, because this is the last time I'll mourn her here with my best friends. I can almost imagine her sitting in the corner, Snoozer in her lap, tottering and woozy with her third glass of sweet wine. I try to get ahold of myself; I focus on my family. CeCi and William and Edmund and DJ are looking at me with an unfiltered mixture of pain and pride, faces that I've seen pieces of for months. It's fitting that it was Rory who finally got us to look up from our own belly buttons and into our friends' hearts.

I see you, fashionably late, entering through the big wooden door, and I'm so happy that you've come, despite everything that's been going on. I'm leaving this letter under the door to your room, so you'll know how much your coming meant to me.

Zell, I hope you find what's right for you, too. Wherever and whatever it is, know that I love you and I'm proud of you.

B

From the Desk of Cecilia Cinder Charming
Crystal Palace
North Road, Grimmland

Dear Zell,

The cooking school agreed to let me take classes as often as I'm able, at least until my tuition credits run out. I can still learn things, even if I don't have a certificate. It was so good to see Phil again. I bought him a whole lot of beer and told him everything. He said it made more sense than his alien theory, though we agreed to keep our tinfoil hats as a cover story just in case. He promised to take me to the movies as often as he could to better understand the Human imagination and help me give even better weekly reports to the Godmothers.

On my way from class back to the portal today, I heard a voice calling to me from a Starbucks sidewalk table. It was Rory's therapist friend, Patricia.

"I'm sorry to bother you. It's CeCi, isn't it?" She brushed her straight red bangs from her eyes. "It's just that I haven't seen your friend Rory around in a while. I was just wondering how she's doing?"

I wasn't quite sure how to answer. We all made connections Outside, but for some reason I never thought about how Rory befriended the people here. Standing in front of me was a woman who'd done Rory a kindness—several kindnesses, actually. I wanted to tell her the truth, but I wasn't sure how.

"Something happened, didn't it?" It wasn't really a question. She stepped closer.

I nodded, gulping down the sudden lump in my throat. "It's hard to explain." Telling her Rory died is a lie, and it would have made her needlessly sad, and yet, from her perspective, her shortened years, it was the truth.

"I don't mean to pry, it's just I've been worried about her, you know, as a friend. I wasn't seeing her in any sort of professional capacity. But she looked so sad. I wanted to do something."

"I know," I said, trying to reassure her I hadn't been judging her. "She told us she asked for your help with Henry."

"I hope our shopping trip helped her confidence. But it didn't sound like her relationship was something that was going to get better on its own."

"You're right. Henry would never have been worthy of Rory. Not all the therapy in the world would've made it so."

She smiled to herself then looked up at me. "You can't tell me?"

"I'm so sorry, Patricia. I'm not sure how to explain. Rory, well, she was tired."

"Oh no." She held one hand to her heart and raised the other to her mouth. "I didn't see. I'm so sorry."

"None of us did. I promise. And we've all been through the what-ifs, Patricia. I assure you, there's no consolation there." I wished I had something to make it better. I dug into my satchel and pulled out a bag of those toy unicorns that you sent for the sign at the restaurant and Bianca's cake. I handed one to Patricia. "I'm not sure that we'd ever be able to explain where it is we're from. Some things you just have to skip over, leave to the imagination, you know?"

She laughed lightly and smiled. There were small tears at the corners of her eyes, but she didn't wipe them away.

"These were, inexplicably, some of Rory's favorite things. I'm sure she'd want you to have one. To think of her."

"It'll go nicely with my lingerie set."

"You were responsible for those!" It felt good to laugh in the sun. I hoped Patricia thought so, too.

She turned the unicorn over in her palm, and it glittered in the light. "We'll have to have a party someday."

I gave her a hug and told her I'd see her the next time I was Outside. It's like we have a garden of family here. We have a garden of family everywhere. And all we have to do is nurture it.

Love,
CeCi

Important Fucking Correspondence from Bianca White
Ocean View Apartments
Santa Monica, CA

Rory,

So, last night Rachel and I go to this place that specializes in *molecular gastronomy*. I ordered asparagus foam with steak sorbet. CeCi will find it fascinating, but it's probably the last iced meat dish I'll be eating for a while.

Speaking of our favorite chef, we're meeting her tomorrow along with Phil's partner, Eric, at the new restaurant Phil's apprenticing for. We're going to drink our way through as much of the wine list as we can afford. Then we're going to the House of Blues to hear a band Rachel thinks we'll love.

All these new things, all these experiences, are why I adore being here. I love the noise and the energy and the possibility and the unknown and the weird. For example, I now have a cell phone. I can talk to Rachel no matter where she is. Well, except at the corner down the street and in the vegetable aisle at Ralphs where there are no bars—cell phone bars, not taverns.

I should also tell you I've had my first driving lesson in a large, empty parking lot. (Well, not my very first. Mr. Toad did let me try driving once, but that was before he got put in jail.) Rachel is unimpressed with my existing skills and says I need to practice a lot or go to driving school (which is like cooking school, but shorter) before I take a driving test.

When I get a car, I think I'll get a red one. With one of those little ledges on the back. A fast one. What do you think?

Did you know that here in the markets, there are entire aisles of ketchup? There are like ten different brands. Some made of berries and balsamic vinegar. Some are outrageous colors. There are big bottles and small bottles and teeny-tiny bottles like we had at the Beverly Wilshire. Rachel is slowly adapting to the fact that I don't know very much about ketchup or anything else. Sometimes it seems like I'll never adapt, but Rachel says all the choices are just as overwhelming for Humans.

She wasn't kidding when she told us my father's name was a common one here. We've found twenty Steve Whites who worked for the theme park in some capacity over the last ten years. Maybe he isn't one of them, but it's worth a try to track them down. Even if takes my whole life. I've been back to the park several times. And I keep thinking I see his handprints on the fantasy world there. I could be making things up, but I wonder if he isn't visiting the parks like this around the whole world, tweaking a detail or two, making sure the Humans are always dreaming us, inadvertently making sure that when you wake up there'll be a Realm to wake up in.

Speaking of sleuthing, I asked Rachel to see if she could find anything out about Fred. Before you get angry, please know that I did it for myself because I was curious. I'm sending a book of poetry along with this letter. If you read the poem "The Sleeping Beauty" and find that nothing rings true, then we've chased the wrong lead. Otherwise, it seems you were never terribly far from his mind.

I keep waiting for the portal magic to wear off in some visceral way, and I wonder if this felt the same for Fred, or my father. I feel the same as I always have. Except maybe a little more purposeful. I'm thinking about training for something that will help me help people. You know, like a missing-people finder or a counselor like Patricia.

Snoozer is doing well. He loves Rachel and has met a lady Great Dane two doors down that he enjoys visiting every day. He gets to go to PetSmart every week for a bath. Zell sent him a unicorn chew toy last week that he's completely destroyed.

He misses you. We all do.

This is only the first of a great many letters Zell, CeCi, and I will be sending you. When you wake up, you'll know we thought of you every single day. We're choosing to keep you as part of our lives—somewhere we can't be, but still with us.

I hope it's a good surprise.

I've also started collecting a bunch of crappy romance novels for you. You'll love this first one. It's all about this guy whose wife doesn't remember him because she was bopped on the head with a falling satellite but then he tells her this story of their courtship and then she remembers and it's all better until he turns out to be an evil zombie but then she's saved by someone named Fabio. It'll be your favorite book, I guarantee it. Or maybe the one about vampires. Or the were-narwhals. I can just imagine the look on your face.

Better yet, maybe *I'll* write a book. I'll call it *For Want of a Unicorn*. All of my characters will live Happily Ever After.

Love,
B

Acknowledgments

Naming every person who supported me in the creation of this book is impossible, but I'm grateful to everyone who believed and inspired and loved and wished and cheered me onward. Extra thanks go to those of you who've exchanged letters with me over the years. Archiving said correspondence was the first kindling for this project.

Thank you to Jason Kirk, my acquiring editor, and the rest of the folks at 47North for their confidence and contagious, unflagging enthusiasm. I am so grateful to my editor, Caitlin Alexander, for ensuring my first novel realized its best self with her expert guidance and patient encouragement. Thanks, also, to Hannah Buehler for copyediting this tangle of whimsy.

My agent, Cameron McClure, believed in these princesses before their stories were finished—even as their narrator drove, lost, in circles around the Portland airport. I'm beyond fortunate to be making this publishing journey with her, particularly since I can't read a map.

Mama and MamaSue, thank you for loving me fiercely, believing in this dream, and showing me the meaning of strength. I'm sure Pops is lifting a glass with us in some great beyond. And love and thanks to the rest of the family: Bruce, Cassie, Rodger, Valeska, Stefan, Serena,

Amelie, Julien, Dale, Kari, Lucy, Jorge, Sara, Jon, Megan, Nathan, Alexis, Jude, Mindy, Bailey, Olivia, Lucy, Jorge, and Little Miss Not Yet Appearing In This Book.

My critique partner, Casey Blair, read every draft of this novel, called me on my shit, and talked me through the *aha!* moment I so dearly needed during the homestretch. Isabella David McCaffrey, Caroline Edwards, Jill Seidenstein, and Rashida Eddie Scholz provided me with not only fresh eyes and new insight, but also continuing encouragement and love. Thanks to my local girls, Rayna Weth and Wanda Ng, for keeping me sane and well watered. Ashlee Peters (aka Besty Friend), thank you for being there for the celebrations and the breakdowns. Thanks, also, to my writing group, my talented fellow VP XVIers, and the Rainforest Writers.

Lisa Nakamura, chef/owner of Allium on Orcas Island, has my gratitude for taking the time to share her culinary school experience as a young woman. Thanks, too, to the valiant Dr. James Babington for his help when an insolent radial nerve threatened to halt the whole shebang.

I'm also grateful to Stephen Parrish and Wendy Russ, senior management of *The Lascaux Review*, for giving me the opportunity to work and laugh alongside them at the magazine. May their futures be ever free from rubber frogs.

And last, but certainly not least, to my beloved Adam: There simply aren't words for all the ways in which I continue to fall in love with you. Thank you for believing in my fairy tale. Let's go see what this Ever After business is all about.

About the Author

Photo © 2014 Jackie Donnelly

Camille Griep lives just north of Seattle with her partner, Adam, and their dog Dutch(ess). Born in Billings, Montana, she moved to Southern California to attend Claremont McKenna College, graduating with a dual degree in biology and literature. In late 2011, she took a hiatus from corporate research to devote more time to fiction. She has since sold short fiction and creative nonfiction to dozens of online and print magazines. She joined the staff of *The Lascaux Review* in 2013 and now serves as a senior editor. She is a graduate of Viable Paradise, a residential workshop for speculative fiction novelists. Some of her favorite things are whimsy, wine, kindness, rain, and bears.